A massive b[illegible] Sebastian Lee felt a shock run through him. A smell of old earth and bad eggs drifted across the water. He stood up and peered timidly at the water. Bubbles rose again, smaller this time, but numerous. It was happening. It was really happening. Sebastian Lee felt his throat contract and his mouth dry up ...

The black water swirled and eddied. Now he was sure there was something there, something that moved. It grew in a milky cloud of yellow silt that rose and stained the pond water.

He tried to run but couldn't. The smell was overpowering. He was trapped by his terror, his evil, the power he had released. Then the black water bellied and shattered, and for a second before he shut his eyes and screamed he saw a figure break the surface; greet him with liquid eyes and swollen face. Then sink again, wrapped in its wet envelope of black.

SUBTERRANEAN

JAMES BUXTON

Futura

For Liane

A Futura Book

First published in Great Britain in 1989 by
Futura Publications, a Division of
Macdonald & Co (Publishers) Ltd
London & Sydney

All characters in this publication are fictitious and any resemblance to real persons, living or dead, is purely coincidental.

ISBN 0 7088 4358 1

Typeset by Leaper & Gard Ltd, Bristol, England
Printed and bound in Great Britain by
BPCC Hazell Books Ltd
Member of BPCC Ltd
Aylesbury, Bucks, England

Futura Publications
A Division of
Macdonald & Co (Publishers) Ltd
66-73 Shoe Lane
London EC4P 4AB
A member of Maxwell Pergamon Publishing Corporation plc

PART ONE

Chapter One

It was kite-flying weather. That Saturday afternoon, as on almost every Saturday afternoon when the wind was strong, the sky above Blackheath was splashed with flashes of primary colour as kite enthusiasts from the surrounding suburbs converged.

They come because Blackheath is broad and flat. There are no houses on it, no power lines across it, and it has been scraped clean of trees, shrubs and all signs of natural growth other than close-cropped grass. They come because the prevailing north-easterlies have swept unimpeded across the flatlands of Essex and rush up the steep sides of the Thames Valley, giving the kites extra lift. They come because there are ponds for bored family members to throw old beer-cans into.

They come because Blackheath has been conquered and sanitised. Once it was the first stretch of wilderness outside London, a place where highwaymen, footpads and cutthroats preyed on the travellers scurrying to the rich farms of Kent or to the Channel ports. But the heath has been purged. Reclaimed. Every minute spent there is a reminder of the victory of order over chaos.

Blackheath is a civilised place.

On the main road coming down from Shooters Hill to Blackheath, Sebastian Lee Miles's father bit out a short swear-word as an ancient Citroën 2CV with a screaming engine pulled out of a side-road ahead of him and its young driver tried to persuade it to accelerate away. Sebastian Lee's father left it late before hitting the brakes and horn simultaneously, judging it nicely so that the driver would be able to lip-read the stream of invective in his rear-view mirror. Then he took a left turn down a narrow side-road which led onto the heath and parked near a small pond, ringed with gravelly soil.

Sebastian Lee's mother spoke: 'Honestly, Ron! Don't be so bleeding macho all the time. Driving like that! What about the children? You scared the life out of them.' She scarcely looked up from the fat book on her lap. Behind her the two children were anything but scared. Sebastian Lee was staring out of the window, his face controlled and indifferent. Shula, his younger sister, was bouncing up and down on the firm springy seats, intently gleeful.

'Out we get, then,' said Mrs Miles, but showed no sign of following her own orders. With a practised movement, and without raising her eyes from the book, she opened the glove compartment in front of her and flipped open a box of Terry's All Gold, her fingers making straight for the caramel. Shula gave one last bounce and jumped out of the car, clutching a small plastic toy horse. She trotted a few yards away, knelt down and began arranging twigs and scraps of paper into something like a gymkhana course. Sebastian Lee slid out of the car and took up his station leaning against the bonnet, hands thrust deep into his pockets, eyes fixed blankly on the middle distance.

By the small pond lay a patch of ground fenced off from the rest of the heath — a small hummock topped by a birch tree and covered with gorse and broom. The grass there was never cut, and in the autumn lay in dun-coloured tangled swathes. It was hardly ever visited except when the occasional couple climbed over the wooded fence surrounding it. Once a hitchhiker had been found there, stone-cold dead, apparently from exposure. Sometimes people dumped old television sets and mattresses there. The strange hummock was a reminder of what the heath had looked like in the olden days before it was cleared and levelled — or so Sebastian Lee had been told in the private day-school his parents sent him to.

The boy closed his eyes and willed away the cars, the

noise, the people and the great grey spread of London which lay in the flat Thames basin below the heath. In his mind, the hummock with its solitary wind-blasted birch tree grew and spread out over the flat expanse of football fields like an overflowing spring of greens and browns.

A keen wind blew in his face as he waited. Far below, where the blue river wound like a bow between green meadows and empty marshland, a three-masted galleon, listing slightly in the breeze, was beating its way upstream. The sun burst through the clouds; gulls skidded through the air above his head. But Sebastian Lee was deaf and blind to all but the stagecoach bucketing down the road, carrying a fat cargo of merchants and gentlemen from London to Dover. As he settled himself more comfortably into his saddle, his loyal jet-black stallion twitched his ears expectantly.

Where to attack? On the heath itself, or further along the road where the gradient of Shooters Hill would slow the coach to a walking pace? But he was impatient. Let it be the heath then! He spurred his horse into a furious gallop, came alongside the coach, held himself there, and plunged across the gap between his horse and the swaying coach . . .

'Lee! Stop goggling. Get the fuck over here and help your sister.'

Sebastian Lee's father was angry, as usual, but Shula was skipping with glee as she tugged at the cord of the great black kite which had been partially assembled and now flapped sluggishly on the grass. Sebastian Lee had wanted a plain red one, but his father had bought a tournament model with a skull and crossbones on it.

His father was flicking the hair out of his eyes as he always did when he was annoyed.

He'll break that kite if he's not more careful, Sebastian Lee thought, as he watched him fumble the last strut into place.

'Well, get hold of the string, then.'

Sebastian Lee shuffled over and picked up the spool while his father held the kite.

'Ready?'

'S'pose so.'

'All right then, RUN!'

Sebastian made off so suddenly that the kite was yanked from his father's hands. He ran for about twenty yards with the kite bumping along the ground behind him. Then stopped and waited dumbly, hearing the heavy tread of his father's footsteps, but not expecting the explosion of pain as a hand descended out of nowhere and caught him on the ear. He staggered sideways then stood still.

'Ronald!' His mother's voice shrilled from the car. Sebastian Lee walked away without turning, face red, eyes watering.

He heard Shula say, 'Could I try, Daddy? Could I? PLEASE?'

His father's voice took on a false note of patience as he explained what to do. Then the kite obviously began to fly, because Shula gave a happy shriek, and Sebastian Lee turned to see his father crouching behind his daughter, pretending to let her take control, while the little girl leant against him, pretending to be excited.

Sebastian Lee went and sat by the pond. The water level was low, much lower than the week before. In the middle was a piece of drainpipe which stuck out vertically. When the water level was high only a couple of inches showed above the surface, but after any long dry spell a good two feet of metal would stand clear as the receding waterline revealed more and more hidden debris: old cans, broken bottles and pint glasses from a nearby pub, and a selection of filthy rubber balls which dogs had dropped in the soupy water.

Sebastian Lee was puzzled. It was late September and the previous two weeks had seen pretty heavy rainfall. The ground underfoot was sodden, and yet the water level was still dropping — as if the water was being sucked out of the pond, or was draining slowly from it through a fissure below the surface.

Something thin and black flashed in front of his eyes. A shadow. The boy threw his arm in front of his face. A split second later there was a splash.

'Bloody hell!'

The kite was floating in the water, the skull looking upwards from under a film of water, the string tangled around the drainpipe.

Shula was yelling happily: 'Kite's gone in da water! Kite's gone in da water!'

Mr Miles gave the string a couple of sharp pulls, but only succeeded in tying it more tightly around the pipe. Sebastian Lee watched him take off his loafers and socks, roll up his trousers then advance gingerly across the exposed pond bed.

'Watch out for the broken glass, Ron.'

Watch out for . . .

A coldness began to grow in Sebastian Lee's groin, moving upwards through his gut and spreading icily into his chest and throat. The coldness sat there, slowly becoming a feeling of dread. It was something to do with the pond, something to do with his father. He shouldn't go in. He shouldn't . . .

Sebastian watched, treacherously thrilled, as his father waded further in. Even in the middle the water barely reached his knees.

He unpicked the string from the pipe, walked carefully back to the shore and began to dry his feet with a handkerchief — then grimaced.

'Sod it! Must've nicked my heel on something.' He yelled for some tissues and the first-aid box, and started dabbing. The blood ran from his heel in a steady red stream, and quickly soaked the first tissue. Sebastian Lee handed him a second and stood close by, fascinated. The blood was very red; the foot very white.

'Does it hurt?'

'Not too bad, son. That'll teach me to go messing about in ponds.'

'Why is it bleeding so much?'

'Feet always do. Pressure. That's what it needs. There we go. Give us a plaster!'

Sebastian Lee stripped the backing off one and handed it to his father who quickly slapped it over the wound then tossed the blood-stained tissues into the pond. The boy watched them slowly unfold and thread delicate tendrils of darkness through the murk.

He felt a hand on his shoulder.

'Come on, son. Time to go home. Sorry I was rough on you earlier.'

Sebastian Lee looked upwards, his face twisted with something he didn't properly understand. But his father misread this and saw hatred. The hand was snatched away.

'Oh, just get into the car, then. Your mother wants you home for tea.'

Chapter Two

'Penny for 'em!'

Cherie Simpson was jerked from a contented day-dream and into reality.

Oh, shit, she thought, not him. Please God, not him.

On Will Ransom's face the wrinkles had been smoothed out, dry skin buffed to unnatural lustre, and everything looked as though it had been plumped up from behind with some waxy substance. He looked like W.H. Auden in pink shrink-wrap and was next-door neighbour to Cherie and her husband Peter. Her flesh always crawled when she met him, but being a kindly and well-brought-up American she always tried to control her revulsion by accusing herself of being age-ist.

It made no difference.

For a second Cherie stared at him. As usual she wondered how he managed to achieve that precise blend of naivety and depravity; wondered too how long she could continue to live as his next-door neighbour without being incredibly, irrevocably rude to him.

'Long time no see, pardner.' His voice was pneumatic and rich. For her benefit he put on a phoney Texan accent.

If only he could say something intelligent to me, Cherie thought, I might even be prepared to include him in the human race.

'In a bit of a brown study, eh? Anything uncle can do?'

Yes, Cherie mused, please please please just crawl back under a big rock. She gathered herself to speak. Ransom interrupted just as she opened her mouth.

'No can do. Hubby might complain. Sorry, old girl.'

To her acute embarrassment she saw that, for want of anywhere better, her eyes had settled somewhere in the region of his crotch.

'Oh, no. I . . .' She pulled herself together. 'Lovely weather. I was just taking advantage of it to tidy up the garden a bit.'

'Ye-es. So I see.' He even managed to make that sound mildly obscene. His eyes flicked quickly over her body, making her feel horribly aware of her tight cut-off jeans, her legs, and the fact that for once she wasn't wearing a bra under her T-shirt. She crossed her arms in front of her breasts, hoping to divert Ransom's eyes. They bulged slightly, were yellowy and bloodshot. Par for the course.

'Is hubby about? Business, you know.'

'Er, yes. I believe so. He's out back. Front door's open. Help yourself.'

'Careful what you say, young lady. One day somebody might! Heh, heh!'

And he was gone up the steps to the front door, leaving behind him a faint smell of tobacco and cologne and the unpleasant feeling in Cherie that she'd just been licked all over by an old dog with halitosis.

She looked down at her garden. She and Peter lived in a narrow terraced Georgian house on a road that jutted into the edge of Blackheath. Their house was a quirk of fate. (Like our marriage, Cherie had written to her best friend back in the States. An oddity that shouldn't really exist.) Two eighteenth-century property developers had started at opposite ends of the little street, but either they had not consulted each other, or had miscalculated, because they had left a gap between the ends of the two terraces, too big to waste, but too small for a large family house.

So Cherie and Peter's house was a sort of infill, a compressed slice of building that squeezed up between the heavy shoulders of its neighbours. It had 'The Sandwich House' painted onto the fanlight, and that described it pretty well. They had one large through room on each of the first two floors, a basement 'flat' which they could let if they wanted, a bedroom with bathroom en suite to themselves and an attic. Cherie loved it, but from a distance. For some reason she never felt she quite fitted in.

There was about ten feet of garden at the front of the house; a pocket-handerkerchief-sized lawn surrounded on four sides by well-stocked borders. No roses, which pleased Cherie, whom they always reminded of over-anxious spinsters, with their persistent efforts to produce blooms all through the summer and into the winter. The pride of the garden was a pair of magnolias which stood on either side of the front steps, and Cherie was trying to get honeysuckle to grow up and around the front door.

She had just finished what she hoped was the last weeding of the year. The earth was dark chocolate brown where she had just turned it, and a little pile of weeds lay neatly in each corner of the tiny lawn. She picked idly at the packed earth behind her fingernails, looking around for something else to do, reluctant to go inside. There was a slight chill in the air, a background threat of the winter to come, even though the sun shone and a summer haze still hung on.

Cherie felt goose-pimples raise the tiny hairs on her arms and she gave them a vigorous rub. She wanted a cardigan but she knew it was in the back garden where the two men would be sprawled in deck chairs yacking away about percentage points or common acquaintances in the City of London. If she went anywhere near them Peter would say. 'How about some tea for our guest,' and Cherie would make it because she had a horror of seeming discourteous.

'Cherie?'

Peter was standing on the steps looking down at her. He had his hands thrust into his trouser pockets and a cashmere sweater thrown over his shoulder. He seemed edgy. Cherie thought he looked like a hypocrite. His face carried a concerned and sympathetic expression but she was sure it was a mask, hiding worry of a different sort. 'What's the matter?' he asked.

'What do you mean? Nothing's the matter.' She gave a little laugh. 'Should something be the matter?'

Peter shook his head. 'Good heavens, no. It was just ... well, Ransom said he thought you looked a bit mis. You know, down.'

'Ransom said that?'

Sarcastic. Incredulous. Overdone.

Peter dropped his voice to a whisper, 'Look, you don't have to take that attitude. You may not like him but he's a pal of mine.' He was angry. 'He wouldn't notice that you were ill or something if he wasn't being thoughtful. He is thoughtful. He's a nice chap. Just give him a chance.'

Cherie thought for a moment, considering whether or not to start an argument. The way Ransom had looked her up and down had not been thoughtful. It had been intentionally insulting. So what was he playing at?

Peter was now looking pleading. 'Come in. Have a cup of tea with us. Please.'

Cherie sighed. Gave up. 'OK. Go through. I'll bring some out.'

Over tea in the back garden she made a real effort to be nice to Ransom, and watched Peter relax in front of her. Ransom reciprocated by turning on a corny sort of charm. Cherie felt that she and Ransom were playing like actors in front of Peter. It forced her into a state of complicity with him that she hated.

He's got some sort of hold over Peter, she thought. What the hell can it be? Or has Peter got something he wants?

'It's so nice for an old stick like me to see two young people so much in love,' Ransom said after a pause. 'Makes me feel young again myself.'

The smile froze on Cherie's face and she could have sworn she saw Peter wince.

'And were you ever married yourself?' Cherie asked, deliberately ignoring Peter's not very subtle signals. To her horror Ransom looked up at the sky and tears filmed his eyes.

'No, No,' he said. 'Bless you for asking, though.'

Bloody old phoney, Cherie thought. You just want us to think that there's some great tragedy in your past. I bet there's nothing. Unless you were jilted at the altar. As soon as she possibly could she cleared up the tea things from the little table, pretending that she had to finish weeding the front, and left the two men together.

She had just begun work again when a movement in the corner of her eye made her turn her head. Ransom's front door was swinging in the gentle breeze, banging softly against the catch, and then opening again. Not liking to shut it, and resist locking him out, Cherie looked around for something to wedge it with. She found a round rock the house's previous occupants had carried all the way back from Brittany and carried it up the steps.

As she bent down to position the stone, something made her pause in mid-movement. She heard a sound that could have come from the inside of the house, or could have been a fly buzzing in her ear. No. Too mechanical for that. It was a sort of whirring that lasted for six or seven seconds — quite long enough to make her hold still completely — followed by a solid click. Whrrrr — click. She couldn't place it, but as she paused a gust of wind caught the door, pushing it wide open, and she found herself staring into Ransom's house. She had been through it often enough, for drinks or for awful and solemn dinner parties. There was the dark hall, painted burgundy and lined with old prints, tunnelling back towards the garden. There was the staircase leading off straight ahead to a landing, then doubling back to the first floor, forcing the hallway to kink around it. At the far end of the hall, which smelt pleasantly of wood polish and pot-pourri, there was a door which led to the garden, its glass panes overgrown with ivy which filtered a dim green light onto the floor.

But what fascinated Cherie were the antique prints which jostled for space above the dado rail. They made up a fine collection of local views: eighteenth-century maps of the parish; views of the stately homes which had once surrounded the heath; Victorian prints of the newly-opened suburban steam railway line. She found herself stepping further and further into the hall, drawn by curiosity and by the chance to browse through them on her own. She painted well and fancied her eye.

Some of the prints were very fine indeed and she examined them with a growing sense of surprise. She had always thought of Ransom as the dirty lithograph type: the sort of man who would hang a few Picasso minotaur repros on the wall and wait until some unsuspecting female guest examined them. Then it would be: If you find those interesting, perhaps you'd like a look at some of these . . .

And out with the porn.

Cherie paused in front of some ancient local maps. They weren't prints, but originals drawn onto parchment. One in particular made her look more closely. It seemed to be of the heath, but it was a bit confusing. The cartographer had obviously let his fancy run wild. In one corner there was a windmill, impossibly ornate; in another a two-masted galleon, presumably to show the area's closeness to the docks. Top right was an ornate cross. Top left . . . Whatever had been drawn there had been crudely obliterated, scored out and then covered with a blotch of black ink. And there too on the heath, between the carefully-rendered clumps of gorse and broom and birch were more black stains, the scratch marks underneath suggesting that the map had been deliberately, yet furiously, censored.

So intent was Cherie that she didn't notice the dark shadow falling on the polished floor behind her.

'Gotcha!'

Cherie gave a tiny scream as a mottled hand closed around her wrist. Ransom grinned, his eyes level with hers.

'Pretty little burglar, eh? What shall we do with her?'

'No! I mean I'm sorry. Your door. It was open. I just came up to have a look.'

'That's what they all say, sweety. Interested in old prints, are we?'

'Well yes. As a matter of fact I am. I was just wondering . . .'

Ransom was still holding her forearm. Now he squeezed it with an unexpectedly powerful hand. 'Well you won't find that in a shop, my dear. No indeed. Nor is it for sale. Unique actually. Been in the family for generations.'

Cherie bridled, resenting the various implications. 'I wouldn't dream of asking you to sell it,' she said frostily.

'Oh, really?'

'Really. I just came up here to stop your front door banging shut.' (Was it her imagination or did he squeeze a little harder when she said 'banging'?) 'Then I saw the prints. Look, I'm sorry if I offended you in any way and now . . .'

She yanked her arm away from him and pushed past.

'Oh, no offence. No indeed. Well, goodbye, my dear. Do come again soon.' Ransom gave a vague wave.

Hateful, loathsome creature, she thought as she walked as quickly as she could away from the house. How can Peter stand him? Had he defaced that print? Somehow she could imagine it, though she couldn't quite think why. It just seemed to make sense.

She shook herself and decided that she was being unnecessarily negative. Think positive, Cherie, think positive, she said to herself. He too has a contribution to make. And you are stuck next-door to him. He is a friend of your husband's. You might be his neighbour for the next fifteen years. So get a grip on yourself. And now get back to gardening and let that anger be turned to positive use. Let it flow into the earth. Watch out, grass, here I come.

And she attacked the tiny lawn's edges with her shears.

Half an hour later she straightened up and rubbed her blistered hands. Her anger had gone, to be replaced with a feeling of tired despair. She stared out across the heath. Scattered over the green flatness were little groups of people, some trying to fly kites in the erratic breezes of the Indian summer, a few picnicking, others just strolling around, children and dogs in tow. She tried to guess how many people would be crowding into Greenwich Park, just the other side of the main road, and decided that on a day like this there would be too many for her to be able to set up her stool and easel and sketch in peace.

A motorist, late for the Dover ferry and irritated by the behaviour of the car in front, blasted his horn in a long angry bellow, more a statement of frustration than anything else, but it acted as a signal to the drivers all around him and pent-up anger burst through the barriers of restraint and moderation. One by one they sounded their horns, the sounds mingling, the noise growing and slowly tailing away with a few last enraged blasts.

Where Cherie was standing the sound was distant, rural and faintly soothing. Like cows, she thought, like poor little cows standing in line. For what, though? So some of them can be herded into big metal boats and taken to graze in the rich pastures of France. So some of them can be milked dry in the tawdry seaside resorts of Kent. So that others can stand locked in traffic jams on the big London orbital motorway on the last fine day of the year.

Cherie squinted across the heath and shook her head. That road. It bothered her, and had done since she and Peter had moved to Blackheath almost two years ago. To her mind it almost succeeded in ruining the quiet village atmosphere of the place. Big sixteen-wheeler trucks (or juggernaut lorries as she'd learnt to call them) thundered up it day and night, when they weren't caught in tailbacks (traffic jams, she mentally corrected herself, when in England do as the xenophobic sons of bitches do ...) as they carried containers to and from the coastal ports of the South-East. In the summer it was regularly choked solid with holiday traffic, each family car desperate, it seemed, to make an earlier cross-Channel ferry than the one in front of it. And yet nobody ever seemed to think of actually doing anything about it — diverting some of the traffic or widening the road for instance.

She'd raised the subject once with Peter, and regretted it as soon as she had seen the all too familiar and rather pompous expression that pulled his boyish features into an unattractive shape.

'It's just not the way we do things, presh. Widen the road? It'd just encourage more grockles to litter up the beaches and ruin the countryside with their horried trannies and roadside picnics. No way. Not over here.'

She hated it when he said 'No way'. It was a silly pretend concession to her being an American, but really only served to emphasise what he insisted were great cultural differences between them.

'Can't have yobbos cutting into the heath. No, sirree.'

Cherie had fallen in love with the heath the first time she'd seen it, a time which coincided with her and Peter looking for their first house, as opposed to flat.

'Good area,' he'd said, after he'd checked with a couple of friends of his who'd become estate agents when the City of London finance houses had turned them down. 'And we should be able to get quite a decent house down here. Area's cheap but coming up fast. If we buy soon we'll make a tidy packet.'

Comments like that always slightly disturbed Cherie, who had been brought up to refer to money as seldom as possible, but even those qualms hadn't been able to dull the excitement of seeing the rows of beautiful Regency, Georgian and early Victorian houses standing around the wide green field of the heath, calm sentinels to a more elegant age. She could still recapture the warm rush of awe and longing she had felt at her first sight of mellow brick blending with faded stucco, of rich green garden lawns seen from the street through wide sash windows.

Blackheath was the first area of London that Cherie had seen which impressed her without intimidating her. She thought Clapham overpriced, Camden too frantic,

Primrose Hill too dear, and Notting Hill just a touch smug. She loved Hampstead, but the village's almost palpable aura of wealth somehow made her feel second rate.

And then she'd found Blackheath. She and Peter had been driving down to see some old friends of his who farmed near Rye in Kent. They'd crawled down the scrappy bustle of the Old Kent Road with its greasy spoon cafés, junk shops, and used car lots, speeding up slightly as they passed through the edges of Deptford and Greenwich. There had been one more agonisingly slow stretch at the bottom of a steepish hill, and suddenly they had burst out of London into a great empty space and were speeding along a straight road with the walls of Greenwich Park on one side, a huge acreage of mown grass on the other; everything overlooked by tall, elegant houses. And above them a great blue dome of country sky.

'Where's this?' she had asked.

'Hmm? Oh, it's called Blackheath, I think. Quite pretty. Henrietta and Tim moved here when she got pregnant. Young mums and politicians mostly.'

But Cherie thought it was wonderful.

Since that first day she'd fallen in and out of love with the heath a dozen times or more; marvelling at the sky above it, alive with clouds; disgusted by the litter, displaced kerb-stones, bent lamp-posts and used condoms which lay scattered about its edges like a crusty scum. Somewhere in the back of her mind she realised that the place was special and unique, and that back in the States it would either have been turned into something ridiculously neat, preserved and pristine, or allowed to go to seed completely.

She knelt on the lawn and began to scoop up the little piles of weeds. England. She'd never understand that either, or what she was doing here. Not in a million years. Not for a million bucks. The longer she stayed, the less she understood and the more those little things which previously she had found quaint and cute reduced her to screaming frustration. And Peter, her own husband, summed the whole thing up. She thought back to the first time she had met him almost four years ago.

'You'll never guess what just happened?' The voice of Cherie's old New York roommate cut across almost half a decade.

'Boston's just swapped the Celtics for the Statue of Liberty.'

'No, you dickhead.' Jennifer's Brahmin accent was not always matched by her language. She had a knack of picking up, and using, street language she only half understood. 'I have just met the most, er, the . . . Oh God, I just don't know how to describe him.'

'Go on, try.'

'He's unbelievable. Totally unbelievable. Tall, blond, dressed preppy, you know, sorta clean and fit. Er, let's see now. Blond hair, sunstreaked. Blue eyes, my dear, of course, oh, and a sort of quiff type thing, but natural, not all greasy, which falls in an arrogant curve down his forehead.'

'Stop already, stop already. You're right. I cannot believe this guy. Just tell me who his hairdresser is. And his plastic surgeon.'

But Jennifer was literally jumping up and down with excitement. Cherie had never actually seen anyone do that before.

'No, listen. Listen! There's more. I'm standing on the corner of Madison and 59th. I'm loaded with shopping, and I mean loaded, and in a state. You know what I mean? Bloomingdales at 11.30 on a Saturday morning? Wall-to-wall consumers. Well I've just bought this suit and some of those cute panties, fought my way out, and missed the lights at an intersection. *Don't Walk!* I could walk? I could crawl. I'm hot. Frazzled. P-i-s-s-e-d, if you pardon my French. Then there's this voice. "Excuse me, could I be of some assistance?"'

Jennifer dropped her voice to imitate it. Cherie interrupted.

'Wait a minute. "Could I be of some assistance" Who is this creep? Little Lord Fauntleroy or Count Dracula?'

'Neither!' Jennifer screamed. 'It's Prince Charles and Michael York rolled into one! It's an Englishman! The real thing! Tweed jacket. Brogues. Everything.'

'None of them is circumcised, you know.'

Jennifer's nose shot into the air. 'None of my family are, either. I mean, is.'

'Listen, Jennifer sweetheart, anyone walking around New York City in tweeds and brogues in the middle of August has to be suffering from an extreme form of clinical neurosis. This man is obviously psycho. Remember where Jack the Ripper came from?'

'No-no-no-no. You just don't understand. He's It! It's Him!'

Cherie gave a little sigh. She had met half a dozen 'Its' and 'Hims' and 'The Ones' since she and Jennifer had taken an apartment together on Manhattan six months previously, she working as a graphic designer with a moderately successful agency, Jennifer as a receptionist, publicist and coffee maker in a recherché SoHo art gallery. It was impossible to imagine how two women of the same age with the same degree from the same New England College could be so different, but Cherie reckoned that was why they got on so well together.

Both were ambitious in totally different ways: Cherie to make a name for herself in design; Jennifer to marry a name in the art world. In the past Jennifer's finds had generally been happily married or gay, or both, and not in the slightest bit interested in Jennifer's nuptial or even sensual charms. She only ever seemed to go for happy, faithful types. Every which way they were generally baffled by the great waves of childish sexuality Jennifer sent blasting out towards them in crowded bars and fashionable restaurants.

And now this limey, Cherie thought. Slimey limey.

But she decided to be charitable, knowing full well that she lacked Jennifer's ability, erratic though it was, actually to meet new people, and that, without her, life would be that much more flat and stale.

'OK, sugarpuss,' she said. 'What's he do?'

'Well.' Jennifer suddenly became sheepish. 'He's a banker.'

'A WHAT?'

'No. It's not like that. He's not all sharp and sweaty. I'm sure he hates executive toys. He's young. He works for an American bank in London. He's over here on a training course.'

Cherie let her charitable mask slip. 'And how d'you find all this out? Telepathy?'

'No, stupid. He whistled me this taxi. It was so neat. Then he opens the door for me; puts me inside; asks me where I'm going; tells the driver; explains who he is and gives me his card. Oh, and invites me — I mean us — to a party tonight, except he calls it drinkies. It was so suave!'

'Suave?' She took the card and read: Peter Simpson. Two addresses, one Wall Street, the other upper east side. One work, one play. On the back was scrawled in what looked like a monkey's hand: '6.30. Drinks. NO BOYFRIENDS.' Just how corny could you get?

But Jennifer was looking hurt and Cherie relented.

'You going?' she asked.

'Are you?'

Suddenly they were both grinning.

'Course I am, Jenny. Everyone loves a lord. If that's the time, you better start getting ready.'

Warbling 'Tea for Two', Jennifer pranced into the bathroom to begin her interminable preparations. Cherie made her way into the bedroom where a drawing board seemed to be taking up an inordinate amount of space. Come up with a novel idea for a shampoo bottle, she'd been told. By Monday.

The only idea Cherie had come up with so far had been a large, squeezy erect phallus. Somehow she didn't think it would have mass-market appeal. Screw it, she thought. I'm going out. She began rummaging through her closet for something clean to wear.

* * *

The room, in a fairly smart apartment block off Fifth Avenue, was bland and filled with small groups of people and a lot of smoke. Cherie waved her hands in front of her face.

'Jesus, haven't any of these guys heard of secondary lung cancer?'

'No. They're English. Isn't it neat?'

Cherie tried, and failed, to detect a note of irony in Jennifer's voice and peered across the room for the drinks table.

Then it happened.

A young man with a ridiculously crooked smile pushed his way across the room towards them, kissed a swooning Jennifer on both cheeks, whispered something in her ear and planted her into a group of surprisingly similar-looking young men.

'One of them really is a lord.' Jennifer mouthed the words to Cherie with an ecstatic smile on her face. The young man caught the message being passed.

'I'm afraid its true. He's broke of course. Father died in a mental home. Mother's a spiritualist. Family home's owned by an Iranian. Charlie turned out quite well, considering.'

Cherie saw the man pass a comment to Jennifer who promptly began to undulate like a waterbed. Cherie winced and was grateful when Peter dragged her off to an improvised bar, made her drink a neat and very cold vodka and suggested they go off and eat somewhere. Alone.

That was how it had all started. From the first Cherie was completely taken by a combination of sophistication and uncouthness she had never met before. Peter never went to the bathroom, he had a piss or a crap. He swore all the time, foully, ate rare hamburgers and steaks like a vampire, and yet managed always to maintain a certain poise. It seemed as if he didn't care about anything, but what he wanted he got with ruthless efficiency.

After that first evening, when they hadn't gone off and eaten alone, and especially after the second, when they had, Cherie fell increasingly under his spell, and when his seven months were up and he suggested that she come back to England with him, she accepted, glad that she hadn't had to ask. She was, she decided, the only thing in the world Peter really cared about. He needed her. She had to go.

But looking back it had been downhill all the way from there. On his home ground the fairy prince had turned into a frog. For a while they had shared a house with a public school friend in a suburban slum called Wandsworth, which she hated and which she was told repeatedly was wonderful. Then they moved into a small flat he bought in another slum called Shepherds Bush, which once again was meant to evince exquisite taste. The walls were paper thin, the floors and ceilings were like loudspeakers, and after three weeks Cherie was word perfect in every Dire Straits song and Verdi aria that came thumping or warbling at her from every direction.

It's like living in a cheap hi-fi store, she wrote to Jennifer. *I HATE IT HERE!!!*

It was all very different from Manhattan.

Their wedding was a bright interlude of white lace, yellow daffodils, mellow Cotswold colours and wonderful village bells, but Cherie heard more and more the braying voices of the class she'd married into, the childish cruelty of its women, the greed and complacency of its men. The dreamy lie she'd persuaded herself was the real England lay pierced and wriggling at her feet, and when she thought like this a line of poetry from God-knew-where drummed in her brain:

My mind's not right. My mind's not right. My mind's not right.

But England was her home now, and Peter her husband. In spite of everything she still loved him and America was very far away. And if Cherie had given up her dreams of taking the design world by storm, she had set herself an even harder goal.

Her latest fantasy was that Peter would lose the sharp, greedy look he carried back from the office each evening, that and about a stone and a half in weight. He would mellow into a benignly conservative 'old thing', would be quietly proud of his attractive, artistic and exotically foreign wife and together they would move around each other in a gentle ballet, surrounded by an autumn haze in a high-ceilinged room which smelt of beeswax and honeysuckle. What she envied above all else was the ability to translate love into comfort, the way other couples seemed to slip contentedly into a long established social hierarchy. God in heaven, the Queen on the throne, hubby in the garden, and Cherie — That was where the story ended.

A cat's paw of wind batted her lightly on her cheek and a police car squittered its way down the Dover Road, siren on. Cherie suddenly began to feel very vulnerable, down on her hands and knees wearing nothing but a pair of skimpy cut-off jeans and a T-shirt. Suddenly she saw that her hands were not covered with life-giving earth but with the filthy residue of years: shit, putrescent flesh, ground bones. She straightened up and shivered.

'Something's wrong,' she thought. 'Something's very wrong. I'm not happy and I don't see how I can be. Not like this.'

Clouds had gathered. Ragged plumes moved across the sun and small shadows scurried rat-like along the flat ground. Around the heath it seemed to Cherie that the facades of the houses had suddenly become blank and inimical. Not alien — she was the alien — but exclusive and secretive, and it seemed to her that it was a secret kept from her alone.

'It's getting cold. You'd better come in.'

Peter stood on the steps again. This time he really did look concerned.

'I've been watching you from the window for about

twenty minutes. You were miles away.'

Cherie looked up at him. For once there was more than just politeness in his voice.

'I'll give you a hand.'

He walked down the steps and started gathering the individual piles of weeds together.

Cherie caught a flash of gold on the little finger of his left hand. It seemed too ridiculous to ask anything as obvious as what it was. But Peter caught her looking at it.

'Nice, isn't it?'

He turned it and it glinted dully in the last rays of the sun.

'I've not seen you wearing it before.'

'Ransom just gave it to me. Bloody fantastic gift. Old family heirloom, or something. He really wanted me to have it.'

'But you can't.'

'Who says?'

Cherie turned away furiously, feeling in some strange and upsetting way as if she had been betrayed, cuckolded almost. It seemed so personal. A ring. And so complete. Between them alone. Exclusive. She felt sick in the pit of her stomach and turned so her husband could not see her tears. Then, dumping the last of the weeds in a pile behind the next-door garden's hedge, she stumbled up the steps and into her house.

Chapter Three

As usual Cherie got up with Peter and, as usual, while he was fussing with his cufflinks and trouser press and shoe polish, she made her way sleepily downstairs, popped a couple of slices of wholemeal bread in the toaster, set up the coffee machine and slumped on the sofa with the day before's evening newspaper. Peter then began his morning routine of pacing the room in a filthy temper, coffee in one hand and toast in the other, before kissing her on the cheek and dashing for the 7.45 to London Bridge.

It infuriated Cherie that he always kissed her goodbye. Firstly, even after two years in England, she believed that kisses should be an expression of sincerely-felt emotion. Peter always called her a bloody hippy when she said this.

Secondly, she knew he only did it because he'd read a report which stated that men in high-pressure jobs who kissed their wives before going to work were statistically less likely to die of heart attacks, strokes, or in car accidents than men who didn't. When she'd challenged him on this he'd merely looked at her and asked if she really wanted him dead that much, and for a second Cherie hadn't been able to answer him. The result was that Peter stormed about in the early morning and then kissed her goodbye, and Cherie stormed or sulked for anything up to an hour afterwards.

Often she took herself off for a walk to clear her mind before she settled down to her painting, and that was why she found herself in the middle of the heath at half past eight on the first cold morning of the year, heading towards the old convent, a large Victorian building which stood in the middle of a green limb thrusting into the dense rows of terraced houses around it. As she approached she noticed a small crowd standing by it, and wondered what they were doing. She also wondered why the house looked different this morning.

As she approached the gates, Cherie was surprised to see a few familiar faces in the crowd, faces she'd nodded at in the village bookshop or greengrocers. There was a good mix gathered: stoutish tweedy types with silk headscarves, signalling hard that this wasn't their sort of thing at all and they were just onlookers; some young mums, smart but casual in pastel dungarees and with expensive-looking pushchairs; and at the front a group of more scruffily-dressed people, middle-class and middle-aged, one of whom was trying vainly to organise some chanting. Cherie pushed through the crowd to the front and caught the beginnings of an argument.

'Listen, Penny, it won't help. If anything you'll only alienate them.' A man with thinning hair and a fawn duffel coat was saying to a woman. He laid an arm on her shoulder and continued, 'Listen pet. We'll all go inside and make up some placards.'

The reply was immediate and sarcastic: 'Oh great. That's really showing them.' The little group broke up and its members all turned to stare moodily at the building. With a shock Cherie saw that half the roof and almost all of the front had been demolished. She could see the sad wallpaper of a bedroom wall. (Why was it always pink and floral? So pathetic.) A floor hung in space, wide boards gaping sadly. A crane idly dangling a demolition ball showed how it had been destroyed so quickly.

'What's going on?' Cherie asked a woman standing by her.

'Oh, don't ask me. Some demolition nonsense. My husband says it's entirely illegal. Well, said that when they started.'

'When was that?'

'Yesterday morning. They started early. Made a complete mess of the building, but that's deliberate of course. You see, they do as much damage as possible before anyone can get a chance to stop them.'

Sunday morning. I was gardening then, Cherie thought automatically.

'Is that what you're demonstrating about?' she asked.

'Oh, I'm not demonstrating. Don't get me wrong,' the woman replied. 'I'm observing. Don't lump me in with this lot. You see, my husband says that it's all a result of the GLC being abolished, not that we held with them or anything you understand. But they used to control the heath, you know, as a GLC park, and now, ever since they've been abolished, well nobody knows who controls what and everybody thinks they can do what they want. I mean look at those demonstrators ...'

'Yes, I quite understand,' Cherie said quickly. 'I was just wondering if you could make out what they were demonstrating about.'

'Well. Don't quote me or anything but we believe' — her voice dropped — 'we believe that it's all got something to do with this building and its being demolished.'

Cherie had got that far on her own, and opened her mouth to speak, but was interrupted.

'You see, we think there's a plan to knock down the old convent and put some flats up there, and these demonstrators seem to want an adventure playground instead.'

'Are they allowed to knock the building down? Isn't it listed?' Cherie asked.

The woman looked at her pityingly. 'You're American, aren't you? You see I can tell because —'

But her voice was cut off by grating thunder as two bulldozers with massive earthscoops started up, blasting great smoke signals of diesel fumes into the air. The woman was still talking, inaudibly. Cherie mouthed 'thank you' and moved off. She wasn't in the mood for being pitied, even if it was because she was an American.

She felt detached. She prided herself on her objectivity at moments like this. The convent had been an ugly building, misshapen really. And now that the demolition crew had been at work on the thin skin of brick it looked positively distorted. Strangely enough the knocking down of one side actually made the building look bigger, not smaller. Inside, all the walls seemed to be arranged at funny angles, especially on the ground floor. It was no great loss, Cherie thought. Perhaps they would put up something better instead. She walked on around it, honestly admitting to herself that all she really wanted to see was the demolition ball swing and walls come tumbling down. It suited her mood. Still, it was a shame. The convent, after all, was a piece of local history, and it was a pity that it should be destroyed. She vaguely wondered where the nuns had gone and resolved to try and find out a bit more about it in the local library. How ironic, she thought, that it takes the destruction of something before I get interested in it. Perhaps that's the answer for my marriage. She rounded the corner.

A bulldozer swung its blunt nose round an outhouse, the sound of its engine and the clatter of its muddy tracks redoubling as it came in sight. The machine paused. Then, swinging jerkily on a single track, it demolished a lean-to shed, revved and trundled straight towards her. Involuntarily Cherie took a step backwards. The bulldozer lowered its massive scoop and began ploughing up the green leaves and tangled stems of what had once been a vegetable and fruit garden. It lumbered closer and closer to the metal fence, ripping strips from the soil.

Then, just as it seemed inevitable that it would smash down the railings and crush her underneath the metal tracks, it spun almost daintily on its axis, and the scoop seemed to catch something that stood concealed in the tall nettles, something that cracked, and fell, while a part of it was knocked loose and flew to the very foot of the railings.

Cherie thought she heard a sigh and glanced around. But there was no one there. The bulldozer ground noisily around the outbuilding and Cherie knelt down to see what it had knocked towards her. She reached her hand under a matted hank of wet grass and grasped something hard.

Time froze. A shutter in her mind opened; the dark grew into a black implosion of sensation. Her conscious self shrank until she was the size of an ant staring at the tableau moving around the inside of her skull.

There are figures marching through the night, a small procession of men, wearing masks and leather aprons. Their faces are lit fitfully by the great flaring brands some of them carry; others have shovels slung over their shoulders. They stop in the middle of a great wasteland of shrub and gorse by the side of a vast pit so deep they have to use baskets to carry earth up to the surface. Cherie looks at the earth lines on the wall of the pit, the strata, and knows it is trying to tell her something.

The men back into the wind and flying rain like mules. They stand motionless until they all turn their heads, as if by a signal. A cart is approaching, loaded up to the rails with things that shift and glisten. Bodies.

Some are dressed and some are naked; some old, some young. All lie still, flesh flickering in the wet and the torchlight. The carter turns his tumbril round so the back is as near the crumbling pit edge as he can chance it. Then he begins to pitch the bodies out.

He doesn't touch them; just rams a great wooden pole between them and levers. The bodies fall from the cart and tumble into the pit, smearing with earth as they hit the walls. Then Cherie sees something that makes the hair crawl on her scalp. One of the bodies lives. She can see it is a young man, in his teens perhaps. He is weak, thin. All he can do is grasp at the pole, his mouth opening and closing like a beached fish. Surely the carter will notice.

The carter does notice. He reaches over to the seat and picks up a cudgel. Before the boy can react, his skull is crushed and he is falling. He is one of the last bodies who seem to clamber up the side of the pit in a broken white heap. The foreman waves to his men and they began shovelling earth into the pit, covering the bodies with a thin layer. When this is done they stand back. The foreman, a middle-aged man with a sour face, takes off his mask, turns to Cherie. She snatches a breath. She knows him. But from where? How?

Suddenly he begins to dance — no, whirl — twisting with grotesque grace on one leg, then another, now jumping, now bending at the knee. His leather apron spins out from him. His thin hair streams out in the wind. Cherie senses a reluctance in all this, but his face is whirling by so fast she can't tell, and the centrifugal force distorts it, spins it from its natural shape. Then he jerks like a dancer, manages to hold a pose, and she sees his expression is blanked out, shocked into numbness. He begins to spin still faster, his arms flung out for balance or because he can no longer hold them in. It's as if he's standing on the head of a lathe. He slows, enough for Cherie to see exhaustion on his face and streaks from his nose and mouth and eyes where the centrifugal force has squeezed blood and mucus from them which now streak his white face like the lines on a barber's pole.

He staggers, then gasps. He begins to turn again and this time there is no let-up. Faster and faster, his legs like one twisting pillar, his arms flung out, the colours of his coat, his apron, his flesh, fading, blurring to white. A white column, dancing and leaping on the grass.

The colours change. The white becomes tinged with a pinkish hue, no RED. Gore starts to spin from the figure like pink sugar wisps at the candy-floss stand. Strands of flesh twisted, stretched, spun into soft fibre whip out from the white column, break off to fall on the grass, twisted like flayed snakes. Now lumps of fat spatter free, hot and burning, coloured entrails like paper decorations, darker lumps of tissue thud to the ground all around. And the blood is spun into its constituent parts and sprays out in a rich crimson cloud, covering everything in speckled spume.

The colours fade back to white. The column slows, clatters, collapses, a heap of bones spun clean and white, bleached on the green of the grass. She tries to move but somehow the strips of flesh have twisted into ropes and, unknown to her, wound themselves around her arms and legs. She falls. The light dims and suddenly there is a naked figure standing by her — Ransom, her next-door neighbour. He says: 'That was then, this is now,' holds up a hand and shows her a horribly elongated and thickened index finger that tapers to a sharp point. Pressing it into the soft dimple of skin beneath his Adam's apple he draws it swiftly down so that his abdomen opens like a fruit and a tiny pale switch of a girl leaps from the deep red cavity onto Cherie's breasts and begins to lick her with an eager little tongue.

'Sheba! Down! Drop! Leave! I say, are you all right. I said are you all right?'

Cherie found herself kneeling on the grass. Wet had soaked her trousers at the knees. An Alsation puppy was licking her face and its owner was trying to pull it off. He looked relieved when Cherie's eyes opened and she nodded her head.

'Come over all faint?'

'Er, yes, I guess so.'

'Never mind. Expect it's the weather. Need a lift anywhere?'

Cherie shook her head. 'No. Thanks all the same. I'll be OK. I just felt a bit dizzy.' Which is the understatement of the century, she added to herself.

'If you're sure.' The man whistled his dog and strode off.

Cherie got to her feet, dimly registering that she had something in her hand. She jammed it in her pocket and walked slowly home across the wet grass.

Back at the convent the demolition foreman was feeling pleased. The protestors outside the gates had proved a useless lot and now most of them had dispersed. Some might turn up again later, but for now the fact that he and his crew had ignored them completely had obviously acted as a deterrent. The demo work was going well too. To all intents and purposes the building was a ruin already. In fact he was surprised at how quickly it had begun to go. Through a hole in the roof he could see the massive water tank. As far as he knew, no one had drained it. When that went . . .

On the other side of the building he heard the bulldozers throttle down. One of the drivers was walking towards him.

'What the hell's going on?'

'Better come and have a look, guv. Something's come up.'

'What are you talking about? Something's always coming up.'

'Looks like a coffin, guv.'

'What? A coffin? Someone's seeing things.'

'Well, that's what it looks like. Behind the building. In the corner there. There's a few steps going down to a sort of basement — but they've been filled in. I just uncovered them. Old. Stone. Not concrete. The coffin's laid in front of them.'

'Come on, let's take a look.'

The two bulldozers stood shivering rhythmically, engines throttled right down, like two tired monsters. Both were in the bottom of a smooth, wide dip in the ground, about twenty feet across, but no more than five foot deep. Some time in the past the earth must have been scooped out and then the dip grassed over.

The bulldozer drivers had no real business down there in the first place, the foreman thought. They were meant to be levelling the ground, not making the holes in it even bigger. Both drivers were obviously aware of this and were standing sheepishly by the machines. In front of one of the scoops, a dull grey metallic object had been pulled half out of the earth. It was certainly coffin shaped, and roughly the right size, but what on earth was it made of? And what was it doing here?

Once it might have been buried deep, but when the dip had been made in the ground, most of the earth covering it had gone. The foreman looked around to see what it could have been used for, trying to find a clue. In the corner of the garden, about twenty feet away, stood a row of old Andersen shelters, earth piled up on their roofs. That was where it had gone.

He waved at one of the drivers.

'Can you get it out, then?'

'Well, not without doing some damage. Del could do it,

though. With the crane.'

He looked wearily around, first at the men, then at the grey object. He shrugged.

'All right, then. It's fucking playtime. But, for Christ's sake, get a move on.'

Quickly a couple of men unfastened the demolition ball, and dragged a loop of chain to where the top of the object stuck out of the soil. The way it looked, it must have been dropped into the ground vertically.

'Carefully now,' he said.

The chain was placed around it. By pulling against the angle, the crane operator managed to loosen it in the earth. Two men then kicked the chain down to nearer the object's middle and waved for it to be lifted again. This time it came halfway up out of the earth, then slipped back in again.

The foreman moved forward and tightened the chain by sticking a bent six-inch nail through the links nearest the object.

This time it lifted clear. It was, as plain as could be, a coffin.

As it touched the ground, a couple of the younger men dashed forward with crowbars, whooping ghoulishly.

The foreman yelled 'Hold it', picked up a crowbar and moved towards the coffin. Then paused. 'Someone nip down to the nearest phone booth and call the police.'

'Er, guvnor, shouldn't you wait until they arrive?' he heard someone say. He knew he should, but then suppose it wasn't really a coffin? Suppose it was . . . well, anything. Right idiot he'd look.

Curiosity drew him like a marionette. The earth he scraped from the surface fell off easily and revealed metal beneath. He drew the sharp tip of the crowbar across the metal and saw it raise a glistening silver weal. Lead. Only lead was that soft.

The voices of the men cut in.

'Weird.'

'Fucking right.'

'Who put it there?'

'And lead, too.'

'What's that?'

One of the men had been idly kicking the mud off the top and now revealed a metal cross, crudely rivetted on. Underneath was some writing, chiselled into the lead.

'Anyone got a steel brush?'

One of the crew went off. The murmuring went on.

'Won't be too hard to get into' . . . 'If we want to' . . . 'What d'you think' . . . 'I know. It's Count Dracula' . . . 'Look deep into my eyes . . . Ha ha ha —'

The man with the brush came back and set to work. Spider's writing. Carved in lead. Inlaid with earth.

Heere stands one who coulde not walke or crawle
So otheres mighte bee kept in thralle.

The coffin was bound with metal bands, almost completely corroded. Used like chisels, the crowbars went straight through them.

'All right?'

'Come on, then.'

There must have been a slight vacuum inside the coffin. The lid loosened with a soft thump. Slid sideways.

A face that grinned. Limbs bent like a mad doll's. Dry flesh, warped, and wrapped like bad leather around the skull and naked body, carrying the chains around the chest and waist which had held it upright for centuries.

And every single major bone in its legs and arms broken. Thigh, skin, forearm, upper arm — smashed.

Here stands one who could not walk or crawl
So others might be kept in thrall.

The foreman was the first to speak.

'Christ allfuckingmighty.'

That's all we need, he thought.

Cherie was home by ten. She was cold and shivery; the

autumn damp had crept into her home. She wiped the clinging wet leaves and grass from her feet, then leant over and turned up the wall-mounted thermostat to 75 degrees. To hell with the consequences, she muttered out loud to herself. She dropped her quilted jacket on the hall chair and moved into the kitchen to make herself some coffee.

She felt awful. Halfway through spooning coffee into the filter she saw that drops of water were falling onto the work surface and into the coffee jar, balling the grains into glistening black spheres. She glanced up at the ceiling to check for drips before she realised that she was crying. Then her hands began to tremble and she walked on rubber legs to the sofa, holding her head in her hands, overwhelmed by waves of self-pity and despair.

Everything was wrong. All wrong. Her marriage. Her life. Her work.

Now I'm imagining things, she thought. Now I'm going mad. Mad. MY MIND'S NOT RIGHT.

Numbly she telephoned Peter. No answer. Called the switchboard. In a meeting.

In a meeting. Out to lunch. Just stepped out. On the other line. He'll call you back. He never did.

Cherie began to cry again.

Jennifer, she thought. I'll call Jennifer. Jennifer my oldest friend who I love and miss. She fumbled in the address book, her heartbeat quickening at the thought of talking to Jennifer, at the transAtlantic hum on the line, at the dear, sweet leisurely and efficient ring of an American telephone.

Ring, ring, ri . . .

'Hello?' A stranger's voice. A roommate?

'Hello. Er, can I speak to Jennifer please?'

'Jennifer?'

'Jenny Taylor.'

'I'm sorry. You must have the wrong number.'

'Oh, sorry. Sorry.'

Misdial. Hang up. Try again. Ringing. Ringing.

'Hello?'

The same voice.

'I'm sorry, I think . . .'

'Oh, it's you again. I just remembered. We used to get mail addressed to J. Taylor. But that was two years ago or so. At least two years. Goodbye.'

'Bye.'

Two years. Out of touch for two years and the phone buzzing in her hand. Her best friend.

Cherie was eventually disturbed by the faint yet lingering smell of mud coming from her fingers. It seemed to have worked its way into the grain of her skin. Then she remembered she had stuck something into her jacket pocket and pulled herself up off the sofa to retrieve whatever it was.

A cross. Oak. Simple, small and squat. She ran her fingers across the close-grained wood, smearing mud. The surface of the cross was black and pitted with age, but showed no sign of rotting. Its decay was slow and mineral, not vegetable. In fact, Cherie thought, it must have been treated with some preservative for it to have lasted outside. For how long though, and why? And was it linked to that vision?

But the details of the vision were slipping fast from Cherie's mind, and the more she tried to remember them the more confused the memory became. A sense of vividness remained, as well as the stark image of the pit, but everything else was becoming shadowy and vague. There was a face, and cruelty, and horror, and that feeling of depression as if a membrane had broken in her brain and misery was flooding her with its black bitter water.

She turned the cross in her hands and her professional interest grew. Cleaned up it would make an interesting knick-knack. There was a hole drilled in the bottom of it, obviously so it could be mounted. Well, it would be nice to do something like that with it in time.

Cherie put the cross in the bottom drawer of a pedestal desk and walked through to the kitchen to wash the smell off her hands. It reminded her sharply of childhood, of climbing trees and rootling around in woodpiles, of damming streams and making mud-pies. It was enough to make her cry again but for less time, and soon she shook herself and climbed the stairs to her attic studio.

The attic floor of the house had been converted into a sort of bedroom by the previous occupants. A decent-sized dormer window had been set into the north side of the sloping roof, and Cherie, on seeing this, had immediately tagged it her 'studio'. She had painted over the fussy floral wallpaper, which covered the walls and ceiling, with white emulsion and pulled off layers of carpet, underlay, newspaper and linoleum to reveal good wide floorboards. One day she would sand and polish them, but until that day she was quite happy to live with the original dark stain.

The room had very little furniture in it: a small double-doored cupboard where she stored all her paints, an easel with a three-legged stool in front of it, a small table, and a plain but very comfortable high-backed chair which stood in one corner. That was where Cherie went and sat when she wanted to work something out, or wanted to get away from Peter.

There was a view of the heath which she particularly wanted to paint, but had not quite understood how to approach until now. From the landing window she could look out over acres of gently rolling turf, divided at intervals by narrow roads. The view she wanted to paint summed up everything she loved and hated about the heath.

First there was the grass itself, so green, so extensive; but oh, so featureless and bare. She could think of no reason why it was kept so monotonous and bald, except that at weekends it was used as a gigantic football pitch complex by local teams. And that hardly seemed a reason.

Surely trees could be planted, lining the roads in tall avenues, and the odd area of wilderness reintroduced — anything to break up the pointless expanse. It was almost as if some ancient race memory lingered on in the minds of the planners, a memory of the time when the word

'Blackheath' was synonymous with wildness, violence and murder.

And perhaps the planners were right. The heath was remarkably free of muggers and rapists. They had nowhere to hide and a long way to run if anyone spotted them.

Cherie pulled on her smock and felt in the big front pocket for charcoal. Then she put a canvas under one arm and her easel under the other, and with some difficulty made her way downstairs to the landing.

She set the easel up in front of a big sash window which was set into a half-landing between the first and second floors. The light wasn't great but the window managed to frame almost every element she wanted to include. There was the ivy-covered fence blazing red against the green; the litter-bin stuck crookedly onto a lamppost, overflowing as usual with cartons, crisp packets, cans and old bottles. The small dead-end slip road was already filled with its quota of salesmen's cars, their depressed-looking drivers staring across to the doors of a popular heathside pub, waiting for them to open. And, yes — there was a group of children from a nearby primary school who were let out at break-time to play on this little corner of the heath. They were what she really wanted to study; the rest she could do from memory.

There were seven of them playing a game together, ridiculously anachronistic figures with their schoolboy hair and grey corduroy shorts. Cherie recognised the game, Ring a Ring of Roses, but was surprised to see that the group was made exclusively of boys, and that they were older than she would have expected.

Then she noticed something else: the game, and the rhyme, didn't stop when it usually did. In fact they seemed to be playing it with distinct local variations.

The first bit was normal enough. Cherie had seen Peter's nephew and two young nieces playing it hilariously over and over again on their parent's green Surrey lawn. Here the boys began to chant, link hands, skip around in a circle, and all collapse at the right moment, but it was at that stage that the game altered. The way she'd seen it played before, the children all collapsed in a heap, before leaping to their feet and beginning all over again. But this time, instead of collapsing heavily, the boys all threw themselves onto their backs, quickly clasping their hands in front of their chests, looking for all the world like the figures on medieval tombs. And then, as soon as they completed that action, all leapt to their feet again, jumping on top of the one who was slowest, chanting what sounded like another verse in a breathless monotone. And each time it happened so quickly that Cherie could hardly catch the words.

She opened the window a couple of inches and let the high clear voices enter the house. Now, they were beginning again.

'Ring a ring of roses,
A pocketful of posies,
Atishoo! Atishoo!
We all fall down.'

Then — and she stuck her head out of the window to hear properly:

'Last one up's an eytie!'

Now that she looked more closely, Cherie noticed that they weren't simply jumping on the slowest member of the group. Each one, in turn, became the last to get up off the ground and the others were not jumping on top of him; they were kneeling down and touching him with their foreheads and only then collapsing on him like the dead, shaking with giggles. Weird.

Cherie bent to her canvas, and tried to gather her thoughts to sketch the last scene before it faded from her mind. Cute.

So why did she shiver? Of course there was nothing wrong — on the surface at any rate — there never was in this country. But it was what went on behind the mask, under the playful facade that frightened her. Children playing: what could be more innocent than that?

Nothing. Except it was all about death. A ring of roses: the first symptoms of the plague. A pocketful of posies: flowers the desperate inhabitants of London kept pressed to their noses to hide the stink of putrefying corpses, and to prevent the evil humours infecting them. Then the sneezing. The onset of fever. The gross swelling of the groin and the armpits. We all fall down. Dead Dead Dead.

'Last one up's . . .'

She strained her ears. No. Not *eytie.* Something else.

And what did that mean? And what about them kneeling in front of the last to get up?

Oh God. My mind's not right. Mad Bitch.

Cherie groaned out loud. 'C'mon,' she said aloud, 'It's kids. Playing. Having fun. Remember what fun is?'

She smiled at the blank canvas, made as if to draw, and then glanced out of the window to refresh her memory

Six children stood in a ring, heads bowed, as the one in the centre stood with his arms outstretched in a gesture of benediction. They all held the pose for a second. Then quickly the group split up and ran back to school screaming with mirth.

Now the heath was empty. Cherie slammed the window shut, shivering in the cold.

Chapter Four

Sebastian Lee arrived at school that same morning with gummed-up eyes and a head that felt empty and light. He'd been woken up by noises from his parents' bedroom in the night and had gone across the hall to investigate.

'Your father's ill. He's got a raging temperature and swollen glands.' His mother made it sound like an accusation. 'Now, go back to bed before you catch anything.'

Sebastian Lee had gone back to bed but had been unable to sleep again. For some reason he kept thinking back to Saturday, to his father's accident in the pond. His fault. And now his father was ill. His fault, too. Everything was his fault. The weather. His school. When his alarm clock went off he jumped. Then he got ready for school.

'Hey!'

Sebastian Lee was standing in the corner of the playground when he thought he heard his name being called. He turned.

Three boys in in his class were standing together and beckoning to him.

'Smegmastian, come over here.'

Sebastian didn't hear them properly. He smiled.

'What is it?'

'Hello, Smegmastian,' said Edward Scruby, one of the boys. Not laughing. Just a tight superior smile on his face.

Suddenly Sebastian Lee realised that he'd walked straight into a trap. For some reason he couldn't wipe the smile off his own face.

'What do you mean? What does it . . .?'

'Doesn't matter really. You came when we called you it. That means you are made of it.'

They all began to collapse into forced giggles.
'Hey! Smegmastian!'
'Over here, Smeggers.'
'Shut up. Shut up!'
'Hey, he's getting batey.'
'Leave me alone, please. Please.'
'Little smeg-man's going to cry.'

Sebastian Lee felt the pressure of tears behind his eyes and his throat become thick with misery. He turned on them, ran at them with his fists flying. He managed to grapple one of them to the ground, and began to thud his fists into the body underneath him, oblivious to the kicks and blows that were raining down on him from either side. He went on and on, ignorant of everything but the fact that an enemy was underneath him and he wanted to punch and tear him until he couldn't hurt him any more. Dimly he registered that he wasn't being punched and pummelled himself any longer. He kept on. The body beneath him stopped moving. Still his fists and elbows thudded into it. He felt exhilarated, free, and powerful.

Suddenly he was up in the air, arms and legs jerking and flailing. A teacher had grabbed him by the collar and lifted him bodily off the ground. Sebastian looked around at the circle of shocked faces then down at what they were staring at. The boy, Charles Knight, lay curled up on his side, motionless. Blood dripped from his nose onto the concrete playground, one eye was already purple and closing, his ear swollen. Sebastian Lee's white face smiled and blood from his split lip streaked his teeth red.

Then the fit passed and he began to shake.

There is no misery as intense as standing in front of your head teacher's desk, trying not to cry. Sebastian Lee had always thought the head teacher very pleasant up until today. Now he was terrible.

'I don't hold with beating, Miles, which is lucky for you and me. I do not know where I would have stopped. Do you know what you've done to that boy? DO YOU KNOW?'

'He called me names, sir. He was teasing me. He always is. I hate him.'

'He called you names.' The voice was sarcastic. 'He called you names. And for that you turn on him as if you were an animal? He's got a broken nose, Miles, two severely bruised eyes which may or may not fully recover, two broken ribs, and severe bruising all over his body. He's in hospital. He might be blind. Blind! His parents are with him. His father has been called from the House of Commons. His mother is inconsolable. Because of you, Miles. It was evil. Do you understand? Wicked. Never have I seen a child behave with such viciousness. We have called your home. Your mother is out. As soon as she arrives home we will ask her to come and pick you up and take you away. You will never come back. I do not want you in my school. Now, do you know where she is?'

Sebastian felt his misery dry up. He felt quite calm now. He couldn't say why.

'She's gone to the hospital, sir, with my father. I think he's very ill.'

The head teacher interpreted this as an ingenious lie. He fancied he could see the boy taking elements from what he had just been told and twisting them into a story designed to gain sympathy. The child was corrupt and irredeemable. Strange that he had always liked him up until now.

'Don't tempt me, boy,' he said. 'Don't tempt me. I am going to lock you in the janitor's office until your mother can be contacted.'

He grabbed Sebastian Lee by the arm and marched him off.

Escaping was so easy, Sebastian Lee assumed they'd meant him to. He simply opened the window, wriggled out and dropped to the ground.

Then he ran.

The school stood quite near the edge of Blackheath. Sebastian's instincts were to run into the middle of it. Fear lifted him. He felt like a full sail, pushed on by terror. He crossed two roads without looking and suddenly the great expanse of green opened in front of him. He ran and ran, uncertain which direction to take, but feeling alive and free. Then seeing the strange fenced-off hummock topped with scraggy shrubs and a single tree he made his way towards it, first at a run, then at a jog. By the time he reached the pond he was walking.

He sat down on its bank. The place was almost unrecognisable from the previous Saturday. In place of the family estate-cars parked by the roadside, backs open, picnics out, there were only a few travelling salesmen sitting in their fleet cars munching sandwiches, windows up. In the distance there was a young woman playing with a small terrier, picking it up, rolling it over and throwing sticks for it, but apart from her the heath was empty. It looked forlorn and barren. A newspaper thrown out of a car window was blown along the ground for two or three hundred yards with nothing to stop it.

Sebastian picked up a handful of pebbles and began tossing them into the water. He noticed that the water level had dropped still further. Nearly two feet of the old pipe stood clear in the middle of the pond, and around the edges the scum of debris had widened perceptibly.

The water lay very still and very black and didn't reflect the sky. Occasionally a breeze would dust its surface with furrows or a small gas bubble would burst. Sebastian took note of the gas bubbles. He had been taught that they were caused by the decomposition of organic matter in the pond. He could tell the teacher that.

Then he remembered that he would not be going back to the school because he was evil. The thought hit him like a blast of pure oxygen. Surely no school would take a boy who was evil. Was that a good thing or a bad thing? A good thing. The evil he had felt in himself when he was hitting Knight made him strong. That was a good thing. To be strong was obviously good. But the evil . . . had it also made his father ill? Then again, his father had hit him on the ear. Sebastian became aware of the terrible responsibility of his powers. His father going into hospital seemed a little bit extreme. An earache like the one he had had would have been appropriate. He would have to be more careful in future. Sebastian took up his contemplation of the pond again. No weeds grew in it, no waterlilies. It was dead soup. An evil pond. Sebastian concentrated all his newly discovered powers on the pond and the headmaster.

'O pond,' he chanted, 'may your evil power of wickedness and my evil power of wickedness strive against he who is ghastly and foul, my headmaster, Mr Appleby.'

Sebastian felt a thrill course through him. A white hot pillar seemed to be burning in his chest. He closed his eyes.

'O ghastly powers of great vile evil, come to my aid.'

A massive bubble burst on the surface of the pond, and Sebastian Lee felt a shock run through him. A smell of old earth and bad eggs drifted across the water. He stood up and peered timidly at the water. Bubbles rose again, smaller this time, but numerous. It was happening. It was really happening. Sebastian Lee felt his throat contract and his mouth dry up. He desperately wanted to pee. The black water swirled and eddied. Now he was sure there was something there, something that moved. It grew in a milky cloud of yellow silt that rose and stained the pond water.

He tried to run but couldn't. The smell was overpowering. He was trapped by his terror, his evil, the power he had released. Then the black water bellied and shattered, and for a second before he shut his eyes and screamed he saw a figure break the surface; greet him with liquid eyes and swollen face. Then sink again, wrapped in its wet envelope of black.

The boy turned. He felt the earth tilt beneath him as he tried to launch himself at the swooping horizon. Then he collapsed.

Cherie, who was walking along the heath, saw the boy

collapse from some distance away. When he did not get up again she ran over and covered him with her jacket before yelling at another passer-by to call for an ambulance. Police and ambulance arrived not long afterwards, thanked her, and took the child off.

Sebastian Lee was taken to hospital for a check-up, and then driven home in an ambulance. He recovered well and was very polite to the policewoman and the doctor.

No, he didn't know what he was doing on the heath or why he wasn't in school. He couldn't remember the name of his school or why he had fainted. He hadn't slept well the night before and he was worried about his father who was ill. He showed a momentary flicker of unease when the policewoman asked him if a man had shown him anything or touched him, but after consideration he shook his head and said no.

Mrs Miles was asked to keep an eye on him and let him rest a day or two. She agreed distractedly.

She had a lot on her mind. Her husband had been admitted to hospital that morning with a temperature of 103 and swellings in his groin and his armpits. The young doctor had been very nice and had reassured her that it was no longer fatal. When she asked him what he meant he had called the disease *pasteurella pestis.*

She had asked him to speak in English and he had called it the plague.

And back on the heath, the corpse Sebastian Lee had seen floated to the surface of the pond again in its own good time, filled by the gases of decomposition. This time the gases did not escape as it broke the surface and the body was carried by a gentle breeze to the shore where it lay with all the other discarded rubbish for a while. It was spotted in the early evening by a man out walking his dog. Fortunately the team who pulled it out of the water wore heavy gloves and boots, for the autopsy would show that it had died of the plague.

Chapter Five

Cherie threw down her magazine and swung her legs onto the floor. Her head buzzed because she had rebelliously turned the central heating up way above the prescribed temperature, almost to greenhouse levels, and she was straining her eyes to read because she couldn't be bothered to turn on the standard lamp. She had promised herself that she would take the rest of the day off, but now, in the middle of the afternoon, she was bored. She wondered if the point about giving yourself an afternoon off was the anticipation as much as the act. On top of that there was something in her make-up which tended to label relaxation as *doing nothing*. She decided to go to the local library.

Memory of the vision had more or less faded leaving an empty tiredness, like the after-effects of a bad electric shock, as well as a growing curiosity about the convent. In fact there were a number of things she wanted to find out more about, that strange game the kids had been playing in their break, for one. She was shocked to realise how little she knew or thought about the neighbourhood, her destiny, her husband . . .

To get to the library she had to cut across a corner of the heath and walk a little way into the village. A heavy mist was lying around, moving in lazy swathes across the turf, and the damp seemed to flow up through the soles of her shoes and creep into her bones. The air was the colour of a dirty pancake and shopkeepers had already put their lights on outside the short parade of shops that lined the heath.

Cherie walked down past the secondhand bookstands

and the Oxfam shop before turning left into the narrow passage which led to the library. It was smaller than she had expected. The librarians stood in a square booth in the middle of the floor. Books lined the walls or stood in tatty paperback stands in the corner. There were sections for children's books . . . biography . . . fiction . . . local history. She picked up a couple of books from that shelf. One was called *Blackheath: Village and Environs*; the other *Heath Views and Memories: Fifty Years a Local.*

The only seats were on tiny short-legged plastic chairs placed in front of the children's section. Cherie lowered her bottom gingerly, wincing as the plastic groaned, and looked nervously at the librarian who paid her no attention at all.

She opened the first book and began to read:

To the casual visitor, stopping in this enchanting backwater as he pauses in his journey . . .

A man began to cough. She had noticed him when she came in; elderly, bearded, heavy wool coat, green Alpine hat, beard. The cough began as a liquid clearing of the lungs, caught like a ratchet, built to a hoarse, gurgling climax and ended with a muffled dribbling as he expectorated into a clean white handkerchief held up to the mouth. When he had finished (the handkerchief neatly folded and placed carefully into the flapped coat pocket), he looked haughtily round the room, asserting his right as an Englishman to revolt whom he wanted when he wanted.

Cherie lowered her eyes to her book again.

Origins of the village are unclear. We first find mention of it in . . .

Cherie's throat began to tickle. She gave a muffled 'humph'.

Certainly its proximity to the great river Thames would have had some bearing on its development but it seems more likely that . . .

She coughed again, automatically and louder. Her eyes flickered upwards. The man was looking away now but she was sure that he had been staring right at her. He's crazy, thought Cherie, he's a malicious cougher. He travels between libraries disgusting people then making them cough. He takes a sick pleasure from it.

The man cleared his throat nonchalantly. Then again. The wet motor started up. Cherie thought she might have to leave.

Within living memory Blackheath possessed a rural, Kentish flavour, now, alas, a thing of the past as the gimcrack suburban tide has . . .

Cherie felt the ominous itch start high in the back of her throat. NO. NOT AGAIN. Hell. Someone walked through the swing doors, breaking her concentration, and a real cough forced its way from her lips. This time the man did look at her. Cherie stared back, transfixed by his watery eyes, the damp pink lips poking out from the dry hairy beard like . . . like . . . Urrgh.

Mad Bitch. But he's going to cough again and I CAN'T BEAR IT!!!

She stared at him, wide-eyed, pale and strained. The man started, then regained his composure, closed the book he was reading, and walked over to the librarian's desk.

'Just the one this week.' He left, a model of propriety, with *Great Naval Engagements of the Eighteenth Century* tucked under one arm. Cherie returned to the book, flicked to the index and ran her finger down the C's. Convent, p. 73.

Though known locally as, and referred to commonly by the name of the Convent, this edifice is in fact more correctly known as The Retreat.

Cherie's eyes slid over the confusing and pompous prose. Concentrate, woman, she thought.

Though records do not exist locally (I will discuss the reasons for this in greater depth below), this author was able to ascertain through his own researches certain points which he believes bear testimony to an interesting aspect of local history.

The Sisters of Mercy and Vigilance are in fact a rare Protestant order of nuns, although belonging to neither the established Anglican Church nor indeed any of the better known dissenting offshoots. At this point the reader might think of some of the more disreputable 'orders' or 'cults' whose frequent exposures in the popular press have led to subsequent investigations by the organs of authority, but he will be relieved to hear that the Order of the Sisters of Mercy and Vigilance has a tranquil history stretching three hundred years into the mists of time, to the glorious era of the Carolean Restoration no less, and in that time no whiff of corruption has ever sullied their reputation, or even as one might even say, tainted their odour of sanctity.

Cherie groaned at this point and went into fast forward. Main order based in Lincolnshire . . . Founded by local landowner with estates in Kent and Lincolnshire in 1676. Unusual . . . Building on Heath actually silent retreat for contemplation . . . Then . . .

A word about the building might be in order here for parts are reputed to date back to the 17th century when the order was founded. There is an oblique reference to be found in the journals of Thomas Liveridge, a merchant of Woolwich who wanted to improve his position by the erection of a country villa in Blackheath, to the paucity of stonemasons in the neighbourhood owing to their all being employed on the construction of the convent. He makes the intriguing comment that when he visited the site to make enquiries he was set upon by ruffians with a large and fearsome dog, and moreover could see no masons employed at work on the building. One can only wonder where they were employed, or perhaps, this author dares to suggest, the famous British Tea Break, unknown in more industrious nations, has its origins further back in time than we suspect.

'Oh, brother,' Cherie moaned aloud, and this time the librarian looked up. Cherie gave her a vague smile and continued to read.

Alas, unfortunate Victorian additions have obscured the original pattern of the house, though the portico remains, as does some of the original brickwork and fenestration on the east wing. Perhaps, however, this is not as unfortunate as it seems as contemporary comments generally centred on its 'lack of grace' and 'unseemly bulk', phrases which suggest that the original was in fact an eyesore.

Strange, thought Cherie, but that seemed to be coming out when they knocked some walls down, as if the original shape were emerging from within. She read on, but there was no more of interest and she turned to the other book, the memoir: *Heath Views and Memories.*

There was no index to this book; it was an affable if vague account of the author's childhood, adulthood and incipient senility in Blackheath. Cherie picked a bit at random.

In those days I remember the air above the heath was alive with birds and in the summer danced with the many-coloured butterflies attracted by the rich gardens all around. For poor boys like us from the Peabody buildings the heath was a magic garden all of our own. We played the length and breadth of it in the long summer evenings, from the stone walls of St Michael's to Point Hill; from the old gorse-filled gravel pits to the old Convent, where woe betide you if you got in for the nuns kept large and vicious dogs patrolling free in the grounds which would have the seat of your pants as soon as look at you.

Cherie raised her eyebrows. Two references to the convent and each one mentioning guard dogs. Logically, she supposed, it made sense. A silent order couldn't very well yell at mischievous kids to get out of the vegetable garden, but it was a disturbing, somehow rather obscene thought, that this oasis of calm and contemplation was only maintained by teeth that could rend and tear.

She skimmed a bit more but that was the last reference to the convent she could find. She flicked through the pages hoping to pick up the odd word that might strike a chord.

Yes! There! Except as soon as she saw the word she had flipped too far forward and lost it.

'Closing please.'

Not wanting to break her concentration Cherie held up a hand, meaning 'please give me five minutes,' but the librarian was dully adamant.

'Time, PLEASE.'

Cherie saw the last reader walk out of the door with a smug expression on her face.

'Sorry, I'm just —'

'No. We really must close.'

Cherie felt quite irrationally angry.

'Look, just give me five —'

'Are you a member?'

'Of course I'm not!'

The librarian stepped back, shocked. Suddenly Cherie realised that she was much angrier than she need be, that in fact the librarian might be trying to help.

She attempted to gush.

'Look, I'm really sorry, but I was in the middle of trying to remember something. I was really rude, wasn't I? I really am sorry. Is there any way I could join, even temporarily? I mean, I'll bring this back tomorrow.'

The librarian sighed. 'Have you got any identification on you, with your name and address?'

'Yes.'

'Well then, I'll do you a card right now and you can take the book with you. But, please, it would have helped if you had done this earlier.'

She scribbled out a card for Cherie who left feeling relieved and guilty. She walked quickly back to her home and settled back down on the sofa.

This book at least made Blackheath come a little bit alive. She read about the impact the new suburban steam line into central London had made on the village, and how the farmlands around had gradually been swallowed up by row upon row of suburban houses, the heath gradually metamorphosing from wasteland to recreational land in the process. The writer pointed out that Blackheath was a sort of no-man's-land between the town and the country. For those leaving London it was the first stretch of wilderness on the way down to Kent and the Channel ports. Until one hundred and fifty years ago, travellers who had just struggled up the steep hill from Deptford must have looked warily at the great rolling waste of gorse and bush and furze stretching out on either side of the road.

But the whole process could be reversed when you entered London from the country. Then it would have been the obvious place to stop before the last push into the City. Henry VIII had met Anne of Cleves here for the first time, and here the peasants of the Peasants' Revolt had gathered, lingering perhaps, and wondering whether or not they should turn back. Here too Charles II had been rapturously greeted by the victorious army of the Restoration.

But whichever way you looked at it, the author concluded, a sort of brooding wildness still clung to the heath's billiard-table flatness. It was a funny place at night, he said.

Cherie turned a few more pages. Then she stiffened.

It always amuses me to read the way other boroughs puff themselves up with famous associations: Keats in Hampstead, Blake in Chelsea, Kensington with its Royals, and the like. All these associations are true, but none of them has a name in their past to touch The White Man of Blackheath, our own local hobgoblin or bogeyman. No one knows his origins but every Blackheath schoolchild will tell you that if teacher does not get you for fibbing, The White Man or Old Whitey will.

There are even rhymes about him that are dying out, more's the pity, but when I was a lad they used to be sung in the playgrounds.

I'd rather hop the way to Neath
Than see Old Whitey on the heath.

I'd crawl to Edinburgh and back
To get Old Whitey off my back.

Cherie put the book down, something nagging at the back of her mind. She glanced at the clock. Oh, my God! The time! Peter's supper. As she got up, her eyes slid along the mantelpiece to where she had propped up the old cross which she had found that morning. The words '*Last one up's a Whitey*' fell into her mind; she remembered the schoolboys on the heath playing their games with sweet seriousness; she remembered the unfamiliar coda to *Ring of Roses* she had puzzled over; Whitey, not Eytie. Twit. Whitey must have been the word she had seen in the library. But as she remembered, something happened. It was like watching a badly edited film. One second the cross was standing upright; the next it was as if the film had jumped and the cross was toppling from the mantelpiece to fall on the floor.

Perhaps if she had not been in such a hurry Cherie would have thought this a bit strange, but as it was she simply put it down to the cross being badly propped up and hurried into the kitchen to start rummaging in the back of her freezer to find the small joint of beef she knew was in there somewhere.

Chapter Six

Dusk was now curling round the corners of the heath. The group of demonstrators who had gathered by the old convent shuffled and stamped like uneasy horses as the temperature dropped a crucial degree and added cold to the tally of their discomfort. They'd draped old sheets daubed with slogans over the railings on either side of the gates — NO TO BIG MONEY; PEOPLE YES — PROFITS NO; WE WANT OUR PLAYGROUND — but the lettering was fast becoming invisible in the gloom. A wind which had been gusting in from the east now became raw and penetrating; a few drops of rain spluttered and hissed on a mail-order barbecue someone had brought out to act as a brazier.

The nucleus of the group was formed by a young couple, Penny Barton and Jake Paxford. Around them clustered a group of concerned citizens who had decided that a 24-hour picket was necessary to gain publicity. In mid afternoon a TV crew from Spotlight South East, a local TV news programme, had arrived but they hadn't really wanted to film unless the demolition ball was actually swinging. In fact the site foreman had happened to see the television van arrive and had told his crew to stop work for as long as they were there. That was the sort of attention to detail his employers appreciated.

The workmen left. Some of the demonstrators shouted 'Scabs' in a half-hearted sort of way. 'Wankers!' the demolition crew shouted back cheerfully.

With the workmen gone, the demonstrators began to lose interest in their vigil. The small group melted away into the night, someone pushing the barbecue along with them. Penny could hear its tiny wheels squeaking across the heath long after the people had disappeared into the darkness. Only she and Jake were left; Penny on a point of principle, Jake because he didn't want to seem weak willed. But after a while he suggested tentatively that they pack it in and get some rest. At least then they'd be fresh in the morning. Maybe they could raise it at a council meeting. There were elections coming up, after all.

'Do what you want. Go if you want.' Penny snapped at him.

'Come on. You must have feelings either way.'

'I really don't care.'

'Come on, Penny, what's the matter? Tell me.'

'Nothing's the matter.'

'Look. You know I'm right. What is it that's keeping you here?'

'You know what it is. I don't believe in giving up.' But she knew that wasn't the truth. It was a bad idea and she was trapped into sticking by it, or at least she felt as if she were.

'Come on, Pen.'

'Come on your fucking self, Jake.'

'Damn this.'

Silence.

'Christ almighty, Penny. I'm not standing here just to be brushed off by you time and time again. If you want support you should begin by trying not to alienate everyone who wants to help. I'm off. You can damn well stop the bulldozers by yourself.'

'Piss off then. It's what you wanted in the first place.'

'Oh God, what's the use. See you in the morning,' Jake stumped off.

'Bastard,' Penny muttered under her breath. Then, out loud, 'And you're not staying in my flat.'

She went back to her vigil, confident that he'd return.

But, alone on the heath, Penny began to wonder whether she'd made the right decision. For one thing the temperature seemed to drop at least five degrees after Jake left; for another the darkness on the centre of the heath stopped being simply an absence of light, and became a shifting and unfamiliar element.

Also, if she faced the shattered ruin, bulking jagged and black against the low clouds, she had her back to the empty and unlit heath; if she faced the heath she became horribly aware of the ruin behind her, its black windows, empty of all reflecting glass, boring into her back like lunatic's eyes.

Penny decided to walk around the house. That should be OK. That way she'd have the heath and the hall on either side and she could look quickly from one to the other.

She did a circuit. Halfway round she could see the comforting cluster of street-lights around Blackheath village and she felt reassured. The fake stage-coach lamps were lit outside a large pub on the edge of the heath, between the ruin and the village, but even as she stared they seemed to shrink to little puddles of yellow, which only emphasised the darkness. Three police cars burrowed along the Dover Road, their sirens wailing and snickering. Even that seemed comforting tonight. Penny decided that walking was better than standing still and it wasn't until her third circuit that she began to feel that she was being followed.

It started as a strange and compelling sense that the empty space behind her was no longer empty but contained something which hated her. 'I mustn't run,' Penny thought, 'mustn't bolt. Mustn't show that I'm scared.' Then she realised that this might be her last chance for getting away from whoever was following her, and anyway who needed that macho stuff about not showing they were scared.

She increased her pace to an irregular half-jog and made for a solitary street-lamp forty yards away. She remembered a ramble she and Jake had gone on during a holiday in Calabria when their way had been blocked by a large and very vicious Italian dog. Hadn't Jake walked up to it, carelessly saying over his shoulder that the thing to do was not to show fear? Hadn't the dog battened onto his outstretched hand with an hysterical scream of pleasure? Hadn't they spent seven hours in hospital while his hand was disinfected and sewn up and someone had been sent to try and ascertain if the dog had rabies? Still that was Jake for you.

Jake! Of course. He must have come back. That must be who she had sensed on the heath.

She was standing in a pool of light about ten yards across. In the light there was nothing, and the night formed such a solid wall outside it that an army could have been performing manouevres beyond and she would have noticed nothing. If Jake was out there she'd never see him. And would he see her? He would have gone straight to the gates, then done the obvious thing and walked round by the railings. The overwhelming desire to get near Jake struggled with her fear inside her.

'Jake! Jake!'

Her voice sounded pathetic and small.

'JAKE!'

No! Not too much noise, just in case.

He must be round the other side. Desire to see him overcame fear, and she made off, still calling. She had to let him know that she was still here or he'd go straight home.

'Jake, it's me, Penny.'

Penny made one circuit, calling his name all the time. Then just in case he was walking in the same direction, turned and went round the opposite way. Nothing. Suppose he'd also changed direction? She went back again; the sense of being followed disappeared.

'So I'm alone again,' Penny thought. 'And freezing my tits off.'

She hugged herself, stamped her feet and began to jog on the spot. Then stopped because she felt ridiculous. She didn't notice that she'd inched back towards the railings, while jogging.

Her foot caught on something. She stumbled.

The arms that reach out from the railings to catch her seem very long. They give an impression of great strength. At first Penny is too surprised to cry out. She feels herself trip and then suddenly is cradled in careful arms.

Jake?

No. There is none of his trembling uncertainty; instead a terrible deliberation as she is pulled backwards towards the railing with a smooth movement which is almost hydraulic. Her head is jammed against the railings, her cry of shock, outrage almost, becomes a grunt of pain as she feels the terrible force try to pull her through too narrow a gap.

And then incredibly she realises that it is not stopping.

No! It's impossible. It just won't fit.

The scalp tears and bone is compressed. And only when the shoulders and chest of the now dead Penny refuse to be squeezed through the gap is the body dropped to the ground and pulled under the railings with the speed and deftness of a conjuring trick.

Twenty minutes later Jake returned. When he saw that Penny wasn't by the gates any more, he marched around the railings calling her name lustily. Then, reasoning that she might have been following behind him on his circuit, walked swiftly in the other direction. On arriving back at the gates, he swore.

For maybe half a minute he stood by the gates, then shook his head and walked back to the bicycle he'd left propped against the lamp post. Furious with himself, but even more furious with Penny for simply pissing off after all that fuss, he swung his leg over the saddle and freewheeled slowly down the hill to Lewisham.

Chapter Seven

'Oh, and, Constable?'

'Yes, Sarge.'

'Get us some fags as well.'

'Just as well we're not in the States, Sarge. You know it means —'

'Yes, Constable. Senior Service.'

'Very butch, Sarge.'

'That'll be all. Oh, and, Constable . . .'

'Yes, Sarge?'

'Don't keep calling me Sarge.'

'Yessir.'

Sergeant Willis wheezed throatily for the benefit of the retreating Constable. Almost every noise he made was throaty. It came from the thick tar of approximately fifty thousand cigarettes which had been coating his voicebox and lungs since his first playground puff aged fifteen. The way you smoke, everybody said, anyone'd think you wanted to die. But Willis didn't want to die. He just didn't want to give up smoking. Couldn't, if he was being honest, and in his book 'didn't want' and 'couldn't' amounted to the same thing.

Willis was popular in the station with his subordinates. Never reluctant to pass on tips, never over-anxious, and uncompetitive. He wasn't nearly as bluff and hearty as he made out, but he knew the image suited him well, so he worked at it.

His superiors saw him differently. To them he was an embarrassment, a good policeman, but an embarrassment. With all his years in the force he could have made a much higher rank, but he had never shown the slightest desire to further his career, opting to remain at the level where he knew he worked best and knew he was happiest.

He didn't give a monkey's fuck if he was a permanent reminder to some of his harassed senior colleagues that their last promotion, the one they seemed to stick at no matter what, was their final foundering on the shoals of incompetence.

'You're promoted until you can't do the job you're given, and there you stay,' he'd tell young recruits. 'Don't fall into that trap.' And they'd walk away feeling older, more mature, and one-up on their superiors.

What made Willis particularly awkward was that he knew more about his job than anyone else in the station, and yet he never let on what thoughts were behind his rough, lined face and his blank tawny eyes. His face was a mask. In fact Sergeant Willis was a moral coward and he hated responsibility. He knew this, but preferred to keep everybody else guessing.

The door to the Mini Metro opened and Constable Havelock got in, a packet of Capstan Full Strength in his pocket and two polystyrene cups of take-away coffee in his hands.

'Where to, Sarge?' asked Havelock.

'We'll just drive up to the heath I think. May as well park there and have a quick recce.'

Havelock started the engine, and, after checking the mirrors with elaborate caution, drove off up the hill.

The Billet Road police station had received a spate of calls during the night from an area of about four streets. The complaints were substantially the same: noises outside the front door, gates opening and shutting, dustbins clattering, and strange scratching sounds. But nobody had reported any break-ins and the panda car which had been dispatched to investigate had not found anything to report. Still, they were honour-bound to follow up the reports. A Neighbourhood Watch Scheme had just been started in the area, and if the citizenry were keeping their side of the bargain, the force really had to keep theirs.

The Constable swung right off Lewisham Hill and pulled up a side road which cut across a corner of the heath.

'What's the procedure then, Sarge?'

'Just routine. We'll ring on doorbells, ask the good citizens about last night, be excruciatingly polite. And see if we can find anything in the cold light of day.'

Willis slurped noisily at the styrofoam cup.

'Ever done this sort of work before?'

'Er, not really, no.'

'Best I don't try and give you any hints then. Be natural.'

'Thanks, Sarge.'

'Think nothing of it. Right then, finished your coffee?'

Havelock had hardly been able to take a sip of the hot liquid which smelt of caramel and tasted like burnt toast.

'No, sir.'

'Two qualities a good copper needs, Constable. Possibly the two most important. Know what they are?'

'No, Sarge,' Havelock answered smartly, anticipating one of Willis's aphorisms.

'An asbestos gullet and the bladder capacity of a horse. You'd be amazed how useful they are.'

'Right sir. Where to now?'

Willis gave him an address and they drove off down the empty road.

At the first house no one was in; at the second the man who answered the door, though patently deaf, said that his wife had imagined hearing the whole thing and it was all a ridiculous fuss about nothing. In fact, he said, he would like to apologise for her having wasted so much valuable police time, because with the streets crawling with vermin, (he knew, he'd seen it), they had much more important things to do than chase wild geese.

Here Willis interrupted him by telling him that a number of people in the street had called independently, asking him to stay on the lookout, and thanking him for his time.

'Notice anything yet?'

'The old sod wasn't very nice to his wife?'

'Apart from that.'

Havelock thought. 'Can't say I did really, no.' He looked around. They were standing in a quiet tree-lined street. On one side stood solid Edwardian houses, some of which had obviously been turned into flats. On the other side there was no pavement, only a brambly bank interspersed with sycamore trees. Behind that towered a ten-foot-high wall marking the ends of the next street's back gardens. Set into the wall at regular intervals were wooden doors.

'What about the doors, sir?' Havelock asked.

Willis gave them his attention. 'Possibly, though I'd guess they haven't been opened for years.'

Havelock crossed the road and checked the nearest one. The blue paint was peeling, and the wood looked pretty rotten. Tentatively he put his shoulder against it and pushed. The door was locked or jammed solid and the wood would break before anyone could open it from this side. He sniffed the air (use all your senses he'd been told). Yes. There was something, a taint, just strong enough to register, but thick too, and when he thought about it, rather disgusting.

'You're right, sir. Nothing — just a funny smell.'

'Yeah, I caught a whiff of that,' Willie answered. 'Something's long dead around here. My guess is that someone's cat just died and they heaved her out of the car window. Ground's probably littered with the bones of dear departed Fidos and Tibbies.'

'Yeah.' Havelock thought a moment. 'Plenty of undergrowth as well. Could have been a gang of kids larking around. Street's badly lit, too.'

Willis nodded. 'We'll see. Let's see if we can get some sense out of someone who actually lives here.'

At the next house they struck lucky. The door was opened by an elderly lady in a good-quality suit with a mauve cardigan thrown over her slightly hunched shoulders. Oh, yes. She'd been awake and had heard quite a lot. Willis asked if they could come in and take an informal statement and she said she'd be delighted. One saw so few people these days. If they'd just sit down she'd make them a cup of Nescafé.

'Well now,' she began, after offering them milk and sugar and digestives. 'Last night. Let's see. I'm a light sleeper at the best of times — most old people are, you know — and last night I had particular difficulty in dropping off.' (She pronounced it orf.) 'Usually I read, but last night I was too restless for some reason or other, so I propped up the pillows and turned on the World Service. It's a great help to people like me. It makes me so angry when I hear of the Government trying to cut it back. As if it were a hedge or something shrubby. Anyway, I listened to a discussion on Islam as a world religion — but I'm afraid I dozed off with Mohammed still having visions in the wilderness because the next thing I heard was the tail end of the news.'

'Which edition?' asked Havelock.

'It was the three o'clock bulletin. Anyway, I wondered what it was that could have woken me up. I'm such a light sleeper that the slightest noise ... Last night I had the feeling that something wasn't quite right. I'm sorry. I don't suppose you're very interested in feelings.'

Willis made a gesture to suggest that they were.

'Well. After the news there was a programme on Satie, the composer. I've never liked him much, and after last night with all those notes dropping around I like him even less. Then I heard the first noise. A dustbin lid coming off.'

'A clanging?' Willis interrupted.

'Not exactly. Those plastic lids clatter rather than clang.'

'Where exactly did it come from?'

'Next-door, up the road — number twenty. I thought nothing of it. A cat. One of those urban foxes we're all meant to be so proud of. But then I heard another sound. A soft thud as if someone had fallen over, and a sort of rustle as if they'd landed in a bush. Clumsy fox, I thought, and got out of bed to have a look.'

'Excuse me a minute,' Willis cut in again. 'Did you turn the light on?'

'Oh no. You can't see a thing if you do that. And besides I was rather sold on my urban fox theory and didn't want to startle it. I pulled the curtains back. It was dark last night. No moon. I didn't see anything. Or rather I didn't see *something*.'

Willis noticed that the tiny muscles in her mouth had tightened, and faint lines of strain appeared about her eyes. He was about to bring the interview to an end when something stopped him. The woman had been careful about fixing every detail in her mind; she didn't strike him as the fanciful type. He gave a sympathetic grunt.

'You mean you saw something, but couldn't make out what it was? Could have been a dog but then again could have been a cat?'

'No, I wish it were as simple as that. Believe me, this isn't very easy to explain and you must think I'm a ridiculous old ... what do they call old people nowadays? Wrinklies. You must think I'm a batty old wrinkly. No. I ...'

She seemed to be struggling for words.

'Perhaps you should just give us your impressions, in that case.'

'Very well. There was a presence out there last night. An evil presence. I'm sorry to sound so silly but that's what it was. I got a very strong sense of it. It was . . . it was terrifying. Not because of anything it did, or looked like, but because of a terrible sense that last night it was just out playing around.'

'I'm sorry, madam, but are you saying you *sensed* this?'

'Yes! I was terribly scared. I still am.' The woman was sitting bolt upright, looking defiant. It was easy to see that telling them this was difficult, not least because it involved a certain loss of pride on her part. Willis noted her difficulty, and though he was anxious to get away, he was reluctant to hurt her feelings still further by leaving too suddenly. She solved the problem by getting up and ushering them to the door. But there Willis remembered something.

'By the way. Do you have any interest in local politics by any chance?'

The woman looked surprised. 'How very strange,' she answered. 'Do you know you're the second person to ask me that in two days. Only yesterday Mr Smith from up the road tried to persuade me to put an election poster on my door. I'm afraid I'm rather apolitical these days and told him so. I agreed but told him I'd be honour-bound to put up any others I was asked to. He didn't seem to mind.'

Willis and Havelock walked up the street to their car.

'Funny old bird,' said Havelock. 'Didn't miss much, did she?' But what's all that nonsense about a 'presence'? And local politics. Oh, I get it! All the houses have got election posters in their windows. You mean it might be someone trying to freak out everyone with that guy's poster in the window?'

'Something like that. Mind you, it's more likely a local heritage society. Look at those posters. They're vile.'

They were. On a shiny white background sat a bright red day-glo cross with the candidate's name underneath. The white and the red seemed to glow and pulsate even on that overcast day.

'Bring out your dead,' Willis muttered.

'What?'

'Bring out your dead. In the plague you put a red cross on your front door when someone inside was dead. Then the carts would know where to stop. The bodies would be piled up on top of them and dumped in mass graves.'

'Eeeurgh.'

'Yeah. Eeeurgh.'

They drove around the remaining address on their list, stopping at each one, asking a few questions. Nobody could add anything to the old lady's statement. Few had anything to say at all. Still, as Willis pointed out, it was a good public relations exercise. Back on the heath he asked Havelock to stop.

'Right,' he said, after lighting up a cigarette. 'This doesn't make anything easier, but we can't overlook it because it's the only lead we've got. Every single house which reported a disturbance last night had an election poster up in a front window. So far I've counted ten in the neighbourhood with this man' — he looked at his notes — 'Peter McQuade's poster up. Of those ten houses, eight were disturbed last night. Nobody who didn't have a poster up reported anything. It is possible that someone's got a grudge against this particular candidate. It doesn't explain everything, like certain things that our star witness noticed, but perhaps she's not quite as together as she sounded. Perhaps she imagined a bit of it, though I must say . . .'

Willie's musings were interrupted by a tap on the window. A worried-looking elderly man, thin and frail and with a tiny pot belly, was stooping down and gesturing anxiously for Willis to wind the window down.

'Officer, I don't want to bother you. I really feel a most frightful fool. It's just that I can't quite bring myself . . .'

Willis set his face into a pleasant and helpful expression. The man put two hands on the window, hooking his fingers round the top of the glass and appeared to gather himself.

'Officer, I've just found a corpse in my compost.'

Havelock was out of the car like a shot. Then he realised that he'd left the car engine running. Willis's exit was calmer and more dignified.

'Now, sir', he said, deliberately speaking calmly and slowly. 'A body, you say. In the compost.'

'Yes, yes, yes. It was, it really was, a most terrible shock. My poor lady wife is upstairs in the spare bedroom wondering what on earth is going on, but I insisted that she wait somewhere that didn't overlook the back garden. I was just going to ask my neighbour to advise me when I saw your car. I say, I do hope I haven't ruined proper procedure or anything. I mean I would hate to impose on your valuable time. I just saw your car and ran out.'

Willis cut him off with a hand movement. The man's

nervous preamble had taken them two or three houses down the road which ran parallel with Frinton Road.

He's found a body and he's worried about wasting time, thought Willis. Some people really did take politeness to extremes.

They were ushered into the front garden of a large, detached Edwardian house, whose back garden, Willis guessed, must actually back onto Frinton Road. Glancing upwards he saw a nervous and taut face staring at them from a window.

'My wife,' the man said. Willis nodded gravely at her.

He led them hurriedly through a square and darkly-panelled entrance hall and into a large sitting-room with french windows giving onto the lawn. The man gestured to the high wall at the end. Willis could see the compost heap steaming gently in the cold, still air.

'It's there. This really is most frightfully kind.' The man's voice had gained a childish tremor.

'There's really no need to apologise.'

'Oh, but —'

Willis interrupted him firmly.

'Would you like to show us, sir?'

'Yes. Yes. Very well.'

Reluctantly.

He led them straight across the lawn but stopped a good ten feet short of the dark mound. 'If you don't mind I'll just stay here. It's on the other side.'

His commentary accompanied the two policeman as they approached. Even over the sweet rotten smell of the decomposing vegetation, they could smell something strong and vile.

'I was just turning the compost, as one must, you know, and was standing to one side, there in the nettles, so I could fork some of the mulch at the back over to the front. Suddenly I, I mean the fork jabbed into something and seemed to stick. I — I leant over to get more purchase and it sort of — ripped. Something tore, I could feel it. And then the smell. This awful smell. I bent over to look and on the fork ends . . . what I saw was . . . oh, my Lord, I think you'll have to excuse me.'

Willis heard the sound of dry painful retching. He led the way to the back of the heap, treading gingerly over neat stacks of earthenware pots and a roll of chicken wire. His junior followed.

It was hard at first to make anything out. Without dusk actually falling, something had gone out of the light and colours were drained. Loose wads of compost covered something, but it was the smell, the unmistakeable stench of ancient meat which told them first that something was there, and was very dead.

Willis spotted an old fork shaft lying in some leaves. He picked it up and flicked some lumps of compost away. It was hard to make out the body, but gradually shapes began to make sense and relate to one another, like spotting a chameleon in a wildlife photograph. They came in no particular order: a shoulder, a hip, a foot, an arm lying like a broken branch. The corpse was curled in the foetal position, or would have been before it had been disturbed by the rude probings of the fork. A dark liquid, Willis hesitated to think of it as blood, was running slowly from a split in the body's side.

Willis frowned. 'Get on the radio, Havelock. Report in. No particular hurry but we can't leave this here all night. OK?'

He moved away, signalling that Havelock should too. 'Come back here as soon as you've done that. All right, off you go. I want a word with this gentleman.'

'Yessir. At once.' As Havelock walked away, his footsteps leaving dark stains on the pale lawn, he felt moved by a sense of awe. His first body, a bad one at that, and he hadn't even gagged. Then he stopped in mid stride. Hadn't even gagged. Hadn't even seen it! What sort of wally would Willis take him for? He'd think he didn't have the guts. He debated for a split second whether he should go back, decided that it would make him seem too much like an eager young rookie, but resolved to have a long look when he returned.

Willis approached the old man, who was still standing in the middle of the lawn. 'Now then, sir, I'll have to take a formal statement from you later on, but for the minute there's one thing puzzling me. When was the last time you went to the compost heap?'

'Two days ago. Yes, most definitely, the day before yesterday.'

'And you didn't notice anything? No smell?'

'No, no. Absolutely not.'

'And would you have disturbed, er, it?'

'Well that's the frightful thing. I think I would. Yes, because I was forking off from the back. You see — oh, it's just too terrible. To think I might have . . . and not noticed.'

Willis led him indoors, and tried to think while the man fussed around with the lights. Willis said he might go up and reassure his wife. Above all he wanted some time alone, so when the old man came back into the room accompanied by Havelock, Willis asked the Constable to start taking a statement, checked his torch and walked out again into the dusk.

It just wasn't the place to find a corpse, Willis thought. He knew that wasn't a particularly sensible thing to believe; bodies often turn up in the strangest places, especially in suburbia, but lots of things seemed to contradict what his senses had told him.

He left the room and stood on the step. A wide immaculate lawn, almost laundered, swept down to the great high wall at the end of the garden. A sycamore had dropped half its fretted leaves which lay in neat piles on the lawn's edge. The flower beds were sparse but weedless, a rose bed bristled with newly pruned bushes. Obsessive maybe, but ordered and protected. There was no way into the garden from the front except through the house. The end and side walls were high. Try as he might he couldn't see the old man manhandling a corpse either through the house or over the walls. Or anyone else for that matter.

He reached the end of the garden again. The torch beam in the twilight somehow diluted the horror of it, picking bits of the scene like official photographs. Willis swung the beam about, more out of habit than anything else, then paused. The beam held on the flaked paint of a wooden door set into the wall, and Willis cursed. He'd missed it the first time around, but hadn't Havelock tested that very door earlier in the afternoon and even commented on the smell?

Delicately he scooped away the dead leaves which had blown around the base of the door. An opening about eighteen inches wide and six high had been torn from the rotten base of the door, and a shallow depression scooped out of the earth. Leaves were piled on the other side as well. Willis tried to gauge the size of the body. It might be possible. Just.

On an impulse he moved over to the compost heap and knelt by it. He slipped a pair of plastic gloves on and removed a handkerchief which he held pressed to his nose and mouth. The smell was so thick you could taste it.

He trained the beam on it closely, then straightened up and reeled back against the wall. He swallowed a cry, felt his legs begin to tremble and blackness encroach on the edges of vision. No. It couldn't be! He closed his eyes and tried to control his breathing. Then he walked slowly forwards, pointed his torch back at the compost heap and swore. The skin was pulled back from the teeth in a wicked grin. One ear had been ripped off in a fight.

It was a big cat, but a cat nonetheless.

How could he have mistaken it? He had been so sure that no second closer look had been necessary. He had seen a body. And now it was a cat. He slumped on his haunches.

Forget it Willis, he said to himself. The old man said he'd seen a corpse. A *corpse*, not a human body. That was why he had been so diffident. That was why he had apologised for wasting time. You just jumped to conclusions. What were you trying to do? Show off in front of a rookie?

But, Goddamnit, I saw a body there!

He shook his head and looked more closely. His eyes seem to blur as if a sheet of water had fallen in front of them. He closed his eyes, feeling for a split second something like a vacuum open somewhere in his soul and suck all his preconceptions out, leaving him empty, flapping, as if he had been possessed.

One liquid eye winked at him. The jaws began to work.

'Welcome,' it said in a high, quiet voice. 'I'll be seeing you again.'

He could feel his face begin to twist. The muscles in his thighs began to shudder. The jaws were opening wider now, tearing the skin like wet paper. Willis's legs would not let him stand up. With a grunt he just managed to tip his weight backwards and fell clumsily on the ground.

Then he heard the sound of footsteps. A grimly enthusiastic looking Havelock was leading a serious procession of his colleagues across the lawn.

The cat carried on grinning.

An hour later he and Havelock were back in the Metro, crawling through the stop-start rush hour traffic. In the long pauses between moving, Havelock would glance concernedly at Willis, slumped against the door and apparently asleep. Eventually he stirred himself, rubbed his eyes and snorted.

'Everything all right, Sarge?' Havelock asked.

'What? Hmm. Not really, no — seeing as you asked.'

'Could happen to anyone. Like when he said corpse, I thought he meant human cadaver. Like I said, could have happened to anyone.'

Willis nearly snapped the boy's head off, but checked himself.

'You think so,' he said. 'You really think so.'

'You weren't feeling yourself.'

Willis sighed.

'Right,' he said. 'Right. The question is: what, or who, the hell was I feeling?'

Chapter Eight

Cherie sucked the tip of her paintbrush thoughtfully. The picture she was working on, that she was thinking of as a sort of allegory of Blackheath, was developing better than she could have dared hope. She had had to squash up the perspective a bit, so that the actual heath was presented from an aerial view, but the people on it, the dog walkers, the tramps, the joggers were mostly shown from eye level. On either side the houses leant away from the grass to try and create a sense of space, a trick which seemed to be working, and now all she really had to sort out was the sky. It was so big and pale in real life and she had so little space left for it.

She prodded around a bit on the palette, trying to find the right luminous milky grey as her mind wandered back over the telephone conversation she had just had with Jennifer, her old flatmate. She had found Jennifer's mother's telephone number in an old address book and had got in touch with her that way.

Jennifer had changed a lot. She was much tougher; bitchier in fact. She was married to a New York Neo New Wave Concrete Conceptualist, or so she had put it, sarcastically, and when Cherie had suggested that he sounded like a man who dreamed of laying cement pavements but never got round to it, Jennifer agreed. What I've always said, she added, is that *avante garde* is French for bullshit. And the old jokes are the best.

Jennifer was now running her own gallery in TriBeCa (natch), and as she put it, 'doing fantastic'.

But when it came to Cherie's turn to tell Jennifer what she'd been doing, she found she couldn't. She'd run out of jokes about herself. Cherie sensed Jennifer's disappointment and had a faint suspicion that she had let her down. They each promised to call lots and visit soon. Cherie made a private resolution to write. It was as a result of that conversation that Cherie was painting. It worried her that their relationship, which had always relied on Cherie getting ahead and Jennifer getting, or trying to get, laid was reversed. Now she was the one who had been laid to rest, so to speak, and she wanted to do something about it.

She prodded at her sky. It seemed rather blank. Perhaps I need something in it, she thought. Some birds perhaps; an aeroplane. Clouds. Big dark ones or white fluffy ones? Oh, I think I'll have some of those delicious-looking white fluffy ones. Dab dab dab. Paint paint paint. Oh dear, I've changed my mind. I don't like the white fluffy ones after all. Could I try one of those

lean
pale
grey
ones?

Thank you.

Prod

Scratch

Smear

I . . .

Cherie stood back, an odd light in her eyes. A shape had emerged from the grey and white swirls, had taken form like the random letters scratched by a planchette. It was a figure, made of clouds, of white. A swirling barrel chest, arms that reached wide and faded to nothing. A face that seemed to shift and change in the textures of the thickly-laid-on paint. Plump cheeks. Hollow eyes. Big nose. Small nose. Hollow cheeks. The children had summoned him, the children who were on Cherie's canvas in stiff little postures of glee. The White Man. Old Whitey. He'd come . . .

. . . the front door bell rang . . .

. . . and he'd gone.

Cherie glanced at the blank swirling clouds she'd painted as she wiped her hands. Gone. All gone. Loony Tunes.

'Daa dada dada dadada dadadadaa. Dadadadadaa da DAAAA,' she sang as she ran down the stairs to open the door.

Peter stood there looking slightly flustered.

'Lost the bloody keys,' he said brushing past her. 'You haven't seen them around?'

Cherie leant towards him for a peck on the cheek, more out of habit than anything else, staggered as he moved away quickly from her, then grabbed his arm as she caught an unfamiliar smell on him, underneath the peppermint and aftershave.

'Peter.'

'Just popping up to have a shower.'

'Peter, have you been drinking?' Slightly playful. Moving closer. 'Peter have you been . . .'

She caught the smell again. No NO NO! It was the musk smell of Peter's body and the smell of someone else. Woman. Mingled they made something new. Sex. But was it? WAS IT?

The smell was gone; Cherie felt panicky. She raised her eyes to her husband's. There was embarrassment there but there was amusement and defiance, too. Go on, they said. Tell me. Ask me. Argue with me. I don't give a shit.

'Are you all right?' His voice was carefully modulated. His face set in an expression of concern. But the eyes, the eyes said: You know what's going on. I know you know what's going on. But if I don't say anything you're not going to ask. Because you can't be sure. If you're right, you want out, and so do I. But if you're wrong, you don't want out, and if you accuse me it'll give me the chance to break away. 'Cherie. You're frightfully pale.'

'I'm fine. I'm fine. (After all, she thought, he often has a shower when he comes in.) Well I guess I'm a little dizzy. But I'm OK.'

'Can I get you anything?'

KEEP AWAY. LET ME THINK. Let me think.

'No honestly. I've been working. Just adjusting or something.'

'Go well today? Oh, good. Great. Well, I'm off up. Shout if you need anything, presh.'

Smile. 'Sure, thanks, hun.'

Sofa. Collapse.

Conversation over supper was sparse. Then, 'Got some local work,' Peter said as he shovelled some steak into his mouth. 'Old Ransom's come up trumps. You know the old convent they're knocking down? Well, the old fox is trying to get in there first, put a consortium together for a development. Don't know what the scheme is but he's pretty certain he can get in there. God knows how the old bastard does it. Sent all the work my way. Purely speculative, of course, but . . . Cherie? What do you think, Cherie?'

Nothing, nothing, nothing, Cherie thought. Why the convent, though? Why, why follow my thoughts like that? Or was I following you?

'Cherie, are you all right? Look, if you're ill I'd better call a doctor.'

'Sorry, darling. I was miles away. Wonderful. All those visits to Ransom were about that, were they? Well they were worth it.'

Peter tapped the heavy ring on the table. 'I didn't . . .'

'Oh, I'm sorry. You know what I mean . . .

Just keep talking.

'Wonderful. Luxury flats. Are they going to have guard dogs? Did you know that the convent always did? Funny isn't it. All those silent nuns, all those big angry dogs . . .'

All those big busty nuns and red-tongued Peter and his wolves.

'You see I was reading about it in the library.'

'Really?' Peter got up from the table. 'Any chance of a cup of coffee? I've got some work to do.'

'Like it strong?'

'No no. And white. I think I'll have it white tonight.'

You'll be spotted by old whitey
If you're caught without your nightie

'One coffee with milk coming up,' Cherie said brightly.

If I really am going mad, she thought, I'm not going to give him the satisfaction of seeing it happen.

Chapter Nine

The doorbell rang at mid-morning. Cherie opened it to see a young man dressed in well-pressed blue overalls standing on the doorstep.

'Mrs Simpson?'

'Yes. Who are you?'

'That would be telling, wouldn't it?' the man said with a horribly coy expression. 'Delivery', and he pointed to a little Suzuki jeep, bright red, gleaming, new, immaculate, that was parked outside.

'Here you go' — he thrust an envelope into one hand — 'and there you go' — he pushed the keys into the other — 'and I'll take my leave' — he winked. 'Blimey, cheer up. It may never happen and all that. It's yours!'

He walked briskly away, looking annoyed.

'Thank you very much,' Cherie called after him. He got into a Range Rover with Surrey Suzuki written on the side, and drove off. Cherie shook her head. A jeep. Hers. She ripped open the envelope. Inside was the log book and a note.

'All my love, Peter.'

A bit brisk perhaps. A bit formal. But he probably had to write in the garage. HE BOUGHT ME A JEEP! Cherie's heart thumped up by her throat. He must love me. I must love him. Things are going to be all right. He bought me a jeep.

She walked down to it, ran her hands over the pressed steel sides.

So we've been having a rough time of it lately. So things haven't been going too well. So I could put up with a few more marital problems if he always made up like this. She patted the boxy red machine again. The phone rang. Cherie ran inside and lifted the receiver breathlessly.

'So, how is it?'

'Peter, it's wonderful. Oh, thank you. I don't know what to say.'

'Super. Nice little thing, isn't it?'

'Oh, it's —'

'Look . . .'

'Let me finish saying thank you, please.'

'. . . I thought it'd be nice to celebrate tonight. You know? So I asked Roo and Squirrel to dins. OK? Glad it's OK. Look, must rush. See you eightish. I'll get a lift down with Roo. Bye, presh.'

'Bye.'

Cherie put the phone down feeling utterly deflated, but cheered up almost immediately. I can drive to the shops, she thought. I can drive anywhere. I can drive around and spend a fortune of someone else's money on supper. Life, she concluded, could be worse. In fact it's coming up roses and I'm just an ol'-fashioned girl at heart. Just think, I might actually have to be working for a living.

The dining-room looked spectacular. They all said so, and Cherie had to admit that it did look a bit special. The fine old oak refectory table (a family heirloom Peter treated with studied casualness) stood in front of the great bay window at the front of the house.

Cherie had polished the table and the windows so the evening light could pour in through the clear glass (old glass too, slightly thicker at the bottom than at the top) and bring an added glow to the dark wood. She'd attacked a pair of silver candlesticks with cleaner until she thought she must be wearing through the plate, and had gone to the extra trouble of buffing the crystal. She'd even made flower arrangements for the table and the hall.

They all arrived together, straight from work, Rupert from the City accountancy he was working his way up, Squirrel from the reception desk of a blue-chip stockbroking company. They were later than Peter had said, and from their breath, Cherie guessed that they'd met up for a not-so-quick drink in a wine bar before driving down in Rupert's Audi. She felt a quiver of anger flick across her face at the thought (pre-jeep mad-bitch Cherie) to be replaced by a warm glow of gratitude and pleasure when Peter mimed approval at the flowers from behind Squirrel's back (post-jeep Stepford-wife Cherie).

Just as she led them all into the big dining-room the sun broke through the grey cloud cover. Its near-horizontal rays added a final touch of splendour to the scene, while outside, a sky which was almost rose red stirred and calmly seethed as deep-bellied clouds sailed across it.

'Red sky at night, shepherd's delight, eh?' Rupert's gruff quack broke the silence of the room.

'You know, I've never understood that,' Cherie said, smiling at him. 'Red skies always seem so, oh, I don't know, kind of sinister. Anyhow, I can't see this one lasting. Look!'

With terrible abruptness a black cloud bank which had gathered in the east began to roll across the sky like a great theatre curtain. For some reason Cherie found herself willing the sun to sink behind the row of houses on the other side of the heath before the cloud bank reached it. But it didn't. The last rays were swallowed by the dark mass and night rolled up the edges of the heath.

'Show's over, folks!' Peter said cheerily. 'Amazing to think that all our spectacular sunsets are caused by factory pollution and the internal combustion engine.'

'Volcanoes,' Squirrel said. 'I thought it was volcanoes. A teacher from school was always going on about dust from volcanoes making the sky go all funny.'

Rupert moved over to Peter, and Squirrel's eyes met Cherie's. I can never think of anything to say to comments like that, thought Cherie.

Rupert began to tell Peter that what Squirrel had said was true, actually. As a matter of fact Krakatoa sent more pollution into the air than human beings, with all their cars and factories and atom bombs and things like that, ever had. Made you think.

Squirrel rolled her eyes dramatically in Cherie's direction in an 'oh, men' sort of way. Deciding that Squirrel might be all right, Cherie rolled hers back, and Squirrel grinned. Cherie decided to try and take the game a bit further. She said, 'Drinks, darling!' in a peremptory sort of way, winked at Squirrel and made her giggle. My God, is it this easy? she thought, as she looked up to see Rupert watching with a fond expression, and the look on Peter's face changed from strained condescension to avuncular pleasure.

Squirrel leaned forward to tap Cherie on the arm.

'I hear that mean old thing you married finally got round to showing how much he appreciates you.'

Cherie wondered if this was the beginning of a crude joke, set her face in a chummy leer, then remembering the jeep switched the expression to one of girlish delight.

'Finally, yes. Oh, it's wonderful, you know. Mind you, it took him long enough to see what I was really worth.'

Was she actually saying these inane things? It was like playing house when you were a kid, talking like a grown-up: Oh, yes, Mr Grocer, I'll have a pound of your very best apples and I think I could manage some of your delicious plums as well.

Anyway it worked, though it did worry her a bit that Squirrel seemed to do it naturally.

Squirrel deepened her voice. 'Treat'em mean to keep'em keen. That's what I say.'

And the two of them started to giggle again.

The doorbell rang.

'Ah, that'll be Ransom,' Peter said quickly. 'Just looking in for a drink. Fascinating chap, Roo. You'll like him. Knows the City backwards.'

He shot Cherie a quick look. Cherie couldn't tell if it was pleading or admonitory. I am a changed person, she said to herself. I am reborn and thoroughly pleasant, and I support my husband in all things. My husband's guests are welcome in this house, I do not loathe Ransom's rotten stinking guts.

She moved down to the other end of the room as soon as she was decently able, to get things ready in the kitchen area, insisting that Squirrel should stay behind because she really didn't think she could carry on her girl talk for much longer.

'You just keep the boys in order,' she said, feeling she ought to wink as well. Squirrel supplied the wink for her and Cherie moved down to the kitchen.

From the other end of the room she looked at the group the four of them made and for a second appreciated it on its own terms. Squirrel and Ransom were on the sofa, she leaning forward and slightly sideways, knees together and legs crossed at the ankles in the classic secretary pose. Ransom was leaning back, legs crossed, with his head turning to the left and right, greatly enjoying the deferential attention from Squirrel on his left, and the two men standing with whisky-and-sodas on his right. It's so relaxed, Cherie thought, it's so natural. They all have a place in relation to one another and they're all part of a pattern. Even the table lamps seem to be unifying them in the same element.

Then it was as if a shadow inserted itself between her eyes and her brain. The scene froze and momentarily darkened as the amber light dirtied. Cherie suddenly found herself looking at four stupid and selfish people: a silly girl who did everything, even talk to another woman in a particular way, to make her husband happy; an aging old bore; two toadying young men whose veneer of charm and good manners hid greedy, petty natures. It was a sham. She knew it. They should all be out there in the gathered darkness, she should be alone in here, protected from their influence by this beautiful amber shell of a house.

'Pete, old man, looks like the little lady's seen a ghost.'

Mind's not right.

Ransom was talking about her.

Mad Bitch. Stop thinking.

She forced a bright smile.

'Sorry, I was just planning a painting. The four of you all looked so perfect, the way you're all grouped there, in the light and all that.'

But the blackness was crawling up the window panes. Glass was creaking. Save me, Lord, and them too.

Stop thinking.

'Well. I should be toddling off then.' To her horror Cherie saw Peter was gearing himself up to invite Ransom to stay for dinner and tried to beam a telepathic and desperate 'no' across the room to him. But he really was going.

'Well, thanks to one and all. Jolly nice meeting you both. Peter, Cherie, super. Be seeing . . . Good God!' The exclamation even seemed to take Ransom by surprise. 'Peter, where the hell did you get that from?'

Cherie followed the direction of his gaze. He was staring at the mantelpiece. Nothing much there, thought Cherie. A Habitat vase, a couple of wedding invitations, that hideous ormolu clock Peter's great-uncle had foisted on them, the cross — the cross!

It was unrecognisable now as the mud-caked piece of wood she had found on the heath that day. In an idle hour, exorcising God knows what demons, Cherie had attacked it savagely with household soap and a nail brush, wondering at the elegant yet strong piece of craftsmanship which was gradually emerging in her hands. She had dried it, then buffed it lightly with a duster — it had not needed polishing — and propped it on the mantelpiece.

The wood was astonishingly dark and hard, and the cross seemed to glow with its own sombre lustre. Cherie suddenly realised that it needed to be seen by candlelight to be appreciated, presumably because that was the only sort of artificial light the original craftsman knew. The flames were picked up and seemed to live in the sheen of the wood and the uncertain light brought the intricate Celtic knot at the actual crux into sharp relief.

Ransom stepped over to the fireplace and cradled the cross in his hands.

'Peter, you old rogue. Had no idea you had this tucked away. What is it? Family heirloom or something?'

Peter laughed shortly.

'To tell you the truth I had no idea that I had it myself. Cherie, is it yours?'

'I . . . er, yes. It's mine. That is I . . .' She was going to say 'found it' but that would lead to questions about when and where. Suddenly she didn't want to tell them the truth.

'It came to me. I was left it. I kept it in an old box in the attic and I just brought it down.'

'So you think it's American?' Ransom was looking at her very intently.

'No. I didn't say that. I've no idea what its history is, I'm afraid.'

'Look.' Ransom crinkled his face into a winning smile and softened his tone. 'I've got a few books which might help us to date it. What say I have a go at finding out a bit about it? *Gratis*, of course. Ha ha ha.'

'No! I mean, I'm sorry. Not right now.'

'Cherie.' Peter's voice sounded rather offended. 'What on earth do you mean? Will, I do apologise. Of course we'd be very grateful. Cherie, surely you know that he's an expert.'

'No. Really. I only brought it downstairs because I thought it looked nice.'

'And to keep the ghosties away,' cut in Rupert with a donkey bray in an attempt to lighten the atmosphere, but Peter would not give up.

'But surely, darling, if he wants to —'

'No no, I insist now. It's my turn,' Ransom put in. He handed the cross over to Cherie with a mock bow. 'What the lady wants, the lady gets, as they say. Pity though. Still, anytime you're interested — the offer still stands.' He shot Cherie a fierce look. 'Thanks again. I'll see myself out.'

But Peter insisted on guiding him to the door and Cherie could hear his soft apologetic voice rising and falling as he talked Ransom down the steps. She just thought she heard him say something about setting up a meeting 'about the other thing', then collected herself and took the opportunity to set up the table for the first course.

'What an extraordinary chap,' Rupert said to no one in particular, then added, as Peter came back into the room rubbing his hands briskly, 'I know it sounds a bit silly but he reminded me of the very best sort of teacher from school.'

I'll bet he did, thought Cherie.

'Know what you mean,' Peter answered, 'but he's a damn good contact too. Actually put the firm up to a couple of good deals.' He paused. 'That is . . .' Then he obviously thought better of what he was going to say, and continued: 'Good man. Damn good man.'

'Everything's ready,' said Cherie wanly.

Chapter Ten

In a large family house just off Frinton Street a family gathering was in the first throes of discontent.

Nigel Warmington, Captain Nigel Warmington, father of four and husband of two, had finally been laid off from his executive position in a small firm of printers, but as he was nearing sixty, he had decided to pretend that he'd opted for early retirement. The party had been organised by his second wife, Poppy. The whole family, including his first wife, Sonya, was there.

'Well done, Natasha. Well done indeed.' His step-daughter from the second marriage had just been found a place to read art in a Midlands university.

'Great stuff, old girl. Right on!'

Natasha winced at his ill-considered descent into dated vernacular.

'Thanks, Nige.'

It was his turn to wince. Natasha moved over to stand by Tommy, her stepbrother. Warmington groaned. He hoped she wasn't going to try and flirt with him. And what was she wearing? Ski-pants? Designer ski-pants? They looked more like tights and revealed as much.

'I think Johnny needs a drink, Skip.' The voice was Poppy's. He wished she wouldn't call him that in front of his first wife.

And in Warmington's opinion the last thing Johnny wanted was a drink. What Johnny wanted was a long sharp shock in a detention centre.

'Drink, Johnny?'

'No thanks, Nige.'

'That's most unlike you.'

'Antibiotics.'

Oh God, thought Warmington. He's probably got the clap.

'Well, now that we're all here . . .' This from Sonya, poised like a plump and rather malicious cat on the corner of the Chesterfield.

'Apart from Helen. We mustn't forget Helen,' said Warmington proudly. As if he ever did let anyone forget her, at least three people in the room thought simultaneously. After a series of expulsions from home counties boarding schools, Helen had amazed everybody by getting herself into Cambridge and taking a double first in economics. Now she was a high-flying commodity broker. And she was always a bit late.

'She's always a bit late,' said Warmington. 'Busy girl.'

'Still,' continued Sonya, 'it's so nice for us all to get together like this on this occasion. And what an occasion. I remember how you always dreamt of this moment —'

'And it hasn't come a moment too soon.' Poppy interrupted.

Sonya looked irritated.

'We've all been waiting for this. *All* of us,' Poppy continued. 'Now there's a cold buffet in the kitchen, so, children, why don't you go in and start helping yourselves? And let's all eat, drink, and be merry.'

Sonya rose, smiling. 'Not until someone tells me about this tremendous surprise the children have got in store for Nigel. I've been hearing nothing but strange and mysterious whispers about it from my two. Poppy, have you any idea what it is?'

Bloody well should have, thought Poppy. I shelled out for it.

'Oh, I've got a pretty good idea,' she said, 'but after the meal? No?'

Then Nigel cut in. 'A surprise? For me? How wonderful? Poppy, you've been keeping all this very quiet. Come on, Tommy. What is it?'

Tommy looked flustered. 'I . . . er . . .' He had no idea.

'Oh, for God's sake let's just give it to him,' said Natasha.

Poppy scowled.

'Very well. Johnny, it's in the bedroom.'

Johnny loped off, Warmington rubbed his hands with exaggerated glee, and soon Johnny could be heard thundering down the stairs again.

'It's piddled EVERYWHERE!' he shouted. Then he thrust a wicker basket draped with a towel into Warmington's hands. A lump under the blanket shifted and whimpered.

''Sfer you, Nige. From us.'

Warmington peeled back the blanket. Then his face lit up.

'A puppy! A puppy,' he crooned. He put the basket on the floor and knelt down by it. 'Oh, the funny little fellow. Oh, the little darling. Hello, little furry chap. Hello!'

The puppy thumped its tail.

'Oh, the clever boy. WHO'S a clever boy?'

Warmington stood up. To Poppy's amazement he actually had tears in his eyes.

'Thank you all,' he said gruffly. 'Thank you all very much indeed.'

There was an embarrassed silence. Then the scuffle of feet outside.

Everyone was relieved; they had been expecting a speech.

'Oh, good. That'll be Helen.'

'I'll go.'

Johnny walked red-faced from the room. He really fancied Helen. He'd open the door before she even rang and give a mock bow. He'd say something funny like 'Milady,' or 'The company awaits.' And she would laugh and he would laugh and then — the future was an exciting blank. He opened the door and bowed without looking.

'Your company awaits, Milady.' Then, aware something was wrong, he looked up.

Instead of Helen's gracious smile, he felt a huge force close on his face. He tried to shout, but fingers, pistons of fire and ice, seemed to have punctured his cheeks and were searching for something down his throat. He felt an agonising pain, then a great black hurt as he was struck on the back of his head. Then nothing.

Happy expectant faces turned to the door as it opened. Johnny appeared, his face quite unrecognisable. He sailed across the room and thudded into the wall opposite, limp as a rag doll.

Poppy screamed.

Then a figure appeared in the doorway, and they all fell silent.

As predicted, Helen was late. Her black Porsche skidded to a halt on the gravel outside her father's home, and she hurriedly pulled a brush through her tangled hair. She felt something trickle down her inside thigh, swore and reached into the glove compartment for a tampon, ripping the cellophane off with jerky movements.

She'd just spent the last forty minutes with an attractive potential client in vigorous copulation. She grinned at the memory of his parting words: 'Well you did say you wanted a big spender.'

He could say that again.

She trotted up the steps to the front door. There was no noise coming from inside — nothing strange in that at one of these gatherings, but it was unlike her father to leave the front door open. She marched into the hall and stood there for a moment, hearing silence.

'Hello!'

A dry echo, like a hoarse, mocking whisper.

'Hello?'

Puzzled she slowed her steps, ready to permit a practical joke for her father's sake.

'Where are you all?'

Again that voice.

'Hello-o?'

'Look is this a joke? Because it isn't funny.'

Silence . . . Then 'Heheheh.' Faint. Like the rustle of leaves behind you in an empty street.

She went into the sitting-room. Her family was all seated. Daddy, Mummy, Tommy, Poppy, Natasha, Johnny. All wrong, ALL WRONG. Slowly her numb brain took in the contradictions. They had all dressed back to front. Daddy's head was staring out from above his back. Mummy was facing the room, but her chest was against the back of the chair. Oh God. Oh God oh God oh God. Their joints had been bent backwards. A cry was strangled by a hot pillar of vomit rising in her throat. Then the door swung back.

First blackness, swirling like a pillar, and a foul stench. Earth and bad meat. Then the shape resolved itself into a man.

He was tall, massively built, with great arms hanging like tree limbs from wide shoulders. He was naked, and his skin pure white, so white it glowed with the deathly light of phosphorescence. Helen's eyes widened. His face was beautiful. High cheekbones carrying the sweep of eyes and eyebrows back and upwards. Pale lips, finely drawn, but not quite meeting over the teeth.

Only his fingers were black-tipped, and his eyes were pools of black, and his teeth black and strong. Horselike. The smell was musk and sweat.

One of his arms reached out and took Helen under the chin. Her body went into an instinctive spasm. She struggled, then went limp, helpless in his grip, and her vitals seemed to empty, the emptiness filled with something like pure lust. She felt a hot void in her womb which longed to be filled, felt the warm vacuum travel up her, emptying and filling her simultaneously. Her belly. Her breasts. Her mind.

White hot.

White lust.

White out.

Her eyes glazed. She swept her hair back, a marionette

coquette. The figure dissolved and she stepped into the mist.

Much later the puppy crawled out from under the sofa. He sniffed at one of the dark, crusting pools on the Wilton and then began to lap. His tail began to wag. Something told him that if he stuck around he could eat and drink as much as he wanted.

Almost at the same time a young man reached the top of Lewisham Hill. He was on his way to The Poacher, a popular pub on the edge of the heath. The night was still and warm, one of those freaks of climate which never show up on any weather map and which only ever last for an hour or two at the most. The young man felt the mild air on his cheek, unzipped his cotton blouson jacket and unconsciously loosened and lengthened his stride. He felt good.

He reached the heath. He could follow the road straight towards the pub or head for the dark bulk of the ruined convent, slightly out of his way. It would be better to do that. His bladder was full of the tea his mother had insisted he take before leaving and he could have a piss against the railings there. It'd be better to do that than wait until he got into the pub and have to go to the bog as soon as he'd said hello. First impressions count, he thought, and his mate's girlfriend had said she'd try to get her younger sister to come along tonight. So he struck out across the grass towards the convent's broken shell.

He stood by a gap in the railings and wondered whether or not he should go through, just in case he was surprised by a dog walker; then decided against it. The railings were bent in a peculiar pattern, as if something had burst through, like you sometimes saw where some idiot had gone off the road in his car. Though the gap was big, it looked as if there was a load of nettles and brambles on the other side.

Sod the dog walkers.

The young man felt the familiar rush of pleasure as the

stream of urine hit and hissed around the nettles. A quick shake, a fumble as he tried to manipulate his buttons on his new jeans into stiff button holes, then . . . a strange sensation somewhere between panic and embarrassment. Someone had been watching him.

They must have been there some time, because it was only as his eyes became fully adjusted to the darkness away from the street lamps that he could see that what he had thought was part of a bush was in fact a figure.

'Got an eyeful, then, have you mate?' the young man said, confident that he'd been spied on by a peeping Tom. 'Bloody dis —'

He stopped as the figure detached itself from the railings and shifted a few feet away with a strangely fluid movement. The young man was about to start swearing when he realised that it was a woman.

There was little light and no moon, but he could see that she was tall and held herself very straight. Her silhouette, which he could make out against the line of orange lights in the background, was clean. It looked as if she'd swept her hair back tightly from her forehead. Lower down the outline was more confused. She seemed to be wearing a suit, but it was ripped and hanging loose. When she smiled it seemed that she had no teeth, but when he started back she only had to raise her arm and show him that her shirt was open to the waist for him to step forward again, transfixed utterly by the sight of her breasts, mottled blue and white in the darkness.

A deep sibilant voice which came from nowhere made him take another step, and he saw that the woman was very beautiful with dark eyes and milk-white skin and hair. Her body moved beneath a thin film of pale light like water under oil. He wanted her. He felt himself stiffen as his innards seemed to melt.

Then she opened her mouth again, and this time she was close enough for him to see that her teeth were strong and black and he smelt something awful, close and old. Only this time it came from behind him. He whipped round and sprang sideways to see the woman staring at a darker mass within the foliage behind him.

And then he ran.

Outside the pub he waited ten minutes in the full glare of a street-light, waited until his breathing returned to normal and he felt he could face the group. His friend was sitting in a corner booth with his girlfriend and her sister but when she looked at him eagerly, and perhaps expectantly, he couldn't meet her gaze. He went and bought a round. Could he tell them? It didn't seem possible. A beautiful woman on the heath had approached him, had caught him pissing in the bushes, had turned out to have blackened teeth, and had been with someone else whom he had sensed rather than seen. He could just imagine their reactions. Forget it, he said to himself. Don't bring it up. Get on with the job in hand. When he returned to the booth he went and sat deliberately next to the young girl. She didn't shuffle away. Play your cards right, my son, and you're in there, he said to himself.

Henry Smith was passing an uneventful evening: a bit of television; a telephone conversation to set up a darts match at a spit-and-sawdust pub (authentic) down in Greenwich; a game of patience and then the News at Ten. After the adverts he pulled himself out of his armchair and announced he was going to give the dog its last walk.

For once, though, the dog was reluctant to leave. Henry stood in the hall in his wellies and duffle coat, jingling the lead. There was no thunder on the stairs. Bloody animal's on the bed, he said to himself, and bounded up the stairs. The dog was under the bed. He pulled it protestingly from its lair by the collar and brushed a dust ball from its nose. Cold and wet.

'What's wrong, old chap? Got the blues?'

The animal cringed.

'We've got to go out, you know. Walkies.'

It just sat looking sad and dog-like, with not even a thump of the tail.

Henry put the lead on and dragged it out, the dog's skin wrinkling in thick folds around its neck. Once they were out, however, he understood its reluctance.

There were no stars and the blackness crowded him like something palpable. The dog, for once, got its business over and done with almost as soon as they were outside the garden gate, but a half-awakened suspicion that animals know best irritated Henry so much that he dragged it along the road, coaxing it at first, then talking to it angrily. Really he was talking to himself. They crossed a road, aiming to skirt the grassed-over gravel pit and walk up and around the convent. After they had gone about ten yards Henry saw figures.

The mind has its own library of expected sights, stored like film in the memory's vast archive. When the expected is encountered there is little reaction, but when something is wrong it can take a few seconds to run through the footage in an attempt to match a memory to what the eyes perceive. The mind is a coward, or very vain, and doesn't like to admit what it is seeing is completely new.

Henry's first thought was that there were more dog walkers out than usual. Rejected.

Then he imagined he was seeing a group of pub-goers on their way home. Rejected.

Warning shivers began to run from the nape of his neck down his spine to his legs. He felt himself tremble and a bloody, metallic taste flood his mouth. Danger.

The figures moved jerkily but strongly, as if used to another environment. They were unitedly aimless, crossing and recrossing each other's paths and sometimes wheeling together like a ragged crowd of huge earthbound starlings. The occasional one would lift its head as if to sniff the air and then resume the walk abruptly. To Henry it seemed like a ghastly dance.

Then one stopped. Though it was too dark to see Henry could imagine only too clearly how the head was slowly turning like flesh radar until it reached him. Then the body would follow, drag round and —

A hoarse cry rattled across the grass to where he stood. Henry felt the muscles along his back, his arms, his legs contract. His jaw was drawn open but no sound came from his mouth. He couldn't move. It was the dog that saved him.

With a cry somewhere between a bark and a yelp it tore loose from his grasp, twisting him round and almost pulling him over. Ridiculously, Henry's first thought was to try and recapture it and he dived for the lead, almost before he realised that he was free of the terror's paralysing grip.

Then panic lifted him and he ran, his legs at first feeling as useless and as heavy as sacks of sand but growing lighter and lighter as he moved. By the time he reached the road he felt as if he were flying.

Faintly behind him he heard the sounds of pursuit.

In a house high up on Shooters Hill a little fat boy called Sebastian Lee Miles awoke from sleep, screaming. He screamed and he screamed until his mother was dragged up from her barbiturate sleep, stumbled into his room and forced half a Mogadon down his swollen throat. Then he, too, fell into a heavy and dreamless sleep.

Henry pulled himself up his short garden path, the exhilaration of panic sloughing off him with every exhausted step. He fumbled for a key, managed to get it into the lock, and fell onto his knees in the hall, kicking the door shut behind him.

'*Twilight Zone,* lovey', he heard his wife, Tricia, call from the sitting-room. Then the door opened and she stood above him.

'Henry! For goodness sake, what is it? Where's the dog?'

'Behind me.'

'What, the dog?'

'No. People! Things! On the heath!'

'People? On the heath? Of course there are, Henry, what *is* going on?'

She broke off as the garden gate gave a tortured squeal.

'Henry! What have you done?'

Henry pulled himself to his feet, staggered to the front door and bolted it.

'Upstairs! Quick!'

There was a hollow drumming against the study window.

'Henry.' She sounded shocked. 'Are you in trouble? Tell them to go away.'

'For God's sake, run! Get away!' He began to crawl up the stairs.

'Well, if you won't . . .'

'NO!'

But Tricia had opened the door into the study.

'. . . I'll give 'em what for.'

She marched purposefully into the room. Henry groaned and slumped on the landing. Tricia reached the study window. Whoever was battering against it was masked by a poster stuck on the inside of the window with Blu-tack. Tricia yanked it away and the glass exploded inwards. Clutching the poster to her chest, wide-eyed, mottle-faced she took two steps backwards as a thin figure leapt through the window and landed on her chest like a great white frog. Black eyes. Black teeth. White face. And the stench of the pit.

Splintered ribs slipped into her lungs and heart. As she died, the light went out in Henry's mind.

Chapter Eleven

'And then the judge says: "Yes, I hate it when they piss down my wellies, too!" Hahaha! Excellent joke actually, well the chap who told it to me at lunch made it sound jolly good. I think the punchline might be wrong though. Should be —'

'Oh, Roo, for Chrissake stow it,' Peter interrupted good-naturedly. 'Even Cherie's heard that one, haven't you dear?'

Cherie nodded with a tight little smile, wishing she could laugh at jokes about men 'having it off' with sheep. And surely the reference to the Scottish sheep farmer was racist? Or was she just being judgmental? Yes, she was, she decided, as she remembered the jokes about Canadians she had found so amusing when she lived in New York.

'Oh, Roo's just awful at telling jokes, aren't you, Roo? I mean he always forgets the punchline and has to get someone to tell him, and when they do the whole joke's completely spoiled anyway because someone's already told you what it is, if you see what I mean. And yet Roo *always* repeats it! I mean it's so funny!'

Squirrel shreaked with laughter, and Rupert threw his head back to give a full-throated chuckle, enjoying his reputation as a good-hearted buffoon to the full. Even Peter gave a series of barks which was the nearest he ever got to laughing.

'Right,' said Cherie, 'who's for coffee?'

'Single malt, Roo?' Peter added. 'Liqueurs, ladies?'

So the dinner was a success, thought Cherie, as they

sipped their drinks. The prawns had obviously marinaded long enough and were delicious, even if the effect had been rather spoiled by Rupert and Peter's rather oafish jokes about pickled shrimps. The roast leg of lamb had been totally devoured, the syllabubs eaten in concentrated silence. Peter grew mellow as more and more wine was drunk and Squirrel bubbled and prattled happily. Cherie neither talked nor drank to excess, but gradually relaxed, so that when the conversation took a turn which suggested that Peter and Squirrel had had a passionate, if brief, fling when he was at Oxford and she'd come up for a May Ball, she hadn't even cared.

They stayed at the table with their coffees and drinks and Rupert began on one of his long army stories. Cherie felt her attention wander halfway through the one which seemed to involve a Chieftain tank, a flattened Mercedes and a Turkish pimp. She found herself staring vacantly at the flat black mirror of the window. They hadn't drawn the curtains. She started as a slight movement, dimly glimpsed through the glass, caught her attention. It was gone before she could see what had caused it. Automatically she got up from the table and went and stood by the side of the window so that she could look out of it obliquely and minimise the reflection.

'What is it?' Squirrel asked.

'Oh, nothing. Sorry. I just thought I saw a movement out there, but it's gone. I probably just saw a reflection.'

'Sit down, presh.' Peter sounded relaxed and happy.

Cherie made to move away, but as she turned her head again she thought she caught a fleeting glimpse of . . . something.

'Oh, for goodness sake . . .' said Peter.

'I'm sorry, but it was just as I turned away. I think I saw it again.'

Peter hauled himself out of his slumped position. 'Look, either you saw something or you didn't. Did you or didn't you? If you did, we'll do something about it. If you didn't, just sit down.'

'I don't know! I may have seen something . . . I'm just not sure.'

Rupert joined her at the window, standing unnecessarily close. 'These eyes miss nothing,' he said at her face, breathing meaty alcoholic fumes. He winked.

I have never, thought Cherie, met a couple who winked so much before.

Then Rupert grabbed her.

'Golly, the lady's right. Something by the Audi. By gosh, I'll bet they're after my speakers. I'm going out. Teach 'em a lesson they won't forget.' He moved towards the door.

'Oh, for God's sake, Roo, don't be so bloody silly,' Peter drawled. 'Just stick your ugly great face out of the front door and tell them to fuck off. Actually, one look at your face and they'll run anyway.'

Squirrel pouted. 'I think I left my cheque book in the car, Roo darling.'

'That does it!' Rupert was into the hall and out of the front door.

'They'd better be careful,' Squirrel said smugly as the front door opened. 'You know, there were some yobbos leaning on the car one Saturday evening after a football match. When Chelsea are playing, they're everywhere around us. So Roo just went out there to tell them to get off it, quite nicely, you know, and they wouldn't, so he chopped one right in the tummy ever so fast. You couldn't see his hand move. It was a blur. They ran away really quickly then! He's very good at self-defence.

'He loves his car,' she added.

Psychopath, thought Cherie. Please don't start anything here.

'He can get quite butch at times, actually,' said Peter. 'There was this time at school —'

'He's disappeared,' said Cherie, who was the only one watching. 'He went round to the other side of the car and he just . . . disappeared.'

'He's such a tease,' Squirrel bubbled happily.

'He's such an oaf.' said Peter. He moved over to the window and started trying to open it. 'Bloody thing's always jammed.'

'It's the security locks,' Cherie reminded him. 'We had them fitted.'

'I can tell we had them fitted.' Peter answered. 'Bloody hell, how do you work the damn things? Haven't we got a key or something?'

'Yes. It's where you —'

'Roo! Stop fucking around like a schoolboy,' Peter bellowed through the glass leaving a film of moisture and few white food fragments on its polished surface. 'C'mon out.'

Cherie rummaged in a drawer for the key and returned to the two of them by the window. Peter unscrewed the locks on one of the sashes and yanked the window up.

'Now we can bawl at him.'

'Roo, pet. Coo'ee. Come on. We can't see you. Oh, I say,' Squirrel said, wrinkling her nose. 'Have you got drains?'

'No, we have not! What is that fool playing at? Joke's a joke, you cretin.'

'Perhaps he's found something.'

'Piss artist.'

'He probably dropped the keys. ROO!'

'Why is he acting like this?'

'That's old Roo. C'mon, Roo. We're getting bored in here.'

'Do something, Peter!'

'No, wait.'

'Sod this. I'm going out there to sort the old lush out.'

'No!'

'You boys!'

Peter left the room. From the bay window the two women saw him go out of the house, walk round to the other side of the car, then quite suddenly — as if his legs had been taken away from underneath him — disappear.

Chapter Twelve

Filthy yellow cloud mist grey stink dry hard soft skin slit bone noise round head round ball eye swell nose red noise noise noise noise sick swim swoop up up up cloud mist yellow dirt down filth rot rip rot rip rot soft swell soft swill earth mud bone splinter wood boat rope rope ROPE . . .

And sweat . . .

But the rope held, and Cherie was able to pull herself out from the cesspit of white nights and black dreams by emptying her mind of all words but rope, and from that word building up pictures in her head: wood fires, chopped wood, maples and sugary sap, high stockades and gallant flags, spare white wood-frame churches and flaming autumn leaves, rocking-chairs, Woody Woodpecker, trellises, flowers, flowers, wreaths.

earth
dirt
filth
swell
NO-O-O-O-O-O-O.

But the sweat saved her from the remorseless words that swarmed like little grey spiders across her brain; sweat that embalmed her each night and twisted the bedclothes into a damp winding-sheet; sweat that lay like a dead cow's tongue between her breasts, that dribbled down her stomach into the matted hair of her pubis, that dried to a sticky layer across her face, dripped like treacle from the small of her back, rucking and hardening the sheets into torturing folds. Sweat it was that drove her from her bed every morning before it was light and sent her (feeling flabby grey and cold) into the shower to sluice the little grey words away.

She had never really thought in words before, always relying on her visual imagination to cope with new experiences and feelings. Now she had forgotten that she could see and she tried not to anyway. The trip to the morgue to identify her husband's body had done that to her, cauterising something in the optic nerve when the grey sheet had slipped accidentally from his waxy yellow skin and she had seen the wide dark hole.

'ole in ther groun' all big an' sort o' roun' it woz

where did THAT come from?

And the dark clots and the white of the bone where the arm stopped halfway . . .

words, words, words. I'm sick of words. *My Fair Lady*? Audrey Hepburn?

Words had been swarming around her face and in her ears ever since, like highland midges. There were no words from Peter's mother and father at the memorial service (the funeral had to await the autopsy) because they hated her, but there were little words from others — the Vicar and all Peter's friends and relations who were prepared to be nice for two minutes before forgetting about her — and big angry bitter words from Squirrel, with her neat little teeth and mad, pinched face, which led to sorry-please-understand words from Squirrel's mother. And then there were Cherie's own words, which hovered in a ring around her head, her own insane autocue; words like break yellow slit soft swell rot which followed her around the house (always too hot or too cold or too dry or too damp) as she waited for something to change, even a fraction.

But as the days after Peter's and Roo's murders changed into weeks, the only thing that had changed was that her misery had become exaggerated by the monotony of days which were grey on the outside and grey on the inside, and by boredom and depression which made up a blacker and fouler emotional liquor than Cherie ever could have imagined.

THE BLACKHEATH MURDERS. THE MASSACRE ON THE HEATH. THE BLOODBATH IN THE SUBURBS quickly gave rise to an enormous press file. Front pages were held, one of the tabloids even ran a second edition at four o'clock in the morning. Picture editors tore their hair out trying to find one interesting photograph of the place (too fucking flat) but had to settle instead for full frontals of policemen standing guard on suburban porches.

'PSYCHO! PSYCHO! PSYCHO!' one headline ran while another went for 'IT'S A BLOODY BLOODBATH', attributing the made-up quote to a shaken baby-faced constable just out of college (though grown men blanched too, they said.) Short editorials under the headline WHO ARE THESE MONSTERS? gave leader writers every opportunity to list what few details of the atrocities the police had released, and to mention all kinds of poignant details like cold buffets standing uneaten, television sets still on, saucepans full of milk boiled dry (red hot in fact). The little puppy with its stained muzzle and barrel tummy was especially popular.

But nobody knew what had happened.

In part this was deliberate policy by the police who felt that they could not release all the details because so few of the facts, apart from the inescapable fact of death, made any sense. And it was this very lack of hard facts that forced the newspapers to search for parallels and to come up with the only one way they could find: the notorious Californian Manson murders. As time went on and the facts still refused to settle into an acceptable pattern, the discrepancies began to be overlooked and the Manson theory of a gang of drug-crazed devil-worshippers began to gain ground as much with the police as with anyone. It was one thing to be unable to find a killer — the public, thank God, didn't seem to demand instant results as long as they felt something was being done. But to be unable to say *What* had committed the crimes, and how, was just asking for trouble. So without ever wholeheartedly endorsing the Death Cult Loony Massacre idea, but by not refuting the story either, the impression grew that this was the official line.

Until the *Metronome* story came out.

Metronome was a small independent listings magazine with an unusually good news team who managed a decent scoop about twice a year, usually the sort of scoop that people noticed. Somehow they had discovered that rarest of creatures, a policeman-who-talks, and over about three weeks were fed a stream of information that completely contradicted the story that was popularly accepted. There were photocopied situation reports, autopsies, forensic reports, and a strange transcript from a boy who had been on the heath that night on his way to the pub and who had seen something.

On 29 October, Henry Smith and his wife Patricia were watching television. She had just put the milk on to boil, he had just come back from walking the dog. At about 11.15 someone or something burst in through their living-room window and killed both of them: Henry by turning his head round 360 degrees on his neck, Tricia by applying pressure on her chest until the ribs fractured and pierced her heart and lungs.

At roughly the same time, six members of the Warmington family were killed by the same methods, although here the assailants used disembowelment on one member of the family. Slightly later, Peter Simpson and Rupert Haugh Hardy left Simpson's house to investigate a disturbance. Their bodies were found half a mile away. Simpson had been disembowelled and further mutilated; Haugh Hardy had suffered removal of the spinal column. Among other things this releases the ribs and causes them to spring upwards and outwards like the wings of a bird.

These were the first hard stories to come from the heath, and the writer went on to explain why.

Ever since the story broke, reporters have been pushing the police for more details about the literally horrific incidents. (Two freelances and a photographer actually broke into the morgue: the case comes up on Tuesday.)

Rumours of incompetence have started to circulate, rumours the police are usually only too anxious to quash for very obvious reasons. This reporter can now reveal why. They don't know what the hell is going on.

The Manson case parallels are in fact a smokescreen the police are only too happy to maintain. The details of this case make the Manson murders look straightforward, if such a thing is possible.

These are the facts.

To turn a human head through 360 degrees requires massive torque, or turning power. Two people might be able to do it with great difficulty, if you can imagine one person holding the torso and twisting it in one direction, the other holding the head and twisting it in another. One person might manage it by kneeling hard on the victim's shoulders to prevent the torso following the neck when the head was twisted. Either way, massive contusions would result, both around the neck and over the body and head where the murderers would have had to grip.

There is no bruising on Henry Smith's body consistent with his way of death.

Breaking someone's ribs is relatively easy, though fractures from applied pressure are usually of the green-stick kind (i.e. not clean breaks). The pattern of the fracture on Patricia Smith's chest is, to quote a reliable source, consistent with the sort of force a train buffer might have on a torso if there were a relative velocity of between 20 and 30 mph. However, such an impact would result in massive tissue damage.

There is no tissue damage, no bruising on Patricia Smith's body even though her ribs were struck with such force that they penetrated the floor boards underneath her. Fragments were embedded up to quarter of an inch in the wood.

* * *

The catalogue of inexplicable injuries continues. The pattern of bone fractures on Peter Simpson's body suggest that some of them were broken internally, as if by massive muscular convulsion. Blood vessels around the cavity caused by the removal of Rupert Haugh Hardy's spine were cauterized. But then most of his blood had been drained anyway, though no trace of it has been found.

The extent of physical injury and mutilation of the bodies in the Warmington household is so extensive that to quote one source: 'It's as if explosive charges were surgically implanted inside the abdominal cavity and then detonated by remote control. Their insides were just dog food. We couldn't perform an autopsy in the normal sense of the word because there was nothing to perform it on. Just an envelope of flesh.'

This bewildering evidence tells us that these killings are in a different league altogether from anything else on record. Whatever went on in Blackheath, the public must be told. No leads have been followed because none has been uncovered. The murderer or murderers, for want of any better term, are still at large. The public has a right to know the extent of the risk to them. And the police force has a duty to tell them.

What we are seeing now is yet another shabby attempt to pull a discreet curtain over the events which overtook eleven innocent people that fateful night. The police, far from pusuing their job of uncovering evidence, are seeking to bury and ignore it. And once again the public is left in the dark.

Much of the article was unfair, as a terse press conference later that week made clear. The police had been unwilling to release the full story for fear of copycat murders (sarcastic if predictable howls from the newshounds) and because they had their hands full enough with the murders without having to deal with the panic that would ensue.

The Manson parallels had not been drawn by the police; the press had made them up.

And no, they would not officially confirm or deny any

factual points made in the article concerning the nature of the victims' injuries.

Of course a witch-hunt then ensued for the unusually well-informed source of the leak, but nobody was caught. Sergeant Willis had covered his tracks well and was owed enough favours by his sources to keep stumm even in the face of increasingly bloody threats from their superiors. And in Blackheath nobody took a blind bit of notice. Sociologists afterwards talked of it as a variation on the Stockholm Syndrome, a not uncommon occurrence when the victim of a hijack or a kidnap begins to identify himself with his captor and even to sympathise with his aims. Call it that. Call it middle-class complacency. Call it a sort of mass catatonia inspired by absolute terror, for when the mind is confronted with the complete unknown it can only shut itself down knowing that it cannot cope. Call it the death-wish of rabbits confronted by a snake.

Whatever the reason, within a few more days the police would be wishing that there had been a panic-stricken evacuation and that a few of those big old houses by the heath had been standing empty.

PART TWO

Chapter Thirteen

Willis stood stiffly in front of the Superintendent's desk.

'. . . so let's not monkey-fuck around, eh? Let's just try to get to the bottom of this nasty little can of worms.'

'Yes. Of course, sir.'

'Well?'

Willis thought for a moment. 'I have nothing more to say, sir.'

The Superintendent leapt to his feet and smashed his fist down on the desk, 'Don't give me that puppy-shit, Willis! Save it for your young friends! The second you walk through this door you leave that fucking attitude behind you, d'you hear? Behind you.' His voice dropped, became smooth. Interrogation-room technique, thought Willis. 'Now, let's just talk this one over like civilised human beings, shall we, and try to get to the bottom of this nasty, smelly little mess. Someone released to the press, through unofficial channels, details of this case that were confidential and whose release to the aforementioned gentlemen of the fourth estate was prejudicial, I believe, to the successful outcome of this case. Now I know and you know that you are the only person around here with enough clout or wallop to corrupt the entire coroner's staff and a few down in forensic. And corruption is not a word I use lightly, Willis.'

Jumped-up little prick, Willis thought. Corruption had to do with the slow collapse of matter, the reversal of all human aspiration, the softening, the slipping, the dissolution of once-taut flesh, the patient, toothless earth-mumbling of bones and hair and teeth ... and little jerk-offs like the one opposite me.

'Know why leaks are called leaks, Willis?' the jerk-off continued. 'Because from where I'm sitting they smell like bowel movements. Not an exact analogy, I know, and I know that your smug superior brain has probably noted that down. But there are more important things in life than just being clever, Willis. Things like loyalty to your mates, which you obviously find funny. Things like obeying the law, which includes not disclosing confidential information. Things like common human decency, which means not telling some posturing pinko rag facts about murder victims which their relatives don't even know about. Thought about that one did we, Willis? Elderly mother and father, just getting over the shock, neighbour pops in with a "Just thought you might want to see this". "Oh, look," says the old man, "there's yet another article about how our son was topped. And how interesting. This one says his spine was ripped out and he was sucked dry of blood. And, golly gosh, it goes on to imply that the police are a load of mendacious incompetents. I say, dear, why have you fainted into the cornflakes?" Thought of that, did you, Willis?'

Willis's glazed eyes came into focus. 'What, sir? Sorry, sir. Miles away. Could you just go over what you said again?'

The Superintendent hunched over the desk, his face white and pinched. 'I'll get you out of this force, if it's the last thing I ever do . . . However,' and he gathered himself, 'enough of that. Jesus wept, Willis. In fuck's name WHY?'

Willis consciously relaxed his shoulders. He was off the hook now. He had a position and he was prepared to defend it, but until he was hauled up in front of an inquiry he was buggered if he was going to give anything away. He thought he could detect genuine curiosity in the Super's eyes, which was perhaps not so surprising. The man was nearly ten years younger than he was, and a dedicated careerist. Not only had he never done anything that could possibly harm his career; everything he did, every act he performed, from blowing his nose to organising the local boys' club football team, was neatly tailored to one purpose: his own advancement in the force.

Cynical Willis, wilful Willis, and now, it appeared, Quixotic Willis could have come from another planet.

'You know my views, sir. I've made them quite clear on a number of occasions, both verbally and written.'

'They amount to a load of camel shit, Willis, and you know it. What I want to know is why a canny old bugger like you, with all your experience,

(flattery, flattery, thought Willis.
Don't try and patronise me, chum)

goes apeshit over a crackpot idea, or rather a lack of ideas, and makes a complete prat of himself in the process. And such a public one at that. You used to be a popular man, Willis. Now they just think you're daft.'

'As I've said before, sir, you may think my views are camel shit but the shit's going to end up on your shoes.' He consciously adopted an air of calm stolidity; a wind-up pose. 'To my mind the facts in this case are so extraordinary that ordinary approaches to investigation will lead nowhere. We have Panda cars swarming over estates in Lewisham, Greenwich and Deptford — incidentally causing a great deal of secondary friction in the process — looking for a gang of blood-stained devil-worshippers with medical degrees who are living in a squat. At least that's the message that's got through. Even now this case is still one big loose end. No progress has been made —'

'Investigations are proceeding, you know.'

'— because no progress *can* be made. And no progress can be made because no one knows what the fuck they're doing. I have repeatedly drawn attention to my reports filed weeks ago concerning the unusual condition of the corpses. There are the two plague deaths —'

'And the body in the compost heap? Thank you, Willis.'

While Willis had been talking the Superintendent had

sunk down in his chair. He tilted it back and stared at the ceiling with a bored expression.

'Sir! I've put my neck out when most other coppers would be crawling around looking for an arse to lick. I admit —'

'You never took that holiday I offered, did you?'

'But —'

'Listen, we've heard it all before. Investigations are proceeding which take into account your, ah, fascinating speculations.' His tone now became icily sarcastic. 'Now, we all know how very proud you were to find your very own body, and we're all sorry it turned out to be a moggy. Incidentally, did we ever ascertain who it belonged to? No? Perhaps you should have tried a bit of sleuthing. However, may I please suggest that it really is a teeny-weeny bit immature of you to try and bring it into every conversation. It's getting dull. You're obsessed. You see dead pussy cats and think they're corpses. And you see patterns where none exist. We are investigating these murders, Willis, and *we* is the operative word. It's a team effort. You've gone from cynical no-hoper to classic paranoid in a few weeks. You've always thought you were a bit special, haven't you? But we've no room for mavericks here. I expect you to take the holiday I've so generously offered you and get off my back. Now I really am a bit pushed for time . . .' If he had had a buzzer system on his desk he would have leant over and called up his secretary.

As it was he glanced up at Willis's furious face and thought: Got you, you bastard.

Willis was furious. It was a long time since he had been caught out like that. Coffee was called for. And double sausage, bacon, double egg, beans and chips. He walked slowly to the greasy spoon round the corner and ran through in his head the way the conversation should have gone. have gone.

I suppose it has escaped your notice, he should have said. Deadpan, slightly bored. No.

I suppose it has not escaped your notice . . . No.

You will no doubt have noticed in that case (that was better) *that none of the theories you have concocted are born out by a shred of evidence? You will have duly noted that there is not a single shred of forensic evidence to . . . to . . .*

Willis felt a cold wind tickle the back of his neck and he felt the sweat chill uncomfortably on his body. The words that had just come into his brain to finish the sentence were: *to link with any human agency.*

He tried to thrust the thought away, but it kept on coming. There must have been . . . No. The forensic reports had been categorical — unusually so. No fingerprints, no traces of sweat, no shreds of cloth so beloved by the men with microscopes, no traces of bruising, no skin fragments, no saliva, no semen. No nothing. No nothing. Double negative equals a positive. Something then. Something, but WHAT?

Double sausage, bacon, double egg, beans and chips arrived in front of him. Chips like stale twiglets, dark grease pooling in the folds of the bacon, sausages pale and surprised-looking, beans like . . . there was nothing like the beans in the known universe. And real fried eggs with the yolks so pale they were white, and the whites so greasy they were yellow. It all made up a lopsided face. Baked bean hair. Bacon nose. Mottled sausage lips.

The two bleached yolks looked up at him like the cataract-covered eyes of his dead mother's old highland terrier.

They blinked.

Willis jumped backwards on his chair with a shout, recovered, then leant forward. He was shaking, and the café owner was looking at him hard. He saw the white strip-lights reflected in the glistening membrane, saw how possibly, if he moved his head slightly, they might create a . . . certain effect.

Blood bloomed in a great stain across them, haemorrhaged from the taut dome of the yolk. Slid down like thick tear drops. Settled redly in the grease. Willis felt the hairs on the back of his neck stiffen, his mouth contort.

'Sorry, mate. Did it get you?' A man at the next table waved a ketchup bottle apologetically. 'Always the same: either too much or too little, and never where you want it. Just like the pol . . . Whoops. Anyway. Buy you another plate if it makes you feel that sick. Can't think how it splashed all the way over there . . .'

But Willis was out of the door. Anywhere, but somewhere else, he thought. Anywhere. He walked quickly down the road away from the café until he came to narrow streets of suburban terraced houses. Lights were coming on in front rooms and for a few minutes the gauze wall of net-curtains would be made transparent by the back lighting, and the contents of the houses made visible, vulnerable to the outside.

Was the Superintendent right? Was he way off track and behaving like a wanker? The whole thing had started with that bloody cat that had seemed to shape-shift in front of his eyes. And the old woman who had said she sensed a presence. An evil presence. It was ridiculous. Totally ridiculous. Had he allowed himself to get sucked into her fantasies? Was he really washed up? Had he cracked?

Willis's walk had taken him round in a large circle. He now found himself back in front of the police station.

He thought for a moment that he would very much like to resign there and then, just leave a note on his desk (*Goodbye. Fuck you.*) and walk out of the door never to come back. His heartbeat accelerated, adrenalin lightened his body. Then — Don't be daft, he thought. Stick it out and fuck the system.

He walked through to his desk and tried to think. Suddenly he felt very tired.

Chapter Fourteen

Shula had been sent away to stay with an aunt who lived in Essex, and Gran, Sebastian Lee's mother's mother, had been called in to look after the remaining two members of the Miles household.

Mrs Miles had been in bed, on and off, for five weeks now — ever since her husband's funeral, in fact. Sebastian Lee and Shula could not quite see what all the fuss had been about at the time. Their father had already seemed distant from them. His disappearance into hospital and the way no one really talked about him had made him disappear from their minds more or less completely.

'Ashes to ashes', an uncle had remarked conversationally to his wife as they left the crematorium. 'Dust to dust.'

And Sebastian Lee, walking unseen behind them in a new suit (wicked smart), had had an immediate vision of his father as he had last seen him, standing tall by the pond holding the big black kite, suddenly crumbling as he stood, crumbling and blowing away in the wind like . . .

'Well, I prefer a good old-fashioned funeral,' his aunt had remarked, glancing up at the tall chimney which even now was venting Mr Miles's body fats sootily into the air. 'All this makes me think of a biscuit factory.'

. . . like Rich Tea crumbs, thought Sebastian Lee. Ashes to ashes. Dust to dust. Crumbs to crumbs.

Even if Sebastian Lee had not been expelled from school, he would have been kept in quarantine for some of the past few weeks. The private hospital which had taken in Mr Miles had completely mis-handled the case. Plague, the *pasteurella pestis* virus, can be cleared up with antibiotics relatively quickly if it is caught fast enough. Now the hospital was taking no chances, and had advised that the surviving members of the family quarantine themselves.

This suggestion had been taken up by Gran with baroque enthusiasm. It was not enough that Sebastian Lee stay indoors for the duration. He and his mother were barricaded upstairs with the skeleton of an old G-plan sofa that Gran had lugged from the garden shed and wedged into the landing.

She felt 'easier' that way, she yelled through a crack in the kitchen door when Sebastian Lee had tried to go down for some cornflakes on the first morning of her visit.

Meals were pushed onto a tray and pushed through the sofa frame. Then, whenever Gran thumped on the ceiling with an old broom handle, Sebastian would emerge from his room and pick up the tray, along with whatever encouraging homily Gran had scrawled on a scrap of paper.

Cheer up! Worse things happen at See!
Smile! Even when your heart is achking!

These didn't make Sebastian Lee feel any better.

As a back-up system there was an old intercom set that Sebastian had been given two birthdays back. The original idea had been to stretch the wire next-door to where his best friend lived, but then the neighbouring family had moved, and his mother had classed their replacements as 'common' and not to be associated with. So the intercom had meanwhile lain gathering dust in the garage until Gran had discovered it and pushed it through the sofa one breakfast-time.

The intercom system was now used to arrange more complex matters than meals: matters like changing the sheets — something Gran was very particular about, and which she managed to turn into an exercise worthy of a Pentagon logistics expert.

First there was the call-up and response code, followed by a terse interchange of code-words that signified the change of sheets. (Gran seemed to think that even talking down a wire carried a risk of contagion.) Having changed into navy-blue dungarees and a World War II gasmask, she would take up position outside Sebastian Lee's bedroom window and whistle three times. This was the signal for the dirty sheets to be let down on a long rope. Gran would then wheel the load to the garden incinerator, soak them in petrol and burn them. Sebastian would watch her prodding at the smouldering remains with an ancient laundry paddle until the last shred of material was consumed. When all was done, she'd give a thumbs-up sign and stump off indoors. The bomb squad had nothing on Gran; the spirit of the blitz lived on in the Miles household.

Sebastian Lee had hardly spoken a word to anyone since his father had died, and strange things were happening in his mind. The only communications he had with the outside world were reduced to a crackle by Korean electronics. Television was a bit one-sided, though it was switched on permanently in his mother's bedroom, and he was allowed to watch about as much of it as he wanted. On top of that he was continually disturbed by strange and elusive memories that centred around the pond where his father had cut his foot. They troubled him and danced in and out of his mind like great dark moths.

He tried to talk about all this with his mother one afternoon, and even thought he was really getting somewhere with her until he glanced at her face and saw that she was asleep. He himself had difficulty in sleeping, and when he did had such awful nightmares that he would cry and scream. But when he woke up he couldn't remember anything about them. In fact he preferred not to sleep at all, and when he did he tried to arrange it so that he nodded off during the day, as his mother did. She was sleeping a lot these days, thanks to tranquillisers, like about twenty hours out of twenty-four, and she hardly ate anything at all.

No, Sebastian Lee thought, he couldn't blame her for not eating. He, too, was getting sick of mince and onions and diced carrots. In fact there was a huge plastic bowl of the stuff in the middle of his bedroom floor which was beginning to grow mould on its grey fatty surface. He didn't know what to do with it. He couldn't really send it back downstairs, especially now it had been sitting around for weeks, for fear of hurting Gran's feelings. Gran set a lot of store by her mince, he knew.

Dreamily he dipped a hand in it, and rubbed the old mince between his fingers. It felt softly gritty. It stuck to his hands. Got behind his nails. Clung between his fingers. Bit gross, in fact.

He looked around for something to wipe his fingers on. There was a small pile of dirty washing in the middle of the floor, but he didn't want to get that too dirty. There was also a bedspread, but he liked that. It had a sort of flattened racing car on it, and when spread properly over the bed the bits that hung down the sides had wheels on them and the bit that hung down the back had exhaust pipes. He'd wanted racing cars and power boats on his wallpaper, too, but his mother had vetoed that idea and chosen pathetic naff clowns.

He smeared a hand across the wall. The fatty gravy left a long straight line that half obliterated one smirking clown-face. Another blob did for the balloons he was carrying, and a few more dabs completely covered the idiotic red nose and the horrible red, thick, shiny lips.

Now, thought Sebastian Lee, I can draw my own pictures. In the next-door room he heard the familiar music of *Blue Peter* start up, usually quite enough to send him trotting into his mother's bedroom where the TV sat on a dressing table, because he was madly in love with one of the presenters: the one with long legs who wore mini skirts.

But not today.

He heard his mother get up from her bed and start to bump into things, but he didn't even react when she fell over. Gran heard it, too, and started to bang on the ceiling with the broom. When that failed she started to buzz him on the intercom. Entranced, Sebastian Lee painted on.

A meaty grand prix was winding its way around his walls, screeching its way around posters, powering through the fitted cupboards. The chequered flag dripped pale streaks of fat onto his pillow. Finished! Sebastian Lee, Champion of the World!

Filled with the sense of anticlimax that follows every great endeavour, he dipped his hand back into the mince and began to doodle aimlessly. He splashed on a thick horizontal line. Blobs of meat from it began to slide down, trailing gravy behind them. To balance them, he painted vertical streaks upwards and finished each one off with a blob on top. Mince trees growing out of hillocks of meat and fat jogged some dim memory, because he frowned and began to fill in the ground at the feet of the trees with bushes. A little hummock, a tree, shrubs. What was needed now was water.

Another part of Sebastian Lee's mind began to register discomfort. His painting hand began to falter. It would stop moving and fall by his side, then drag itself up again like a puppet's arm. Without properly realising it, he began to cry. His hand began to shake, and he could no longer control it. A compulsion gripped him that went deeper than will. His hand began to dip into the basin of putrid meat with the regularity of a piston and darted like a lizard all over the wall, filling in details with a skill that was not his own. The tree was now plainly birch-like, and the dark shape in front of it suddenly seemed to sharpen and define itself. A pond with short gravelly banks. Half of Sebastian Lee was fascinated by these new Rolf Harris skills; but the other half was terrified by the shape that was emerging, slowly but with increasing definition, as his arm, now aching and tired, splashed in and out of the emptying basin and glided over the wall.

Sebastian Lee felt a moan start somewhere in his tummy. It wobbled around there for a while then decided to move upwards, finally squeezing itself from his lips as his brain registered what he had been painting.

The clouds that had gathered above the pond suddenly re-formed with a few deft strokes of the hand. A figure had taken shape, brown and white, but quickly reversing out to negative on Sebastian Lee's retina.

A round face, white as the moon but blander. Pebble eyes. A great barrel of a chest that seemed to heave and swell, bulge, expand, writhe as if there were creatures beneath the mantle of white which were trying to escape. And as this thought hit Sebastian Lee, the pale disk of the face split open into a huge smile, wider and wider, tearing itself apart, and the white sprung from the great hole, leapt the gap and entered the boy's brain like a tornado of foam. For an instant he felt terror and strength flood him. Then he collapsed.

He awoke in a fog and sat up. Not a wispy, tendrily gothic fog, but a roaring block of dense paleness so bright that it hurt his head to look at it. A corridor led through it. He could see down the corridor but only down there. If his eyes strayed from the narrow boy-wide passage, the blindness and the roaring pain took him, and he had to focus desperately and in agony on the passage again.

Then the pain started behind his head. He took a step forward. He had to. And another. And another. Faster. Slower. He found the speed. The passage through the howling fog led him downstairs, over the barrier on the landing and through the front door. Outside it was night — a bit of his brain dimly registered that.

He turned right onto the street and followed it to the end. He took a narrow path between two gardens; dog-legged through a smart modern estate, and then walked on, sensing the ground beneath his feet change from paving-stone to grass.

Then he stopped. He swung his head from left to right like a blind animal, flinching as he waited for the pain to punish him. Cautiously he unscrewed his eyes and saw a ruined building above him, jagged and black against a moon haze.

A voice was calling him from a dark hole punched in the building's side — a voice that sounded warm and thick and kind. It sounded so kind he wanted to cry, and he proved too weak to resist. He followed his feet to the darkness, which was now beginning to glow with a sinister, pale opalescence.

Chapter Fifteen

17 Heath Hill Row
Blackheath
London SE3

2 November 1987

Dearest dearest Jennifer
We all promise to write, we promise to phone, but we never do. Thank God I called you the other week. If I hadn't I don't think I would be able to write. Please bear with me. Keeping hold is not easy.

I went to church once when I was a child and we were vacationing up in Maine near Portland — I suppose my mother thought that I'd better see the inside of a church just once — although she didn't approve at all. Anyway, the priest gave a sermon about those in peril on the sea. The story was that there was this ship and there was this captain and there was this storm and it began to look as if the ship was breaking up. Waves were all over the deck and the masts were down, the rats had left, and everyone went down to the saloon to hold a prayer meeting. Then someone noticed that the captain wasn't there. They were all pretty upset and went looking for him so he could say the prayers for them because then that would carry more weight. They found him on the bridge, lashed to the wheel, and said: 'What do you think you're doing? Why the fuck aren't you down there helping us pray? You ARE the captain after all.' Anyway, the captain just looked at them and said: 'When the weather's good I pray and say "Thank you, God, for the fine weather." But when the weather's bad I don't think of God at all. I just try to stop the ship from sinking. Now get the hell off my fucking bridge and let me sail the ship.'

Cute!

Anyway, the upshot of this small early dose of religion (actually the priest didn't swear) was that when my parents were drowned a couple of years later, out boating, I didn't pray and I didn't ask anybody for help because I thought it was wrong. I couldn't even ask my relatives for help because I hadn't been properly appreciative of them before I needed them. Fortunately my aunt and uncle, who you met once, were very nice, and operated on the assumption that I was barking mad.

I think that sermon really fucked me up, and I suppose what I'm getting round to saying is that if I hadn't called you the other day. I wouldn't be writing to you now.

Perhaps you heard about the murders here? Well, Peter was one of them. I mean of the victims. I know that sounds a little bald, I've tried to think of the best way of putting it. Peter's dead. Whichever way you phrase it, I might as well be saying: The weather's nice; I like apples; my husband's dead; I hate my hair the way it is. I feel I should apologise for telling you all this, like I'm ruining your perfect day. There's a commercial they have here to stop people taking drugs. The punchline is Heroin Screws You Up. Well, death screws you up. It screws up the survivors. The heroin addicts I knew at school seemed pretty happy. It was all the other guys, who didn't want them to die, who suffered. It's other people dying that screws you up. It screws you up in a lot of ways, but the worst thing is that instead of going around crying and screaming, you go around the whole world apologising for still being alive. Come on, Death, take me instead.

It was awful. We'd nearly split up and nearly got back together again. I thought he hated me and I was probably right, and I probably deserved it, because deep down he was very conservative and traditional and old-fashioned (all the things I thought were shocking and outrageous and exciting in New York, like him pissing in the sink, are just normal here and really disgusting). I should have known. I always blamed him for being immature, but in fact he was just himself and I couldn't see. That makes me immature. Just before he was killed he tried to make up, and now I can never tell him that it was all my fault.

There. I'm sounding like a victim again. I hate him for dying, too, and things really were pretty awful before because I was cracking up and *he couldn't have cared less.* I was going mad, Jennifer darling. I was seeing things. Having visions. Everything was dirty and awful. The washing-machine overflowed and all the foam spilled out of the top and I flipped. I thought it was chasing me. I was crawling across the floor going: 'White than white. Whiter than white.' That's an old soap commercial here.

So everything's a bit on the intense side at this very moment. Now, of course, there's just a horrid buzzing inside my head like all the thoughts are rushing around and cancelling each other out. White noise. But I'm better now, really I am. I'm writing to tell you that I'm back in the land of the living dead (joke, ha ha).

This will be one hell of a letter to get. Thank you and sorry. I mean thank you for being there for me to write to so I can put all thoughts together. (What thoughts I don't know.)

How are things with you? *Please* write and tell me you're fine.

All love
Cherie.

She licked the envelope and stuck it down. The glue left a faint brown taste on her tongue. Not altogether unpleasant. She put the envelope on the hall table to be picked up later when she went into the village for a bit of shopping. She went shopping every day now. Sometimes she went twice or three times a day (though never to the same shop). At times she would look up from the pavement and encounter a face like hers, a white mask of misery, a bit puffy around the eyes and with deep lines running diagonally from the edge of the nostrils, pulling the mouth down at the corners.

But the village hadn't changed one bit. It had worn mourning weeds for a fortnight, then got bored with looking solemn. By the time Cherie was able to go out of the house, the shopkeepers had taken off their solemn faces and put on their jolly pre-Christmas ones. A minor TV celebrity was booked to throw the switch on the Christmas lights, and some posters went up about it. The colours red and green began to appear everywhere, and while at times these made Cherie think of Father Christmas and Christmas trees, at other times they brought to mind blood on the grass.

But the worst thing of all was the boredom.

Every pointless step from room to room was recorded in her mind. She focused with fierce concentration on the petty and the banal, and yet at night, when she lay in bed and sweated for fear of what sleep might bring, she could not call to mind a single action that could have filled a minute, or one solitary detail from the empty hours as the day dragged its dead feet from brown morning to white night.

Cherie looked at her watch. The sitting-room was too big to sit in comfortably; the kitchen was too dirty. She trudged upstairs and collapsed on the bed, then decided that she wanted to change her clothes, and she went to the wardrobe. Her husband's dark suits hung on wooden hangers like rows of empty men. They even had names: Valentino, Ralph Lauren, Versace. Cherie began to pull them out and pile them on the floor, but as her hands closed on one she felt something in the breast pocket. A wallet. His wallet. Season ticket. Credit cards. A memo: *Call J.* Five and ten pound notes. Access card receipts. It was the suit he had been wearing at work on the day . . . the day . . .

As she held the wallet, Cherie began to cry with heaving, racking sobs which soon settled into an easier rhythm that rose and fell on each breath. Blindly her hands felt deeper into the pocket. There was something else there. An envelope.

She pulled it out, crying even more, crying so much that she did not register that it reeked of scent. She ripped it open with fingers that would not stop trembling. Empty. No. Something in the corner. Holding the envelope by the bottom, she shook it over the bed.

Hair. A strange small lock of short hair tied in a tiny red ribbon. Blond hair. Crinkled. Crisped. Coarse. It lay on the duvet like a little dead animal.

No NO NO! A scream of horror and outrage rose in her throat. NO-O-O-O-O

She stopped it suddenly. Wrinkling her nose and gagging slightly, she slipped the envelope under the small sprig of crinkled hair as if it was a spider, and carried it to the lavatory. She dropped it in, pressed the flush, and watched the first and last hard evidence of her husband's infidelity race round the wide white eye of the bowl and gurgle down the waste pipe.

Something broke in her and followed it down into the sewers. Something relaxed in her face; some tension went out of her shoulders.

On the way back from the post office where she had posted the letter to Jennifer, she dropped off a great black bin-bag of expensive men's clothes at the Oxfam shop, and walked home feeling better than she had done for a long time.

Chapter Sixteen

The letter-box snapped. There was the solid clunk of something heavy hitting the mat. Cherie went into the hall. No letters — just another sample of the endless variety of free newspapers that the British had invented to bore people with. They even emphasised the class system. In West London people got treated to big fat glossies bulging with seductive full-frontal home ads and recipes to cure champagne hangovers with yet more champagne. In South London they got tat. Is this the country that once ruled half the world? she asked herself. Would Queen Victoria be amused?

She picked up the paper out of habit, the newsprint smearing on her hand, and wondered idly what the headline would be.

COUNCIL HOSTEL IN DRUGS SCANDAL, for instance?

RUGGER CLUB ROWDIES UPSET WIDOW, perhaps?

Or SAVE MY HENHUT (*pleads retired caretaker who awoke one morning to find burly municipal workmen tearing down the wooden structure. 'I spent 17 years of my life building this to give my hens a decent home,' the shaken pensioner told our reporter. 'Nobody told me I needed planning permission'.*)?

But the main story concerned some wrangle over school funding, an issue Cherie had long since given up trying to understand. However, there was an article on the second page with a photograph that caught her eye.

She read the caption: *The Blackheath Convent As It Was.*

It was an early photograph: it had that clear, scratchy appearance to it. The building stood surrounded by young trees and well-tended shrubbery (which looked like rhododendron) and Cherie realised with a sort of thrilling shudder that part of the reason that it all looked so strange was that today the trees overshadowed the building, as they had now grown so tall, and the rhododendron shrubs had become high, waxy walls of heavy, rustling green.

The building itself was almost unrecognisable. Instead of the strange and asymmetric wings, the high gables and the spiralling chimneys, there was a weird and misshapen central hulk with small wings, probably just outbuildings, sticking out uncomfortably on each side. The convent had originally been plain — no, it had been hideously ugly. All Cherie could compare it with was the top of a water-tower. In fact it looked like a tank: it was far too square for a house; too high-shouldered. But as she looked more closely she saw that square was the wrong word, too. As far as she could tell, the old convent had been built in the form of a pentagon. There was a definite break in the wall, a different depth of shadow, although the flat roof did seem to be square, so that corners of the walls stuck out underneath.

But what struck her most forcibly was the fact that the modern building, with its typical Victorian neo-gothic flourishes, paid no attention whatsoever to the original house. Hadn't someone told her that these were just additions? If they were, that must mean the original house was *inside* the later Victorian facade. The thought made her queasy, and she realised why she had felt that the building looked somehow bigger when it had been knocked around a bit. There was another building inside it, trying to get out. Why hadn't they just knocked the whole lot down and started again?

The article itself was really only an excuse to print the illustration. It was thought to be the only picture of the original convent in existence, and had been sent in by a reader who had come across it while emptying the attic. A footnote said that the reader's great-grandfather had been a builder and perhaps he had worked on the alterations (her word), so had kept the photograph as a memento. The article went on to say that the demolition work had been suspended indefinitely. The police had held it up initially, as they were combing the area for a gang of drug-crazed necromancing surgeons, and after that the Department of the Environment had stepped in tardily with an emergency preservation order, once it had been established for certain that the main structure dated back over three hundred years. A spokesman from the demolition firm had said mysteriously that he did not know what was going on, but he'd been told in no uncertain terms by his employer to keep away. The reporter then tried to spice the story up with a ghoulish report of an ancient lead coffin being found in the convent grounds.

Cherie wondered vaguely if the detail about the coffin was true. If it was, she didn't really want to know much more about it. If it wasn't, she wondered how the hell reporters got away with making up things like that.

It was still morning. The sun was low and bright, and it came in through the fanlight in the hall and struck the side of Cherie's head, bathing her in a warm orange glow as she put on her anorak and adjusted her headscarf in front of the mirror. Cherie looked at her face for the first time, it seemed, in years. Wide-apart eyes, a slightly pointed nose, high cheekbones (hollow cheeks) and a mouth that had seemed normal by American standards but which English people told her was large and sexy. The eyes stared back at her; they didn't slide away. The mouth had lost it sharkish droop at the corners. The mellow sunlight even gave her the illusion of a tan. She became aware of a pain between her shoulders which had been with her for weeks, and she found that by straightening her spine and holding her neck further back on her shoulders the pain lessened. You're getting better, she said to herself, and this time, instead of heading towards the village with its shops and warmth and relative anonymity (as long as you didn't send your children to one of the schools, or belong to one of the choral societies, or own a dog) she turned towards the wide open space of the heath itself.

She wasn't surprised to find herself heading towards the convent. The sun lit up the old ruin half obscured by the high rhododendrons and wild shrubbery around it. Cherie thought she could catch a glimpse of mellow sandstone through the foliage, and wondered if this was one of the original walls, exposed now that the red-brick Victorian skin had been broken. She had a strong desire to get closer.

There was a break in the fence so she stepped inside, folding herself in among damp leaves, half aware of the rank smell of nettles. Her foot hooked up a bobble hat from under the grey tangled grass. The noise of the traffic dropped to a distant hum. She pushed forwards, ignoring the wet that dripped on her head, unaware of the denseness of the air which wrapped the building in silence . . .

She was standing on a lawn. Ahead of her a path of mossed flags led towards the convent. Following it, her eyes were fixed on the wall in front of her. This side of the building had been left untouched by the wreckers. A great pointed window was set in it, crudely bricked up. The mortar looked fresh, but already the lichen from the surrounding stones seemed to be spreading over it, touching the breeze blocks and making them look as if they were sweating green. There were black chinks in the blocks — the darkness was dripping out.

Cherie followed the path around the side of the wall. It turned a corner and kinked round a towering hedge of yew. Here outbuildings stuck out from the back of the house like an afterthought, built of the same depressing colour of brick as the convent itself. There were no windows in the buildings, only a line of narrow doors set maybe six feet apart. One of them hung open.

Cherie stuck her head inside, recoiling immediately from the smell of animal. But it was a stale smell, and something told her that whatever had been kept here had gone — gone with the nuns. Her eyes slowly grew accustomed to the gloom. A rough concrete floor showed itself through a thin layer of straw. A stable perhaps? No feedbox set high on the wall. Only a great steel hook and a chain with a spring clasp lay heavy against the plaster and snaked across the floor. Two enamel bowls. Dog — it was the smell of dog.

Cherie backed out, feeling fear prickle up and down her back, her mind going back to that story she'd read in the library about the gentleman, almost three hundred years ago, who had been set upon by large and vicious dogs. These were the kennels then, and they had still been inhabited until not so long ago. Dogs kept in the dark until night time, until they were let loose into the dark outside. For what, though? To protect what? A house full of silent nuns padding through the corridors, intent only on their salvation, while the dogs were intent on . . . Murder?

Cherie took deep breaths to steady herself. This was getting absurd. Of course they needed some protection. But one — two — three – four . . . she counted ten kennels. The air stuck in her lungs like cotton wool and she felt herself panic. She had to get away from that row of empty, stinking kennels.

She ran from the yard. The building bobbed and wheeled above her like a huge cliff dancing. The yew hedge blocked her. So tall, so long, so dark and dusty. There was no way through. The ground began to break up. It became rutted and pitted and white vapour clung to the dark puddles that lay in the rough folds of the brown earth. Cherie glanced up. The sun was wavering behind a layer of clouds. She stopped and looked up at it as it flickered out like a gaslight, leaving only a glaring stain on the grey clouds that flowed across the sky. She looked around her.

To her left lay another lawn, wide and empty and terribly exposed to the blank eyes of the building to her right.

A great hole had been smashed in the wall.

Cherie recoiled, then remembered the demolition work.

Pull yourself together, girl. You're jumping around like a lobster on a griddle.

where did THAT come from?

She forced herself to approach.

The wreckers' ball had knocked out a great archway in the masonry. It hadn't shattered the bricks. They lay still cemented together like a jagged pink tongue on the wet grass. Inside all was confusion. And dark. The wall must have taken some of the floor below with it, for Cherie could see a black gap in the floorboards which suggested a deep cavity, a cellar perhaps, below. Above, the boards of the first floor drooped, offering up a view of little rooms, doors to the corridor tightly shut, but exposed from behind. Cherie had the sudden absurd thought of a gust of wind blowing up the skirts of a stout old lady and showing her bloomers. That was the effect it gave. But the cells reminded her uncomfortably of the kennels. They were tiny. The beds came down from the walls on hinges. A potty had skidded from under one into the middle of the little room.

The ground floor was dark. The gap was narrower here, and all Cherie could see was a corridor, wood-panelled with doors leading off it on each side. The corridor was quite light and she saw that while an electric light hung from a cord in the ceiling, swaying gently, the ornate gas fittings were still there, set into the wall at regular intervals. It was as if the convent had been kept in a time warp. She stepped over the gap in the floor and walked inside.

Immediately to the left and right of her a narrow room, almost a corridor, led off from the passage she was standing in. She realised with a thrill that her supposition had been right, and that the Victorian addition was actually a mere skin built around the original house that stood, that was still standing, inside. In fact the inside corridor wall would be the original outer wall. She touched it, a strange feeling welling up inside her which she took a little while to recognise. Then she realised that there was no one that she could tell all this to — in short that she was lonely. It was a sobering thought, and she suddenly began to wonder very hard what she was doing there.

She stepped back into the passage, meaning to take one more look down it before heading straight home. Then she saw that the door at the end was open, and that light was coming from it.

She remembered a story she had once read in which two children were taken to a vast ruined city in another world. While wandering through it they came across a bell with a poem on it, the gist of which was: *You may think you're too scared to hit the bell, but if you don't you'll spend the rest of your life wondering what you missed.*

Cherie walked towards the light.

The door opened easily to her touch. She stepped inside and found herself standing beneath a great domed skylight in a tall many-sided hall as high as the house. It was like a glassed-over courtyard, five-sided, with a wooden stairway zigzagging up one wall, and bannistered galleries all around on all three floors. And in the middle of the floor was a figure.

He was lying on his side, propped up on an elbow, with his back to her, and seemed to be idly scratching in the dust. As Cherie approached him, a pigeon exploded into flight from one of the galleries and began to crash against the skylight; the boy looked round and saw her. He stood up.

Cherie had never seen eyes so black or a face so white. His gaze was blank and uninterested.

'Hello?' he said.

'Hello.'

'What are you doing here?'

It was a simple, unloaded question, Cherie had difficulty in answering it.

'I guess I was just curious. How about you?'

I . . . I . . .' the voice began to distort like a record-player slowing down. 'I live . . . I live here.' Now the boy's face was distorting with the voice. It was swelling, bulging, shape-changing — as if there was a rat beneath a latex sheet. The nose would develop a great swelling which would then shift to the forehead and down to the cheek. Cherie stared, too surprised to move, too amazed to feel scared. She had a ridiculous impression that she was seeing a conjuror go through his tricks in a desperate attempt to find the right one.

Then the boy began to scream: 'Stop it! Stop it! It hurts. Leave me alone! PLEASE!'

The dreadful moment stopped and he stood there looking exhausted and resentful.

Cherie stepped towards him. He moved back, petrified, eyes darting to and fro. Then he stopped.

'You'd better leave,' he said.

Suddenly Cherie recognised him. Weeks back she had been walking on the heath and had seen a boy collapse by the pond. This was the boy, though he looked slightly different now. She struggled with fear and revulsion. Suppose he went all boneless again? She moved towards him, realising with a shock that his pallor was not natural but a smooth, ivory sheen of whiteness.

'I've seen you before,' she said. 'You fainted or something by the old pond in the middle of the heath.'

The boy seemed to wince.

'Go away,' he said. 'We don't like you here. We don't . . .'

But as he spoke he began to dribble, and a thick white foam blocked his words. His face hardly changed. It seemed as if he was still talking, oblivious to the thick white liquid his jaws were chopping. The liquid, light and foamy, floated through the air like spindrift and balled in the dust at Cherie's feet. It smelled of old meat.

'Oh my God. OH MY GOD STOP IT!'

He stopped. 'Please go. Please,' he said.

'Come with me,' said Cherie.

There was a whistle and a sudden dull thump at her side. The pigeon had fallen stone dead inches away from her shoulder. She glanced up.

Whiteness massed outside the dome of glass above her.

'GO!' he said.

The whiteness began to fold itself thickly in the gaps and crevices of the outside walls.

'Look I can't just leave you! You're sick! Let me . . .'

Thicker, heavier tendrils began to force themselves through — where they hung and grew downwards like stalagtites. She sensed that shapes were gathering all around.

'At least let me tell your mother or father where you are. At any rate give me your —'

The shapes were moving, shooting towards each other like mad stars, imploding, growing, spinning a web of whiteness that slowly began to gain a form, the form of a towering composite body, many-sided, many-faced, bent over with intentness and pain, and glowing with the dead dull gravelight of the moon.

'— your address. Your name!'

The white began to form a curtain between them, Cherie grabbed Sebastian Lee by the wrist and ran from the hall.

She stopped.

The door swung shut behind them.

He was walking towards her. The White Man. It could be no other.

The passage walls narrowed into lines of focus that ended with his face. Face-place, but no face there. Or were there too many of them?

Eyes, cheeks, mouths, all seemed to be rushing to the surface of a transluscent plasma, like fish in an aquarium. All trying to get out.

All trying to look at her.

There were old and young faces. Eyes that seemed desperate. Eyes that seemed sad. Eyes that leered at her. Peter's eyes held hers for a second: half mocking, half pleading. Some of the eyes turned her on. The shape began to mutate slowly into a pale column of flesh that ended in a deep red pit. The one eye. The red eye that began to weep.

But the figure was both male and female, a composite

compression of hermaphrodite chaos. On the pink shaft breasts swelled, hung, drooped, deflated. Legs writhed to the surface, blisters on the membrane. Vulvae opened like delicate, gaudy tropical flowers . . . Cherie's head swum with fear, expanded with a throbbing desire to surrender to black waves of pure lust.

She felt her herself empty out, spread and expand like a great hot-blooded flat fish. She sank to the ground, still faintly aware that she should be holding the child in a last-ditch attempt to be protective —

(the boy was looking bored and slightly embarrassed)

— or holding her arms out in the sign of the cross. Back Cunt Dackulick! On my back! Wrong words.

Her tongue died in her mouth. Her arms and legs felt as if they had been filleted; her brain-pan scoured and bleached with boiling water or . . . oil.

A cleft opened in her forehead and something slipped in through the oil and began probing deliciously in the warmly filled balloon of space.

In front of her the figure disintegrated, dissolved, spun upwards like a tiny tornado, then resolved into a woman of vicious clichéd beauty who took Cherie for a second, mingled with her, pierced each cell with needles so that she exploded in a fountain of pleasure, then passed *through*, and dropped her wet and trembling on the ground.

'It is not your time,' she sighed in a zephyr voice of razor blades, and breath that smelled of violets and the butcher's block. 'But we all loved having you. Come again soon.'

Cherie blacked out.

It was discomfort that woke her up. Her arm was being pulled high above her head and her left hip was scraping along the ground. Opening her eyes and straining round, she could see that the boy was pulling her outside with grim determination. The last thing she could remember was walking into that weird glassed-over hall and seeing him there.

'Hey.' Her voice felt thick and out of practice. Everything hurt. She jerked along the ground some more. 'What's going on?'

'Are you better now?'

She was looking at a plump child's face. Sad, rather too wise, but nice.

'I think you fainted. I was just getting you out into the fresh air. You see, I don't think we're meant to be in here.'

'No. OK, you can let me go now. Just give a shoulder.'

Cherie stood up and, with one hand on Sebastian Lee's shoulder, made it outside to the fresh air.

'Ogh! My head. Thanks. What happened?'

The boy was leading her round to the front of the building, where the damage was the worst. He wheeled out a BMX bike that had been propped behind a wall. Inside the building the floors were thick with dust and rubble. Noticing that disturbed Cherie for a moment.

'I think you fainted. I was just poking around, and I saw you come in. Then you went over — clunk! I hope you're all right.'

He was now leading her through some shrubbery to a gap in the fence, the same one she had come in by.

'Yeah, I'm fine. At least I think I am. Thanks for getting me out'. She glanced back at the building. Surely there was more to say.

'Well, if you're really all right I should be getting home. Oh, I found something you dropped. I put it in your pocket.'

He mounted the bike.

'Wait a minute!' Cherie called after him. 'I know you. I knew there was something about you. I've seen you before. You fainted or something by the old pond in the middle of the heath. A few weeks ago. Well, I'm the one who found you and called the ambulance.'

I've been here before, she thought.

The boy's face was very blank.

'Yes, I did faint there. I'm afraid I can't remember very much about it. Thank you very much.' He brooded. 'It's nice isn't it? You help me and I help you.'

'Sure. Take care. See you.' Something was tugging at her memory. Something about history repeating itself. That *déjà vu* feeling.

'Bye.' The boy fixed lights onto his bike and cycled off into the dusk.

Into the dusk. It had been morning when she went out. Had it? Could it have been? She put her hand into her pocket and felt something small and heavy in there. She pulled out a heavy signet ring. By its feel it was solid gold: Although it certainly wasn't hers, it seemed familiar. The boy must have found it on the floor and assumed it was hers. Ah, well, she could take it to the police.

As she walked up the steps to her house a new thought hit her. She had entered the convent by a hole in the wall which led to the corridor. Strange, then, that there had been no tracks on the lawn from the crane. But even stranger was the way the bricks lay. In the rest of the building they had lain in great broken piles on the floor, where the demolition ball had knocked them. There, however, they had fallen on the grass.

Whatever had made that great tear in the building's side had been forcing its way out, not smashing its way in.

Chapter Seventeen

The moonlight is lying across the bed in pale strips. The curtain is moving very slightly because I left the window open a crack. The person sitting at the end of the bed staring at me and not moving at all but just waiting is my trousers and my shirt and a crumpled sweater that looks like a hat, and I laid them out like that on a chair before I went to bed because, like a moron, I forgot that I always wake up in the middle of the fucking night and see spiders in the twig shadows of the moonlight on the duvet, or tree shadows waving at me against the curtain where the street light projects them straight onto my brain. And then there's always the footsteps outside in the empty street that *stop* whenever I hear them, and they would stand still looking up at my bedroom window — like a dog waiting — if I didn't turn the light on to send them away. And then there's always the sound the central heating makes when it cools down, and the pipes make a hollow sound or two and the floorboards go thump-boom-crump-creak like footsteps crossing the floor — that's normal at three in the morning — LIKE FOOTSTEPS WALKING ACROSS THE FLOOR, FOR CHRIST'S SAKE, THREE HOURS AFTER THE HEATING'S OFF. LIKE FOOTSTEPS — I'M NOT HERE I'M NOT HERE I'M NOT HERE I'M NOT HERE I'M A MOUSE AND THERE'S SOMEONE IN MY HOUSE. I HAVEN'T DONE ANYTHING go away go away go away pleeeease

JUST LEAVE ME ALONE!

What do I do when the bedroom doors swings open? Oh dear God, what do I do when the bedroom door swings open? Do I scream? It's like the bomb on the underground. Do you pull the emergency switch with the train swaying through the darkness? Or do you watch it? Wait and just watch it? And when you're playing possum in bed with THE man's breath on your neck and whistling damply down your ears, suppose HE doesn't play dog. Suppose HE doesn't walk away like a proper well-behaved animal. Suppose he grabs you by the hair and drags you down to the floor. Suppose you can't scream by then because it's too late, and his knee's on your throat and his dick's in your face.

Silence.

Cherie heard all the sounds she normally made but usually didn't hear. There was the dull humming roar of blood in her ears. The sound of air whistling slightly in and out of her nostrils. The sound of her heart; a tiny gurgle from her gut; the rustle and creak of the mattress and bedclothes as she forced herself not to bury her head in the pillows.

There was someone in the house. There had been someone in her house. They were gone now. It was all right. The house was safe. She was safe. Silence. Can't you hear? No noise at all. The house is yours — again. Go to sleep. You're fine now. Until the next psycho makes his way in through the swinging french window, the jemmied window, with the axe. Cherie Simpson, *in* the bedroom, *with* the axe. But not the murderer in this game. Just the victim. Just the victim. A victim? Me? Never . . .

Try to stop breathing. Try to stop that heart beating.

Silence.

Not even a mouse

Whimpering, Cherie swung her legs over the edge of the bed and tiptoed across the room to the door. It was open a crack. She paused and put her ear to the gap.

Silence. Still.

She felt the cold for the first time and had to tiptoe back to where a man's dressing-gown lay across the foot of the bed. She listened again at the door. Nothing. But as she stepped across the landing she felt cold trickle across her insteps and ankles and she realised that a draught was swirling around her feet. From the open window. Somewhere at the bottom of the stairs.

The stairs did not creak. She lifted her hand with each step as she walked down so it would not rub against the wood of the bannister. The hall was cold. Moonlight swam through the fanlight and pooled on the carpet. Crossing it made Cherie feel very exposed.

And as she stepped through the door into the living-room, Cherie knew she had been duped, knew that all the time there had been someone in there, somebody more silent than she was, who had heard her sit up in bed, had waited while the thoughts ran like black beetles through her brain, had heard her tiptoe across the floor and down the stairs. Quiet as a mouse. A dead mouse.

She felt the presence. She heard the breath. And as she whipped round, the wind whistled past whatever hit her and the world exploded into splintered shards of white. For a split second she remembered the telephone by her bed and briefly wondered if calling from upstairs would have made any difference. The blackness gurgled up from the drain at the bottom of her mind. She had a brief moment of relief that at least the fear would be gone while she was unconscious. Then she crumpled up and lay still.

Daylight broke into her mind like a thief and stole away what little comfort she had. She was lying where she had fallen. The blinding pain which filled her head gradually separated into two areas of intense agony: one behind the left ear where she had been hit, the other over the left temple where she had fallen. She lay still a while, then sent probes down into the rest of her. Arms still there; check. Legs not mashed: check. Spine not removed: check check check, click click click. Beaten up? No — Raped? No — Possessed by demonic forces? No — How do you know? Well, not possessed any more than usual.

OK. Get up.

Can't.

Won't, you mean.

Can't can't can't.

What would anyone think, seeing you all curled up there?

Don't want to.

Don't want to what? Get up? Or see what they've done to your house?

Oh, no no. Please no. Not that as well.

Cherie got up onto all fours, her head hanging down like a sick animal. She still had her eyes tightly closed. Now she opened them.

The pain increased and dark blinkers loomed and flashed weirdly in the corners of her eyes, threatening to spread across her line of vision entirely. It all seemed OK. Some drawers pulled out. A few things on the floor. A table lamp had been knocked over, but it wasn't smashed. It was cold though. Out-of-doors winter cold, but inside. Cherie pushed herself achingly to her feet and weaved her way across the floor to where the french windows into the garden swung open. The lock had been jemmied messily. Splinters of wet wood stood out sharply against the white gloss paint. Cherie pulled the doors shut, wedging them together with a folded-up *Sunday Times* recipe she had torn from the colour supplement and never used.

She turned back to the room. Saw what had been written above the mantelpiece. Above where she had lain. Big letters. Red. Dripping.

I'LL BE BACK. SEE YOU, PRESH

Oh God. Peter. She just made it to the sink and was violently and painfully sick.

Willis was on duty when the call came through, and was one of the squad sent up to the hysterical Yank's house on the heath. An improvised emergency team had been set up for cases like this one, or for anything which could conceivably throw some light onto the murders. As the woman's husband had been one of the victims of the Blackheath massacre, and as she seemed to be suggesting over the phone that her husband had broken into the house the previous night, coshed her and then written to her in blood, it seemed a good idea to investigate. While Willis wouldn't have missed the trip for the world, it was just his luck that all the women were out or off duty when the emergency call came through, and he would have to conduct the interview.

The ambulance had got there first. The woman was sitting on an armchair while two ambulance-men tried to persuade her to come back to the hospital for an x-ray. She was holding a plastic bag of ice behind her left ear, and a bruise was just visible below the hairline on her forehead. One of the men looked at Willis and shook his head.

'See if you can persuade her to have a check-up. Otherwise we're off.'

'No.' She was quivering.

'She's still in shock,' the ambulance-man said in a stage whisper.

'That doesn't make me an imbecile.'

The two ambulance-men walked out, after shrugging ostentatiously to Willis. Cautiously he took a seat opposite her, eyes taking in the daubed message above the fireplace. Suspiciously red. Suspiciously shiny.

'We would just like to . . .'

He gestured to the fingerprint and the forensic experts who were doing their usual courteous but tight-lipped act.

She nodded. 'Don't tell me,' she said in a slightly

cracked voice. 'It's red paint. I know. I touched it.' She held out her hand. The palm was red, 'Who'd do that to me. Why? Why me?'

She looked at Willis, naked and desperate appeal widening her eyes momentarily. Then a shutter fell and closed her face off. She took Willis through what had happened the night before. He tried to make her remember whether or not there had been more than one person in the room. Had she smelled paint? What had woken her up? Cherie answered the best way she could, staring at the message on the wall. She broke off in the middle of an answer.

'How the fuck did he know?' she asked in a harsh voice.

'Know what?'

'That that's what he called me. My husband always called me "precious" or "presh". It was like some people say "darling" or "sweetie-pie". He called me "presh". Someone must have known.'

'It's not that unusual. It could be a coincidence . . .' Willis was instantly ashamed of his feeble rationalisation. The woman sent a blast of scorn and anger across the room towards him. He sensed resentment, too, and suddenly thought that he had let her down, that the whole country had let her down. Ridiculous. She must have made a decision to move here. All the same, the poor little thing must have gone through hell. Husband murdered. House broken into. Coshed.

I wish he'd stop gawking at me, thought Cherie.

'You've been through a lot,' he said.

'Meaning?' Quick. Snappy. About to snap.

Meaning, thought Willis, I feel very sorry for you. But I can't say that.

'Meaning all this must seem like some sort of horrible pattern, but I'm sure it really is just coincidence.' Oh God.

'Coincidence? COINCIDENCE?'

The fingerprint man turned round and raised an eyebrow, then got back to the job.

'Jesus, you fucking Brits. My husband's murdered by lunatics. Some fucking nutter comes into my house and pretends to write a message from him in red paint on my wall. And you say "coincidence". What's the matter with everyone here? Why do I get all the nutters?'

Willis tried another tack. 'Could anyone else have heard anything? A neighbour? Who are your neighbours?'

'Family on one side. Can't remember their name. Guy called Ransom lives there.' She jerked a thumb at the connecting wall. 'He's away, though. Been away since the . . . the . . .'

Cherie buried her head in her hands and began to cry. Which made her head hurt even worse which made her cry more.

Willis knew his limitations. He let her get on with it and went over to join fingerprints, who was looking at the polished dining table.

'There are a lot,' he said in a low voice. 'Four sets: two men, two women. There was a supper party here the night the two men got topped.' He looked over at Cherie, who had her head in her hands and was shaking. 'Can't very well ask her though, in her state. Why couldn't they have got a WPC though?'

Cherie heard them talking and stared across the room at them with dull wounded eyes. Very attractive in a pathetic sort of way, Willis found himself thinking — if her mouth didn't droop down like that at the corners. Wonder what her figure's like.

He nodded at his colleague, impressed by his sensitivity, and slightly disgusted by the thought of the fingerprints themselves, minute traces of sweat and grease and person, lasting so long after the person was dead. And there would be so much of a person around for so long. Not just the possessions, but the skin on the bath towels, the dust under the bed . . .

The message on the wall caught his eye. Someone was either very malicious or just lucky. He wandered over to the french windows. The wood looked as if it had been chewed. That surprised him. French windows usually gave way easily. Outside, in the high-walled garden, a set of wrought-iron chairs dripped onto the dewy grass. No footprints. He was reminded strongly of the cat he'd found in the compost heap — again.

Why had a burglar chosen this house? It was right in the middle of a terrace; the back garden was surrounded by a ten-foot-high wall. It must have been a bugger to get into. Unless . . . unless . . . He looked speculatively at the wall on Ransom's side, then walked back into the room.

The woman looked a bit better now. Willis sat down again, finding himself drawn towards her for some strange and no doubt highly unprofessional reason — and being drawn into this job as well. There were officers who claimed that grateful women clients were always the easy lays, but he had never bothered to find out. Too much involvement all round.

'Just a couple more questions, if you're up to them.'

'Yeah, I can manage. Then perhaps I should get down to the hospital.'

'We'll run you down.'

'Thanks. Fire away.' She gave a rather bad attempt at a plucky smile.

'Have you been able to notice what's been stolen yet?'

'I had a quick look. I think a set of apostle spoons went from the sideboard. And maybe — no definitely — the candlesticks. Silver. Old. A camera — Willis automatically checked for television, video, hi-fi. All were there — 'Oh and . . . I don't suppose it's important, though . . .'

Willis made encouraging noises while agreeing with her tacitly.

'There was an old wooden cross I found. I polished it up. It was beautiful. That went.'

'Was it valuable?'

'Well our next-door neighbour seemed interested in it. He said it was most unusual.'

'Ransom.'

'Yes.'

'Is he in?'

'No. I said he's away. He has been ever since that terrible . . . that terrible night.'

Cherie was clearly about to faint. Willis cut short the questions, helped her to her feet, and got her to the car.

As they drove off to the hospital, he glanced up at Ransom's front door. Another coincidence? Perhaps. But it did seem a little bit strange that Ransom's handsomely panelled front door was painted exactly the same shade of red as the message scrawled above Cherie's fireplace.

At six o'clock that night Willis was parked outside Cherie Simpson's house in his own very battered Datsun, wrestling with a problem. Another man might have been wrestling with his conscience, but Willis had suffocated his about twenty years before with tortuous and energetic rationalisations. Now it didn't bother him any more.

The problem was complex — and new. A career of studied non-involvement was about to come to an end. Meeting Cherie Simpson had clinched that. He did not want to bed her, and anyway had a suspicion, or rather was 110 per cent certain, that she would laugh in his face if he suggested anything of the sort, now or ever. But he was attracted to her in a very strange way. All this was further complicated by the case, which again was beginning to obsess him, and here at last was a lead. Whether the Simpson break-in was related to the massacre or not, someone had tried to make it seem that way.

He had done a bit of checking up on this Ransom as well. He'd found out the usual things: background, career, bank balance, and then had had a stroke of luck. While flicking through *Who's Who* he'd come across the name and been directed to look under Leaford. Lord Leaford's family name, he discovered, was Ransom, and the present Lord lived down in Kent. Different address: Leaford Hall, no less.

Then Willis remembered a vague whisper of scandal. He glanced at the date on the spine of *Who's Who*. 1961.

He pulled out a few more editions of *Who's Who*. The one for 1967 seemed to have the last listing for the name. That was strange in itself. Had Leaford or Ransom renounced his title? Was that enough not for him to be listed any more? Or were people struck off the list for crimes against their class?

He pushed all these thoughts to the back of his mind and tried to concentrate on the job in hand. How could he establish a link between Ransom and the break-in? Ransom had shown interest in one of the objects that had been stolen. Big deal. His front door was painted the same shade of red used by whoever had written over Mrs Simpson's wall. His garden wall was low at one point, and he could have got over it into the Simpsons' garden. Not exactly overwhelming evidence, but three strikes, at any rate — or whatever they said in America. Unfortunately Willis knew that a search warrant would be out of the question, but he was still certain that the case was worth investigating further.

And so is Mrs Simpson, said an irritating little voice inside his head.

Chapter Eighteen

After she had slapped yet another coat of white paint over the red message, Cherie stepped back. She noticed with dismay that large blobs of paint were forming into ragged tears and dragging themselves down the chimney breast to pool on the top of the mantelpiece, the result of too many thick layers of paint put on too quickly. Though it was illegible, the shape of the letters still showed through: a faint shadow-stain on the white.

She ran upstairs to her studio, where she knew there was an old sheet hidden away in a cupboard, ready to tear into rags. When she was halfway up the stairs the doorbell rang. She continued up, grabbed the sheet, ran down again, half fell into the hall yelling, 'OK! I'm coming!' — and then realised that she didn't want to let anyone in.

Shit. She stood there for a few seconds. Could she get away with it? Then the letter-box rattled and a voice came through it asking if she was all right.

'Who is it?'

'Sergeant Willis, from this morning.'

Big man. Slightly bored-looking one minute, sharp and intense the next. He'd driven her to the hospital and got her into x-ray in double-quick time. He had left his name and telephone number in case anything came up.

There was a dull thump and a clatter. Muffled. Coming from upstairs? Cherie rushed to the front door and pulled it open.

'Yes, yes. I remember you. Come in, please. I think I just heard a strange noise upstairs.'

Willis nodded and proceeded slowly across the parquet in a stairwardly direction.

'What sort of noise?' he asked.

'Muffled.'

'Like what?'

'Like something heavy and soft falling . . .' Cherie's voice tailed off as she realised that she was sounding melodramatic.

Willis didn't seem to mind however. He fished a torch out of his rally-jacket pocket and walked up the stairs.

'Er, be careful.'

He turned and gave a mirthless grin.

The stairs went up the back of the house. The nicotine-knight made the first-floor landing with barely a wheeze. It was a decent-sized landing hung with oil paintings, and two doors led off it. The first was the airing cupboard, the second a bedroom. Both were empty and quite untidy. White clean style; what Willis thought of as 'modern', though he knew that word was out of fashion. He looked for the latest John Le Carré paperback by the bed and was surprised not to find it. Instead there was Bulgakov's *The Master and Margarita.* Willis pursed his lips; he'd read it once on a self-improvement drive. Feeling out of touch, he'd gone into a bookshop on Charing Cross Road and bought up almost every paperback on the rack with the word 'important' mentioned in the blurb on the back cover. At the end he'd still felt out of touch, but had not cared so much. Most of what he'd read was rubbish; the Bulgakov was a welcome exception. But he'd been relieved to get back to Hammond Innes, Trollope and pulp Westerns, his favourite literary cocktail.

From the landing the stairs narrowed and steepened, and led directly into an empty low-ceilinged attic room which took up half the floor. The door from that led into Cherie's studio. Willis took a quick look round, and checked the cupboard. Canvasses were stacked facing the wall. There was a painting on the easel, draped with a cloth which he twitched off to reveal a heath scene done in the style of an American primitive. It worked well, though the sense of wonder that the originals conveyed by their apparent childishness and awkwardness had been tinged, or even replaced, by grotesque ironies.

In one corner of the picture a parked car with steamed-up windows stood by the heath, and an elderly man tried to look in inconspicuously while tying a shoe-lace. In another section two dogs were copulating while their owners, man and woman, sized each other up. Behind them a man was flying what looked like a cross between a kite and a baby. The pushchair beside him was empty. Something like a body was floating in a pond.

In the centre of the picture there was a group of young boys playing. They looked energetic, but still and awkward, almost as if they were taking part in some charade. The sky above them was a blinding grey, with strange shapes emerging from the clouds. The handsome terraced houses looked on with blank windows.

It was a good picture, Willis could tell, and it told him a lot about the artist. He guessed she had been working on it for some time, which suggested immediately that she had been somewhat disturbed before the murders, or if not disturbed, at least apprehensive about something. What, he wondered, and he set off back downstairs, whistling to show he was still alive.

Cherie was energetically rubbing away at the mantelpiece with the old sheet but every time she cleared up the sticky goop it started to run down somewhere else.

Willis suggested that she just leave the sheet on the mantelpiece to catch the worst of it, and then sandpaper the surface smooth again when it was dry.

'There was no one up there,' he added.

Cherie nodded. 'I must have made a mistake. Perhaps my neighbour's back and was moving things around.'

'Have you seen him?'

'No. Why are you here?' The question was open and direct. Not even particularly aggressive.

'I wanted to

(*see if you were all right*)

ask if anything had come back to you. You

were in a bad way when I was round here this morning.'

Cherie was sure that he had come round to see her for other reasons, and she was not confident she could handle that.

'Is that all?' she asked.

Her question connected with what was going on in Willis's head. For a moment he was flustered, and he confessed one of the other things on his mind.

'To be honest, Mrs Simpson, I am pursuing some investigations of a . . . general nature. Well, to be completely honest, we have made little progress into the events of that night your husband and friend were murdered, and I don't think, I'm afraid, that we're going about things the right way. So I'm trying to look into every strange occurrence that we could possibly link with the murders.'

He looked at her. 'It's OK,' she said. 'I don't break down every time I hear the word. It was just that last night was possibly the worst experience of my life, bar one, and it all seemed a little unfair.'

Oh God, no, she thought. I shouldn't have said that. Unfair always has this effect on me. And she felt her eyes begin to prickle with self-pity.

Willis lumbered across to the kitchen, visibly embarrassed, and began to fiddle with the unfamiliar complexities of a coffee machine, which at least gave Cherie the excuse to get up and send him back to the other half of the room.

Strangely this broke the ice between them.

As they sat down with cups of coffee, Willis pulled out his cigarettes and Cherie was about to protest (nasty dirty habit) when she suddenly found herself asking for one, then coughing violently as the Capstan Full Strength hit the back of her throat.

'Puts hair on your chest,' Cherie said, eyes watering.

'Puts hairs down your throat,' Willis answered.

They laughed. Then Cherie grew thoughtful. 'OK,' she said, 'I'll play. It's not exactly evidence, but for about three months now I've felt that there's something, I don't know . . . weird going on here.'

'I saw the picture,' Willis said.

'Oh, upstairs. Right — I mean good. So you saw the clouds I was trying to do? With that shape? Listen, did you know that this neighbourhood's got its own bogeyman? He's called the White Man and . . .'

Something's moving, Willis thought. God I'm cold, it's on the wall, the fucking wall's moving . . . down. He saw the paint that Cherie had slopped on fall to the floor in a great wet sheet and begin to twitch and writhe on the rug like a vast white flounder. And the words on the wall had changed.

SCREW HER WILLIS BLACK AND BLUE THEN I'LL SCREW YOU RED AND WHITE

And Willis whipped round to Cherie but nothing had changed and she was still talking. In the blink of his eyes the paint slapped itself back onto the wall. Sucked on. White lips pouted at him. Eye shape winked. Then gone.

'. . . he just appeared in the clouds I was painting above the kids playing,' Cherie was saying. 'Autosuggestion or something, but it's — Oh, I almost forgot.'

And she wrestled at her jeans pocket.

'Here.' She held out the ring Sebastian Lee had given her in the convent grounds. This kid found it and thought I'd dropped it. Anyway he ran off so I couldn't give it back. It isn't mine. Do I hand it in somewhere? Funny, actually, it looks a bit like the ring Ransom gave Peter, my . . . late husband. Some bribe or other, ha ha.'

Willis gave her a scared eyeball look and took the ring. Had the paint moved? He'd seen it, but she obviously hadn't. Was this how people cracked up? He glanced at the ring then stiffened.

'Wait a minute.' There was a crest on the ring. A building. Beneath it the metal had been dug into a hole which was now caked with earth. Unlike the fine metal work which described the house, this gave the impression of having been roughly and crudely done. It reminded Willis of something. Then he remembered. When he had first been a bobby on the beat, one of his patrols had taken him past a school. It was one of the schools local boys got into if they worked hard: a foundation school or something. Some fee-paying boys and some scholarship boys. A clear picture of the school now came into his mind and of the board outside. The Leaford School for boys, and below it a crest. The same crest.

'Ransom,' he said.

'Ransom?'

'The Leaford School!'

Cherie looked puzzled, then took back the ring he was holding between his finger and thumb.

'But that's what the convent used to look like,' she said. 'Before it was changed! There's a photo in the paper. Look —'

They both heard the door slam outside and footsteps run down to the road.

That was Ransom's front door, Cherie thought, and stood up to have a look at the street. But Willis had got there first and was trying to peer round the corner.

'Blast. Missed the car. Away, did you say?'

'Well, yes.'

'And he gave your husband a gold signet ring which just happens to be like this one?'

'Which looks like the old convent looked once.'

'Which has the same insignia as the Leaford School.'

'I know the name. I must have walked past it some time.'

'It's his name. Your next-door neighbour's. Before he changed it — or dropped the fancy bit.'

Willis paused.

'Look, I want to talk to this Mr Ransom. Either he's in and will answer the door, or he's out, in which case a concerned neighbour asked me to investigate mysterious noises coming from his property when he was away. Right?'

Cherie was slow to catch on.

'I said, right?'

'But I —'

'Look, Mrs Simpson, your next-door neighbour's front door is painted exactly the same colour as that writing on your wall. That's point one. Point two: there is a place on your garden wall where someone could conceivably climb over from Ransom's garden. Point three: he was interested in your cross — the one which was stolen. You told me that this morning, so it's no good shaking your head. Right, now tell me about that cross. Where did you find it?'

Cherie frowned.

Oh God, thought Willis. I pissed her off. Why is nothing simple? Settle down. Don't push. Don't bully.

He held his hands out in a placatory gesture. 'Look, I'm sorry. I don't mean to push, but I've got to know.'

Cherie raised an eyebrow. 'Relax. I was trying to think of something. You know, I didn't exactly find it — the cross, that is. I mean, it seemed to find me. It was just outside the old convent. It got knocked at me by a bulldozer. And I . . .'

Willis shook his head. He wanted more. But Cherie, white-faced, wide-eyed, stretched-skin, said: 'God. It's like someone's in my brain. It was about to remember something then. I was about to remember that face. It's like I had this dream . . . There was a man . . . and he began to spin . . . and dissolve? Sort of disintegrate. And there were a lot of clean bones and blood. I think.'

White and red, though Willis and felt sick. He glanced above the fireplace. Nothing.

'Oh God, this is dangerous. I know it is. What does it all mean?'

Suddenly Willis wanted very much to go home and leave this pale intense woman who had somehow got involved in something that made paint move off walls and writing appear that revolted him, and yet touched a deep-buried root in his psyche. Set it wriggling. Right now the thought of becoming a store detective at Tesco seemed attractive.

'We'll have to ask Ransom about all this,' she said.

Willis answered, 'You stay here. I'll go and do that.'

Chapter Nineteen

The door banged gently on the latch. Open. Willis struck the knocker three times, stood back and waited. Cherie hopped and shivered on the step below, wishing she had brought her quilted jacket out with her, hugging herself while Willis stared impassively at the front door. She longed for a good American outdoor outfit, thick shirts, thermal underwear, the works, with such unexpected intensity that she had to stop herself from running back into her own house and changing. She had them somewhere, she was sure.

They waited a full minute in front of the door before Willis pushed it open and called, 'Hello! Anybody there? Hello?' and Cherie had to suppress a ridiculous desire to tug his jacket and whisper 'Ssssshh' to him with her finger to her lips.

'Can we go in?' Cherie whispered instead.

'Don't see why not,' Willis replied at normal speaking level. He touched the catch screwed onto the wall. 'Faulty,' he said, wobbling it with his fingers. 'It's loose. Door must have jumped out when it was slammed. He should have used the Chubb.'

Cherie, caught between fear and excitement, wanted to laugh.

'He must have been in a hurry to get away,' she said. 'I wonder why.'

'Do you know the house?' Willis asked.

'Hardly. There's a dining-room and a kitchen on this floor and a sitting-room and a study on the floor above. But I've only been into the dining-room and the sitting-room. Oh, look!'

She pointed to one of the prints: the one she had been studying all that time ago when Ransom had disturbed her. 'Sorry, I just thought of something, but it's gone. Wait . . . Got it. That big black patch there.' She put her finger below one of the black inked-out patches that disfigured the map of the heath. It was bigger than all the others, and the paper underneath had been scored more vigorously. 'Look at the way the roads lie. Well, supposing they've stayed more or less the same, that's where the convent is now, isn't it?'

'Yes.' Willis looked interested. 'Yes. The convent. I wonder . . .'

'Wonder what?'

'Sorry, nothing. I'm just trying to think what those patches mean.'

'If they mean anything.'

'Yes. True.'

The dining-room looked unused. There was a dust-cover over the table. But in the kitchen there was a cold pot of tea on the table, and a half-full cup, the milk streaking its surface. The sitting-room was exactly as Cherie remembered. Heavy leather armchairs, Chesterfield sofa, wingbacked chair next to the fire. Books, books, books everywhere. The study was untidy but ordered.

'Supposing that thump you heard as I came in was from this house, where do you think it would have come from?' Willis asked.

'I guess this floor or the one above. But nothing's been moved from here.'

They paused. In the silence they heard each other's breath and the creak of the floorboards under their feet. And something else: a sound which was half in the silence and half out of it — that was repetitive, familiar.

drip drip drip drip

Cherie turned round and screamed. Willis was standing with his back to the wall, and a halo of blood had suddenly bloomed from this head. It was dripping through the ceiling and flowing down the wall, where some freak in the structure had spread it out in a broad-veined aureole. A single red drop hit the crown of Willis's head before he realised that something was wrong. Cherie's expression told him that he didn't want to turn round. But he wheeled, saw the spreading rosy stain, and lumbered out of the room and up the stairs, with Cherie following.

They reached the landing together. Willis hesitated. Three doors, all closed. Cherie stood by him. 'It'll be that one,' she said. Willis turned to her.

A voice from somewhere arrived in his mouth.

'Ladies first,' said the voice, and he opened the door with one hand and politely but insistently pushed Cherie into the room with the other.

Yellow light came in through the window from a street lamp. There was a chair with a loose cover. There was a towel horse. There was a washbasin. There was a ceiling light with coolie shade. And there was a bed.

It was a typical spare-bedroom bed: short and narrow. Blankets were piled up at one end, neatly folded; bare pillows with their striped coverings at the other. Strangely, a pale rug had been thrown carelessly across it, at an angle.

A rug that smelt like . . .

that flapped in the breeze like a spaniel's ears . . .

that snuffled? . . . whimpered? . . . Mewed . . .

The orange light of the streetlamp made the ceiling quiver. Cherie fixed her eyes on the thing draped over the bed, and her arm reached out for the light switch.

She thought first of a shop window display — the sort where they laid empty clothes across the floor in artistic patterns.

sweater

trousers

s s

o o

c c

ks ks

mohair sweater

mini-skirt

s s

t t

o o

c c

k k

i i

n n

gs gs

Then she thought of a flattened inflatable doll.

Then she noticed the way that a dark liquid was draining from the splayed ends of the long yellow dangling things that hung over the edge of the bed.

Then she saw how round one of the dangling bits was and that it was half covered with hair. Skin like leather.

Her scream was cut off by thick bile that rose up her throat like a geyser. She was chucking up her stomach into the washbasin when Willis walked in.

The first thing that Willis thought of was the flat chickens you see in the windows of some Chinese restaurants, boneless chickens that look like surreal frying pans. It took him a split second longer to say to himself: boneless human. He whitened. His knees nearly gave way. But all the time he was saying to himself: I am going white, I am trembling; and he forced himself to unscrew his eyes from the back of his head and confront the thing on the bed.

Take yourself out of the context, he kept on repeating to himself. It's the context that screws you. He took a step closer.

The fingers had been neatly severed at the top joint, which was how the blood was escaping. Apart from that the pelt was unmarred, though crumpled as if it had been carelessly dropped. The head had folded across the nose, more or less, and as far as Willis could tell, it had belonged to a young woman, dressed in a big woolly sweater, mini-skirt and white stockings. The sight catapulted him back to his days as a young man, when with too short hair and a swagger he couldn't lose, he'd spent the odd afternoon in the Kings Road, Chelsea, trying to swing. A dolly bird? There were large irregular lumps in the torso which Willis numbly identified as vital organs. Behind him Cherie staggered from the room and collapsed in the corridor outside.

As Willis turned to follow her, he spotted the woman's bones stacked tidily on top of the cheap wardrobe. Neatly put away. The skull grinned a chimpanzee smile. Exit Willis pursued by . . .

He walked out into a full-beam stare from Cherie, her mouth starting to work before he even closed the door (firmly) behind him.

'What did you do that for?' she screamed. 'Why did you push me in like that? What the fuck were you playing at?'

Willis shook his head. 'It wasn't me. It was something else.'

Eyes dipped. Then back. 'Oh my God,' she said. 'What did that? What could do that —'

There was a crash in the room, and a gust of wind blew into the corridor.

Cherie's face began to work again. 'It's done enough to me. IT'S DONE ENOUGH TO ME!' She flung the door open.

Drained now, the body was rising from the bed,

rippling slowly like a weed mat on the ocean swell. Wind buffetted it softly. It hovered for a moment and then floated out of the shattered window leaving a trail of pale pink fluids glistening behind it on the floor.

Once in the night air it turned and seemed to stare at Cherie, a flat mask face, strangely beautiful, moon-shaped, and Cherie had to follow it to the window, somehow carried with it.

Words too faint to hear murmured deep in her mind, with a growing sense that the figure was familiar to her. Then it all became too much.

She mouthed the night. 'Don't look at me like that,' just breathing it. 'Don't look me like that. Horrors can't plead. Can they?'

The arms and legs formed a star like a mermaid's purse, and a light breeze caught the empty sail of flesh, swelling and bellying it slightly. It drifted away, incongruous, insouciant and filled with grace, over the trees and over the grass towards the dark bulk of the ruined convent.

Cherie leant out of the window and stared after it, until it disappeared against the darkness. Then she closed the windows and leant back against them. She felt as if a door into the dark had been closed in her mind. She and Willis looked at each other.

'Poor thing,' she said.

'Something got her.'

'Twenty. No, twenty-five years ago.'

'I saw the clothes.'

Cherie paused. 'Something's changed,' she said. 'You know, if I'd come up here and that poor . . . thing . . . just dead — that would have shocked me. I'd be crying, screaming, that kind of thing. But this time. . . I can't say why but I wasn't zapped. Sure I was shocked and revolted, but I wasn't zapped. Not like when I saw the — what the fuck was it? . . . Anyway it missed. Whatever it is, it missed. For some reason I'm thinking of conjurors. Too many special effects.'

'Speak for yourself.' Willis answered. 'I'm thinking of murder. That wasn't any special effect that was . . . filleted, and laid out on the bed. That was a person, once.'

Cherie followed him out and down the stairs. She knew he was right, but she just felt that her discovery was more important. In the hall she touched his arm.

'You're right, I'm being insensitive. I can't explain it. One minute I'm throwing my guts down the drain, the next I'm feeling like Wonderwoman. Forget about me.'

Willis looked uncomfortable. Far from feeling like Superman, he thought he was about to faint. 'The basement', he said.

'Sure', said Cherie. 'Want me to go first?'

Willis pushed past her and clumped down the narrow stairs.

'What are we looking for?' Cherie had started whispering again.

'Anything. Anything at all. Look for things that seem to have moved around. Anything out of place.'

'Like that?'

A corridor ran down one side of the cellar. Two rooms led off it, while at the far end it had been partially bricked off. Bricks now lay scattered on the floor. The cavity behind was dark.

Willis pulled a torch from a jacket pocket and flashed it in, half expecting to meet the red baleful glare of the mutant ancestor chained to the wall. The cavity was dry, spotlessly clean, and empty.

'Sod it.'

Willis shone his torch into the corners — nothing nothing nothing — while Cherie wandered down the corridor, drawn to one of the two closed doors. Both were tough and solid-looking. The one she was looking at was painted purple and had three heavy bolts set into it, all drawn back. A section two or three inches high and about six inches long had been cut from the bottom. She fumbled for the light switch.

'Wanna swing, baby?' She whipped round as if stung, but there was only Willis, with his mouth open, gawping.

It was perfect 1965. The walls were hung with silver embossed wallpaper. Three frosted plastic lamps hung at different heights from a mahogany boss. In one corner there was a spherical white plastic chair. The rest of the furniture was G-Plan, upholstered in green plaid tweed. The carpet was purplish, thick, and swirled. Dust lay like a thin grey fur everywhere. The only window had bars on it.

Cherie wandered aimlessly around. Dust-coated cigarette stubs in the dusty ashtray, an empty mug with something black and cracked in the bottom of it, a magazine. She drew her fingers across the title. *Queen* 1966. Jesus. She flicked through it, the dusk working its way up her nose and into her throat. Mini-cars, mini-skirts, mini brains. Pudgy spoiled faces. Black eyes. White lips.

Records stacked by the sofa: Johnny Halliday, Kenny Ball, the soundtrack to *Breakfast at Tiffany's*; TV's Dr Kildare, Richard Chamberlain Sings.

Out of curiosity she walked over to the old record-player, switched it on, and dropped the record onto the spindle, then swung the old-fashioned arm across, and switched it onto automatic. The machine whirred and clanked. The record dropped, but when the arm swung over and down, the only sound was the tinny hissing of the stylus.

'Give it time to warm up. That's an old valve set,' Willis said. The music seemed to approach them from a long way away, getting louder, gaining definition above the scratches and hisses.

'True Love', from *High Society*, sung very slow and slightly flat.

I give to you . . .

Cherie began to look around the room again, and this time her eyes immediately fell on a dark wooden box, old and rather battered, standing on a desk at one corner. She looked at Willis. He nodded.

True love

'Has it got a key?'

The key was lying on the side of it. Cherie inserted it and turned.

True love

It was full of documents; old documents and what turned out to be modern transcripts of some of them. Many of them looked like old bills. There was a roll of negatives. Then she found some sheaves of what looked like parchment, carefully fastened together. And hidden beneath them, the wooden cross.

'Jackpot,' she said.

For you and I . . .

'Jackpot. Could you turn this crap off?'

'OK.' Cherie got up and pressed the reject button.

Love forever —

'What do you make of this place, then?'

Cherie took another look around it, noticing this time the enormous mattress spread with cushions and furs in one corner, and the mirror set above it in the ceiling. At its foot, pointing at the centre of the mattress, stood a Leica on a tripod.

'Tacky.'

'Someone knew how to have a good time.'

'Ransom.' Cherie spat the word out.

'Those Ransom's?'

Willis pointed to a row of cosmetics that stood on a shelf above a small washbasin.

'Probably kept them for his conquests,' Cherie said. 'Come on, let's get out of here. What's that?' Her feet had kicked something — a book. 'Now that's strange.' It was a copy of the second book she'd read in the library: *Heath Views and Memories: Fifty Years a Local* — the one she'd quite enjoyed. It somehow didn't seem to fit in. Then she remembered. It had referred to 'Old Whitey'.

'Well if you ask me it's a girl's room,' Willis said suddenly. He picked up the chest and moved towards the door. 'Come on. It's giving me the creeps.'

'Wait! Please, just a few more minutes.'

'It's getting cold. I want out. Now.'

'But we must find out —'

Suddenly Cherie realised that she couldn't stay there. Not yet, she thought, and began to feel terror wind chill fingers round her throat.

As she made for the door a veil seemed to lift from the corners of her eyes and panic began to gather there — panic that if she rolled her eyes and looked she could just see, massing like a fog in her peripheral vision. Don't run! Walk! Don't look behind you! But walk quicker . . . quicker. Up the stairs into the hall, across the floor, don't look back, look at the door. LOOK AT THE DOOR! It was receding down a long tunnel of white. Don't run, don't panic, just walk fast . . .

Willis came up the cellar steps and nearly bumped into Cherie, who was staring at the front door with a white face. She was goosestepping on the spot: crash thump, crash thump. Her heels were thumping into the floor; her eyes began to stream tears of frustration. Sweat stood out on her upper lip and forehead. Willis waved a hand in front of her face but there was no response.

Placing his hand in the small of her back he pushed her gently towards the door. She marched forward into it, back, into it again, back. Like a broken toy.

Willis jiggled with the lock and got the door open. Cherie goose-stepped down the steps and stopped on the pavement, then she slumped and almost fell. Willis glanced back inside the house. The Turkish rug on the floor wriggled, bleached, swelled into a mini-skirted woman. Long fringe, dark eyes, string top, no bra, big black belt. She looked at him and began to dance, tossing her head from side to side. Willis could see her small breasts and pink nipples jerk and wiggle through her vest. She moved towards him, lay on the floor. Shook her pelvis at him.

He slammed the door shut and heard the house laugh.

Cherie was shaking her head as if to clear it.

'What happened? I was in the hall. But I couldn't get any nearer to the door. The faster I ran, the further away it went. I was trying not to panic. I was trying . . .'

'You were walking on the spot,' Willis said. 'No wonder Ransom got the hell out when he could. I wonder what he saw.'

Wonder what *I* saw, he thought.

Chapter Twenty

'This one looks the most interesting,' Willis said. He had laid the old sheets of parchment out on the dining table. They were remarkably well preserved. The handwriting, though crabbed, was decipherable. It seemed as if the writer had taken extra care to make it legible. Cherie brought over a jug of coffee. She looked pale. Half of Willis wanted to tell her to go to bed; the other half wanted her to stay up with him and read. He finally decided that she would be offended if he suggested she go to bed, and it would do their relationship most good if he stayed silent.

Cherie came and sat by him and they began to read.

It has never been my practice to linger over-long in one place. Experience, alas, tells me that my patients, or their families, persist in attributing too many powers to the poor apothecary, and when, in the course of nature, nature takes her course, the instinct in the bereaved is often to find causes other than the inexorable workings of providence or fate. Moreover, human nature being what it is, namely perverse, vindictive and cruel, that cause is often ascribed to me.

I digress, but I must explain. When, after a period of fat, I was beset by a period of leanness and penury, and reduced to peddling my wares from a mere wagon, I was offered the chance for stable and regular employment, I put aside the misgivings given above. I was, as I have made mention, in a state of flux, both as regards my social station and also because, having been forced by the action of various creditors to reduce the extent of my business, in short to sell much of what I had accumulated, useless though it would be in the wrong hands, I was homeless. Though by nature perambulatory, my wealth had allowed me the purchase of a fine town house near the Strand, whose unfortunate destruction by the great conflagration and whose lack of insurance, moreover, reduced my circumstances still further.

How, you may ask, did a poor apothecary wax prosperous? How did a humble peddlar of healing balms and lotions come to this elevated station and learn to play the great man? The answer is simple: the Plague. The enemy of mankind was kind to the healer, and though my concoction, brewed and distilled from plague flesh (reduced to ash and ground), piss (my own, but anyone's would do provided it had been allowed to stand in the pot three weeks) and a special and delicate balance of rare herbs and oils, could not promise a cure once the deadly disease had been contracted, merely an alleviation of suffering, it was the only effective prophylactic available, as countless fortunate clients, rich enough to purchase a vial, could testify.

Alas, my house destroyed, and my business wrecked by the growing health of the city (God strike me down if I should complain), a change in mood moreover that tended to favour certain dangerous modern cures and eschew the methods handed down from the mists of time, yeah even from the time of the Pharaohs of Great Egypt, of Moses the Great Magician, of Abraham, yea even of pagan deities whose wisdom in the art of healing is well known, I was forced to leave the capital. In short, I was bankrupted, and forced to ply my trade away from the slick corruption of the city and make for the ruralities, where though the rude peasantry is perhaps over-expectant, at least they are prepared to be persuaded.

This I did for many years, covering many miles, curing many ills, enduring much hardship and hard words beside. Then, passing one day a great house which lay a few miles from London, on the Dover Road which leads to Kent, I was surprised to be greeted by a woman, a servant, who said that her master was ill.

'What master?' I asked. 'Why none other than the great Lord Leaford, knave,' she replied — that fountain of charity, great benefactor, founder of schools and such-like nonsense, none of which I then believed but recognise now as the truth.

I held my peace awhile, It has long been my contention that the greater the patient, the greater the opprobrium attached to the poor doctor should an ill befall him, but she mentioned a price at which my services would be hired, and I agreed to at least examine the patient. As we passed across the wild moorland which lay between the house and the road, my mind seethed with questions, but I soon learned that this stout-hearted matron was as straightforward in her dealings with men as she was buxom, and demanded that I state my questions forthwith. To summarise:

I had been heard to mention, in an inn at Deptford the night before ('shout out in beer-sodden stupor' were her actual words, for which I chided her for being contrary), that I would be passing this way. A stable lad from the hall there visiting passed this intelligence onto the housekeeper, who, knowing that the master was ill, came out herself, no less, to apprehend me as I passed.

'What illness?' I asked. 'Why, fever,' she replied, 'but something else seems to be troubling him withal, but whether that be sickness of the body or the spirit I know not.'

And here I fancied she shot me a cat's glance, sly and sideways.

'Why me?' I asked, as boldly as requested. I sensed equivocation in her reply. There were aspects of the illness, she said, which made the calling of a local doctor something they would as lief avoid.

'He is delirious?' I asked. He is, she stoutly replied. And at once I understood, knowing full well that in delirium devils are conjured by the brain to carry the evil humours from the body to the pit whence they come, but that sometimes a doctor's help is needed to expel them, as the demons, gaining entrance to the body, and especially when that same body has shown a tendency to evil in its past, reside and call out like legion from the patient's mouth. Well I understood the need for discretion.

Cherie and Willis were riveted. Willis even forgot Cherie's proximity. Occasionally they would hesitate over a word rendered indecipherable by the crabbed hand, but these hesitations grew less frequent as they became more familiar with the antiquated penmanship.

'This is an amazing document,' Cherie said. 'It should be in a museum or something.'

'I can think of a good reason why it shouldn't be,' Willis muttered.

'It might incriminate somebody?'

'That's what I think. And of course there's no reason why anyone should hand their family's dirty washing over to the public to paw.'

'Unless it concerns the public.'

'Especially if it concerns the public, love,' Willis said. 'This is England.'

I found the patient in a great draughty chamber: the windows unshuttered, unblinded, sunlight pouring in. Well I knew the effect this would have on the devils within him, who need to be coaxed out by the making of the air around the patient as similar as possible to the realms they inhabit. Forthwith I ordered the windows, which were open, to be closed; and the shutters bolted. I caused the fire to be lit, and called for sulphur to be introduced to the flames. He was an old man of pale complexion with thin white hair. A striking face, but a stern one, and concentrated about the eyes and the mouth.

I called for my chests.

It has long been my contention that an innate sympathy exists between man and disease. Otherwise why would healthy people grow ill? It therefore follows that to repel disease or sickness of any kind, the sympathy must be replaced with antipathy. Therefore I have concluded that the matter which a healthy body expels, that is, its waste, must be in itself antipathetic to disease, which itself is so attracted to the natural and healthy state of the body. The rotund logic of my arguments hath confounded many a critic. Now I had an opportunity to put them into effect.

With the air in the chamber approaching near perfect conditions, and a good sweat appearing on my patient's body, I called for the housekeeper and demanded that the contents of the master's night pot be brought to me. She paled, and would have made to protest, but was overcome by coughing (by now the patient was coughing too in an attempt to expel the demons — already my cure was working!) and I confounded her with my logic. Minutes later there was a knock at the door and the chamber pot was thrust in.

Moderation. Experimentation. These are the two pegs on which I hang my art. I took no more than a one half ounce of the patient's faeces and mixed these into a brew with a portion — a gill perhaps — of his piss. To this I added a drop or two of arsenic to induce vomiting, and some salt to aid the emetic effect.

I forced some between his lips. At once he gagged! Indeed, so effective was this stage of my cure that the patient regained full consciousness and was staring about him with wild eyes, a sure sign that the demons were rising within him, leaving the breast and entering the head. I saw that trepanning might be necessary, although sometimes leeches applied to the ear and scalp will suffice.

He spoke: 'In God's name, what are you?' 'I am here to rid you of demons,' I said. 'And this is purgatory?' he asked. I merely laughed at this suggestion, a laugh which seemed to disturb him, for he started. He asked after the smoke, which I said was inevitable, given his situation. At this he went white and began to tremble.

'But if you wish to tell me of the demons,' I said (for what are words but the exhalations of our soul, and what are descriptions of demons, but their exhalations, and being exhalations part of them), 'talk.'

'Talk,' he said? 'Confess?' I held my hands out. 'Lighten your load,' I said. 'It will help you.'

'Help me leave purgatory?' he asked.

At this ready shaft of wit I laughed long and encouragingly, but anticipated too readily his return to robust spirits for he cowered and began once more to tremble. I regained my composure, and with all solemnity bade him speak. I put down his words for they were a veritable torrent, and a true testimony to my skill, and nonsense though they were, I realised that such ramblings might *appear significant to one who might have wished my patient harm.*

'God or devil,' he began (a sure sign of possession), 'hear me.'

'My name,' he said, 'is Thomas Wainright.' (The man was mad. It was Lord Leaford who spoke). 'Would that I had never risen from that state of simplicity to this state of corruption.' (Here my eyebrows rose.) 'Would that I had never set eyes upon this blasted heath' (the man was waxing poetical), 'this accursed waste that I have made more accursed than ever before.' (This is how he spoke.) 'The pits! The plague pits!' (Here he leant over and grabbed me with a bony hand. His dark eyes glittered fiercely as he spoke.) 'Devil, confessor, whatever you are, look beneath the ground. Look beneath the ground!'

'What lies there?' I asked.

'Murder!' he replied. 'Murder.'

(He paused, then began again.)

'I was young, foolish, ambitious. That was all. I wanted a position. I wanted power. And the old man was so foolish. He had a son. He had a title. But he had no money. The estate was rotten, wasted. He was in debt. I came to him as a clerk, but soon found that the estate manager was corrupt. I denounced him and took his place. Under my hand the estate's fortunes improved, and the old man was grateful, oh, so grateful. He called me his son. He called me his son, and grew to love me. But still there were pressing debts.

'And then the plague came. At first I merely saw how, by using a corner of my master's land for burial, money could be made. Then I saw how I could be paid for having the streets of London cleared. Bring out your dead! Bring out your dead! But a penny a corpse was not enough, not for that stinking work. It was not enough. We deserved more, so we took it.

'Thievery at first, no hard task when half the city's away, and the other half's too scared to move, or too sick, or dead. And then one of my men was caught with his hands in some widow's linen chest. He struck his captor a blow, and killed him. It was so simple to put the body on the cart and throw it in the pit. That was the first. Then another, then another.

Soon we were killing more than we could carry, but who would look too closely at a body? And who would come too close to men who carried them? And so I grew rich. The old man was pleased. I offered to put money into the farms, to pay off the debts for a stake. He accepted, but his son was jealous. His son and his son's wife: he a vile and malicious creature; she a picture of beauty and propriety. My Margaret. My little fruit. My Cherry I called her, My little Cherry.'

Cherie felt almost like vomiting when she read this. Something seemed to drop through the pit of her stomach and she began to feel dreadfully exposed.

'Somehow that brutish son found me out. He accused me! There was a fight. I killed him. I killed him, and buried him secretly in the pit, and gave out that I had seen him leave, riding. The body was never found. Not where I hid it.

'And the old fool, my master, he adopted me in his son's place. He gave me his widow. He gave me the title.

'I had everything. And when the old man died, I became Lord Leaford, I, a Lord, with a wife, and a child in her belly and a fortune. But my wife grew ill. She began to look at me askance, she who had shown only obedience and meekness. I pressed her. I spoke gently to her. I argued with her. I pleaded with her to tell me, she whom I loved. And one night she did.

'She was beset by dreams. She saw a great pit on wild moorland. She saw naked bodies falling into it! Some still lived, and those that lived she saw men club with great cudgels. She saw a man grow rich off this, and that man she said was me!

'I protested. But she insisted. She said that the earth talked to her in her first husband's voice. She said she saw the earth move and gaping lips open and talk to her. She said she had heard him say he was murdered in his own house, murdered by the man who now lay with his wife, who took her nightly, whose child lay in her belly. "YOU," she screamed at me, "YOU. YOU KILLED HIM!"

'I struck her and she fell, and before she could speak further her waters broke, and her contractions began. I left, but saw her

staring after me with murder in her eyes. She thought she would be safe, surrounded by women, and then she could accuse me. I waited — an agony of waiting. Ten hours it took, and finally delivered to me was a baby boy. She lay there asleep, exhausted, and while all were distracted I killed her. There was so much blood. So much blood that no one suspected.'

(Here he paused, as well he might, for he seemed gripped by a demonic force so great that I was quite amazed. Such a story! Then he seemed to faint, so I fed him more of the potion. He started. His eyes stared! His mottled skin lost even what little colour it had and he spoke again. Thus:)

'I tried . . . tried. But still they came. The devils. The demon. The pale prince and his bride leading an army of the dead. Together. Wedded together. In white, IN WHITE. Oh, let me atone. Let me! The sisters. The sisters of vigilance. They will keep watch. Their prayers will silence them. I will build a nunnery over their grave! The sisters will watch. BEWARE THE WHITE!'

(Here he screamed and died.)

Such a story I never heard, and I resolved to record it so that I might better consider the issue. If —

REMOVED FROM THE POSSESSION OF ANDREW SMITH, FRAUDULENT DOCTOR AND MURDERER OF MY FATHER, WHO DID ADMINISTER TO HIM A POISONOUS MIXTURE OF FOUL AND UNNATURAL SUBSTANCES, THUS BRINGING ON A FIT OF MADNESS AND ULTIMATE DEATH, REMOVED FROM HIS ROOM, SEVENOAKS, WHERE HE WAS RESIDING PRIOR TO HIS ARREST.
MAY GOD HAVE MERCY ON HIS SOUL.

'A nice can of worms and no mistake,' Willis said, leaning back in the chair. He heard the back beginning to crack, and hurriedly jerked forwards again. 'What do you make of it?'

'It's the ghost. It's that white ghost. Wedded together . . . Don't you see?' Cherie was shaking badly. 'And it's coming for me. It wants me! Oh, my God, what can I do?'

'Nonsense.' Willis tried to sound reassuring. 'It doesn't make sense. Look, I don't know what's happening, but I think it's trying to . . . I don't know . . . show you something.'

'*Show me something*? Show me people disintegrating! Show me bodies! Oh, my God, the pit. The pit. It showed me the pit, just like it showed the woman! It's possessing me! Just like her.'

'Wait a minute! Wait a minute!' Willis jumped up. 'Of course. What are we talking abut? It's ridiculous this thing about ghosts. OK, I admit something is working through us — something very strong. But it must be part of us that's making it, too.'

'Like that thing on the bed? You saw her, too, for Christ's sake. It can't be just working through us. We both saw the same thing!'

'OK.' Willis sat down again. 'I'm too tired to think straight. I need to sleep.'

'Me too. Look, just sleep on the sofa. I'll bring some bedding down for you.'

Cherie went upstairs. Willis waited a second then heard the thump of a duvet and pillows being thrown down the stairs from the landing.

'See you in the morning' Cherie's voice floated down. Willis began to make up a bed.

Chapter Twenty-one

Cherie lay in bed and gazed at the featureless sky through a gap in her curtains. She had not got to bed until after three, and then had found it difficult to sleep. She badly wanted to drift off again. The bed was just the right temperature.

Willis — Damn! She'd forgotten that she'd offered him the sofa to sleep on. It had seemed like the obvious thing to do at the time, but now the thought made her feel uncomfortable. She grabbed the bathrobe that lay across the foot of her bed, keeping one eye on the door in case he burst in, and she tied it crossly round her middle.

I have a policeman sleeping on my couch. I only met him once before. For all I know, God talks to him and he wants to beat criminals, personally.

She felt increasingly crumpled and sinusy as she went downstairs.

Willis was already up, sitting on the sofa and poring over documents he had spread out in front of him on the coffee table.

'Sleep well?' he asked.

'Yeah. OK.'

There was a pause, while Cherie wondered how she could get him to leave. She wanted the morning to herself, to think. But the pause was getting too long.

'Couch OK?'

'What? Oh, the settee. Great. I slept like a log. The old brain does funny things when you're dog-tired. There I was lying on my back saying to myself: "Don't go to sleep. Whatever you do, don't sleep" — when all of a sudden this little voice said: "Oh, don't worry. He won't worry with you. He's busy elsewhere." And I thought: "Great. I can have a nap." You know, it's like when the alarm goes in the morning and you get up, have a wash, get dressed, have breakfast . . . And then you wake up properly, still in bed and you're half an hour late. Your brain can play funny tricks: always wants to get its own way.'

'Find anything interesting in that lot?' Cherie shuffled over to the kitchen end of the room and began to clatter around with the coffee maker. Willis looked over to see if the bathrobe would open when she leant across to the coffee tin.

'There's a lot here. Haven't worked it all out yet, mind.'

'D'you mind the radio on?'

'Go ahead.'

'What have you found?'

She pulled the bathrobe tightly around her and went to stand by the window. There was a sullen mist hanging over the flat turf. Even the grass looked grey. She shivered. Underneath that sanitised, flat, unnatural surface there were real secrets, dark horrible secrets, she thought. It was so English: the civilised surface, the horror underneath. The bland smile, the skeletons in the closet. And yet they do it so well, and nobody ever questions them. Nobody ever thinks: why has nobody built houses on the heath? Nobody ever says: why is there this great field, so flat and featureless, with nothing, absolutely nothing on it apart from a rash of goal posts every Sunday morning? There's just a feeling that builds up, some community memory, some garbled rumour that eventually becomes enshrined in some local byelaw that the heath must not be built on. And that's that.

No other country could be so reverent about its past, and yet so deeply careless of it. And then she thought quite clearly, the sentence properly formed and precisely articulated: but the heath *has* been built on.

'Of course!'

Cherie was surprised by her own outburst. Willis looked up with a grunt.

'What?'

'It *has* been built on!'

'What has? What are you talking about?'

'The heath? Don't you see? I was just thinking to myself that it's never been built on because of some, I don't know, some race memory about the plague pits. Except it *has* been built on. It's staring us in the face. The convent! Last night we read something about the nuns. The Sisters of Vigilance. Of course. They lived in the middle of the heath, right where it was all happening. Then someone comes and knocks their blessed nunnery down and all this starts to happen! They must be the key! It's all so obvious!'

'One problem,' Willis said. 'They were a silent order. Nobody knew anything about them. They came, they went.'

'Let's see if there's anything here.' Cherie began to rummage through the remaining piles of papers.

'I've been through them,' Willis said. 'There's nothing. It's all old receipts, records. Boring really.'

'Just old receipts? What's this?'

She held out a piece of paper, ancient and dry. 'For the purchase of four acres of land in the village of Wragglesby in recompense for the Sisters of Mercy so they might —' The rest of the writing was covered by a large dark stain.

'It must be worth a try,' Cherie said.

Two hours later the congested roads of East London were behind them and they were humming along the M11, bound for Boston in Lincolnshire. Cherie stared in dismay out of the window as the countryside around them flattened out and the sky grey bigger and blander above them.

'What the hell's going on here?' she asked, as Willis thoughtfully pointed out the Gog Magog hills outside Cambridge. 'Those aren't hills. Those are pimples. It's so flat here. Who'd want to live in a flat place like this? I thought England was hilly, sort of rounded hills, with big houses and little villages and trees.'

'And you've lived here how long?'

'A couple of years actually. But we only ever went to the West Country.'

'You've no idea how silly that sounds,' Willis said.

'What do you mean? Do you expect people to come here?'

'There are people who *live* here. It's said to grow on you.'

'It'd have to.' Cherie muttered.

They ate in a pub outside Cambridge, then Willis took over the driving. Away from London, Cherie's mood deteriorated. She began to study the map and noticed that the long straight canals marked on it were called drains. Outside Boston she stuck her head out of the window.

'We're in drain country all right,' she said in a John Wayne drawl. 'Just smell those drains.'

The air hit her face like a handful of freezing gravel. There was a bite to the wind, and a vicious arthritic dampness to it that shocked her into silence.

'It's so bracing,' Willis said. 'I had a very bracing holiday here when I was a lad.'

Between Boston and Skegness they turned off down a single-track road to towards Wragglesby. Crawling across the naked, flat landscape, with the reeds shuffling together in the dykes and winter trees leaning into the black soil, she suddenly began to feel exposed and vulnerable. Then Willis brought the jeep to a halt. There was a small cross painted on a board by the side of a gate. An unmetalled road snaked across the middle of a field towards a great dark clump of trees.

'They don't exactly advertise themselves,' said Willis.

Cherie was staring at the sign. 'That cross. It's just been repainted. Look.'

The fresh enamel glinted wetly in the dying light.

'We're on the right trail then, pardner.' Willis was staring stolidly out of the window.

'Yes.' Cherie did not feel like joking anymore.

They had arranged that she would do all the talking. Willis would come along if he could, or would wait in the car if he was not allowed into the grounds. He had finally tracked down a police station which knew about the nunnery, but had been told precious little, except that nobody knew anything much about the mysterious order, and that the locals would not disclose much to strangers. Willis received the distinct impression that this included him, too, so he had wound up the conversation quickly.

The track wound across the field and crossed a wide dyke. On the other side of the dyke there was a ring of tall trees: chestnuts and a few elms. The nunnery stood within the ring, surrounded by a high wall. Inside the ring of trees all you could see was a couple of steep gables and a tall chimney stack leaning slightly to one side, dark against the afternoon sky.

Cherie rang the bell-pull that hung beside a high gate, and waited. A small latch shot sideways and two slightly rheumy eyes peered out. They looked at Cherie, then flicked sideways to Willis who was sitting hunched over the jeep's steering-wheel, trying to look inoffensive and kindly. Nobody spoke.

After a while Cherie realised that quite possibly the nun behind the gate had taken a vow of silence and that it was up to her to introduce herself.

'We have come up from London,' she said, speaking very slowly and enunciating as well as she could. 'We have important news for the Mother Superior' — the two eyes frowned — 'as well as some questions. Would it be possible to see her?'

The hatch slammed shut. The wind rocked the jeep on its springs. Cherie and Willis waited in silence.

Chapter Twenty-two

It was the pilot of a light aeroplane chartered by one of the London radio stations who noticed it first. He tried to point it out to the young journalist who was peering out of the window at the traffic jam extending on either side of the Blackwall tunnel. 'They're not going in and they're not going out. Northbound and southbound, we've got a rubbernecking bumper-to-bumper jammaroonee stretching back two miles in each direction,' he announced in an accent in which the jagged edges of Dagenham and Brooklyn snagged and half-meshed in a mid-Atlantic drawl — hard work when you were a nice public schoolboy from Windsor.

The pilot had seen something strange. The heath was crossed by white trails centring at a few patches which lay at odd intervals on its surface. The trails were not straight. They curled like the lines you get when you sprinkle iron filings on paper and slide a magnet underneath. The pilot thought of that because he had a ten-year-old son who was doing magnetism in physics. *Why, Daddy? Why?*

Now looking out of the window the pilot was inclined to ask the same question.

Mr Hoyle had been on the heath for years. He'd seen masters come and masters go. His first boss had been the local council. Then the Greater London Council had taken over, and now power had devolved once more on the local authorities, two this time, who divided the heath between them. A victory for local democracy they said, but a pain in the arse to administer. The wind cut through his brown suit, but he ignored the cold through force of habit.

He had a pleasant weather-burned face, and was completely wrapped up in his thoughts as he speared more litter with his metal spike and slid this anaemic kebab off with a gloved hand into a black plastic sack.

One thing had changed, and that was for sure. People were messy buggers nowadays, and no mistake. He skewered a sheet of newspaper as it attempted to scurry away.

'Oh, bloody hell,' he spoke out loud. There was a trail of litter curving off to a great pile of the stuff in the middle of the heath. And another. And another. He could see them clearly. There was so much rubbish that they looked like pools of the stuff. It was unbelievable. It had to be the gipsies. Bloody gippos.

It was vandalism — no other word for it. And what was more, the wind would soon blow it all over the place. Sheer bloody vandalism. Angrily he speared another leaf of drifting newsprint that danced away playfully from his darting spike. Got it!

Something was wrong, but Mr Hoyle was too pissed off to notice exactly what it was. He was planning his revenge on the gippos, wherever they were. Another piece of paper moved. And another. Hoyle stabbed them both, oblivious to the fact that far from blowing around in the wind, they were actually moving against it, crawling with ragged, inanimate determination towards the spot about twenty yards away — the spot to which Hoyle himself was being relentlessly drawn.

Hoyle stood on the edge of the main concentration of litter. He was feeling strange, sick, as if something was loose inside. There was a thwump and he glanced down to see a herring-gull heaving and twitching on the ground beside him. It must have fallen out of the sky, he thought. Could have killed me. Never seen anything like it.

Tentatively he stretched out a hand to the struggling bird. It whipped its head round and scored a deep gash in the back of his hand, then it seemed to collapse — flatten. Still hissing though — or deflating.

The crumpled litter around took on a bloom of red which drained suddenly to a milky white. Somebody laughed, and Hoyle felt his ankles chill. He looked down and saw the impossible. Damp paper had gathered round his feet, and it parted into two thick liplike folds. As he looked, they pouted, funnelled and smacked up to his knees. He screamed and dragged himself free. And ran.

It was an elderly couple who first noticed the birds from their sitting-room window. They were wheeling in strange patterns. Gulls, pigeons, and sparrows were circling in untidy flocks above certain bits of the heath, all flying in the same direction in a motley vortex, like water gurgling around a drain. As those closest to the apparent centre of this spiral crossed a line, they would tumble and fall as if stricken. A great flock of chattering starlings flew over and the whole flock suddenly wheeled downwards. Some broke away and fluttered scrappily off, but the main body of the flock began to fall like dirty snowflakes to the grass. The old couple dressed themselves carefully in warm clothes, and by the time they were out on the heath they found themselves merging with a small crowd of curious dog walkers and baby walkers.

Muffled against the cold, the humans stood and watched the birds die. A white cloud began to gather over the convent.

Chapter Twenty-three

The gate in the nunnery wall opened smoothly and silently.

Willis looked at Cherie. 'Is that an invitation?'

'Perhaps a posse's about to ride out. Or the four horsemen of the apocalypse. You know: Death. Famine. War . . . What was the fourth?'

'Pestilence.'

'Sometimes I get the impression I'm living my life to a theme.'

'I thought all your generation ever wanted was a lifestyle.'

'Ha, they can write about me in the Sundays. I'll be sandwiched between the CDs and Dinky duvets. Cherie Simpson: London's first Plaguey.'

The nun whose eyes Cherie had seen through the peep-hole put her head round the gate and beckoned angrily. Willis started the jeep and they drove in.

Willis was ushered into a room just inside the main door, and there he was locked in. Cherie was led down a brown lino corridor by the hard click of the nun's heels. The nun threw open a door at the end and almost pushed her through. She blinked in the warm bright light and at the figure who marched towards her across flame-red carpet tiles, with hand outstretched.

Her habit fell in well-ironed folds and her posture was upright and alert. Two dark intelligent animal eyes glinted in a pink, parboiled face, and she radiated a sort of disquieting energy. The accent, when she spoke, was modulated North Country.

'Come in, come in. There's a mountain of work on the desk and the central heating's about to blow up again — at least that's what Mr Henry says. He's from the village and helps us out with odd jobs when we can't, or won't, manage ourselves. But we so seldom get the chance to meet anyone from the big bad world that I'm more than happy to drop the paperwork and see how I can help. We get so little news here. Driven far?'

The eyes suddenly lanced Cherie then danced skittishly away.

'From London, as a matter of fact.'

'London, London, London. Fancy that. How lovely. I always think of it as a very *lively* place. Very alive. You must be so busy there with the theatre and the cinema and all those lovely art galleries, you lucky thing. Of course, we sometimes venture into the throng, don't you know. A group of us went to see *Agnes of God.* We rather liked that one. Oh, and also *Children of a Lesser God* — very disappointing we thought, so sentimental. And, you know, we still like some little luxuries; you just can't get material like this up here. They try but . . .' Here she plucked flirtatiously at the pleats of her habit. 'But there I go, rambling on, and I expect you've come to ask me something, haven't you?'

She stopped suddenly and Cherie felt herself flounder.

'Well, yes.'

The nun strode round to the other side of the desk, and sat down with her head bowed and her eyes obscured. Cherie decided that she should bluff this one out. Suddenly she wished that instead of bickering with Willis on the way up here, they had tried to sort out some line of attack. As it was, they hadn't talked about anything since the morning. 'I live in Blackheath,' she began, 'and, well, I found out that the old convent, what we call the convent used to belong to your order. As you know, it's being demolished, and I just wanted to find out a bit more about it.'

'Well, how extraordinary. How absolutely fascinating.

Now let me see, you've been researching?'

'Yes.'

'A keen student of local history. You know, I didn't know there were any public records. I must find out from you later where you found them, because that really would be interesting. Very interesting. Well now, how can I help you?'

Cherie began to feel her flesh crawl. Resistance she had been prepared for, even outright hostility, but this was like talking to a sentient spin-dryer.

'I picked up a reference in a local history book actually, in the library. But I was wondering what was the nature of the relationship between this branch of the order and the one that used to be on the heath.'

'The nature of the relationship? Now I wonder why you want to know that. But, no matter, it's quite simple. What you call the old convent was in fact named the Retreat. It was a silent retreat for the members of our order, a place of silence and contemplation. What else do you want to know?' The eyes said: And then you can get out.

'Well, why did you close it down? And, I suppose I should ask *why* there was a retreat on Blackheath?'

'Oh, dear, do I detect the slightest hint of snoopishness? Just a little bit of the amateur detective. No, of course not, because you're asking me wonderfully frank questions like a little soldier. No offence — just my little joke. No, there's no reason why I shouldn't tell you, just as there's no reason I can think of why I should. Still never mind. We closed it down for a number of reasons. Firstly, it was very expensive to maintain. Do you know what the heating bills are in a place like that — or what you pay when the roof caves in? No? Times have changed. There was a time when we were given endowments. Of course the largest came when we added vigilance to our duties. One local man completely rebuilt the place for us in the nineteenth century. Now, that's generosity. Those days have gone, though. Now we just moulder away. But I digress.

'Secondly, none of us wanted to go there. We like to get out and about, not shut ourselves away. We are far more community-orientated these days, you know. We really like to get involved and it all seemed a bit "behind the times" to lock ourselves away like that. Well, quite frankly we had had enough you know. We wanted to move on. We are a progressive order you see.'

'Move on from what?' Cherie found that if she didn't look at the nun's eyes she could think more clearly.

'Well, well, well. I am being picked up on little things, aren't I? Well frankly we now find all the superstitious mumbo-jumbo rather embarrassing. All that silly old watching and waiting. We're changing our name. We're no longer the Sisters of Eternal Mercy and Vigilance, you know. It's such a mouthful. We're the SEMV, now. Much more up-to-date. We've got it on the side of our van. Moving with the times.'

She picked up a collection box from the desk and waved it at Cherie. 'Only if you can afford it, of course.'

Cherie fumbled in her pocket and found a pound coin covered with damp biscuit crumbs. As she dropped it into the box she felt as if she was feeding a meter. How much information will a pound buy me, she wondered.

'So the name actually meant something? Eternal Vigilance. You were actually keeping vigil?'

'Oh dear, you really don't know, do you? You're not just another boring folklorist trying to fish for new stories. We had one here about twenty years ago who asked a lot of *very* boring questions. My dear, we were praying for souls. *Souls.* They need tending, you know. Though why we had to remain silent while doing so, I could never understand. Anyway, as soon as we could, we pulled out.'

'But —'

'Don't say it. I know what people think. But let me tell you. That pledge really was superstition of the most dangerous sort, and there were aspects which were, well, frankly distasteful to a modern community.'

'No, I wasn't going to criticise. I was going to ask why

you didn't pull out before?'

The nun rose to her feet. 'The Foundation, you silly goose, the Foundation. A more ridiculous, outmoded, fuddy-duddy old thing I never heard of. We were pledged to stay there or the lands we were given back in the seventeenth century would revert to the Foundation. Three hundred years, from the year of the plague to 1966. After that the lands would revert back to us. Well, now we're free of it, free of all our obligations, so we can move with the times. Now, it's been delightful talking to you but I really have to work.'

Cherie was led firmly to the door. 'Your friend will be waiting for you, and no doubt delighted to see you. We seldom put the heating on in that room.' The nun put a hand on Cherie's forearm. 'I was going to ask you how you found out where we were. From a library? I hardly think so. A book might have mentioned us, but you actually found us. If it wasn't a library, I can't think how else . . . Well, can't be helped.' She gave Cherie's arm a firm squeeze and looked at her very hard. 'It's men, you know. They make all the mistakes and expect our sex to get them out of the mess. Do be careful you're not doing the same, yes?'

Cherie, though by now outside the door, was determined to make one more effort. 'Was there ever any rumour, or story, or anything about a ghost — a haunting. Anything like that?'

The nun laughed brightly, but was already turning back into her room, so that Cherie could not see her face. 'My goodness me. How *imaginative.* Don't you see, you silly goose, that's just the sort of thing we try and fight. Funny girl.' And she laughed again before closing the door firmly.

The nun who had admitted them was waiting for Cherie on a wooden folding chair. She led her away.

While Cherie had been having her interview, Willis had been left standing in the coldest room he had ever set foot in. He heard the key turn in the lock and looked around. The room was large, with an elaborate plaster ceiling and heavy dark panelling on the walls. The floor sloped gently. It was old and so worn that the hard curled knots stood proud. In the middle of the room stood a modern metal-framed veneer table with plastic stacking-chairs arranged around it. Plastic lilies drooped from an orange earthenware vase set on it.

He pulled a chair out and sat down, standing up suddenly as the cold soaked through his trousers to the backs of his thighs. A tall coiled radiator stood at one end of the room, sweating greasy beads of condensation. Willis was surprised that they hadn't frozen. His breath made thick white steam clouds in the air.

He walked up and down the length of the room, swinging his arms and stamping his feet, until his attention was caught by the fireplace. There was wood in it, and it was neatly laid. He patted his pockets and located the Swan Vestas in his shirt breast pocket, almost unreachable under the rally-jacket and thick sweater. The first two matches he struck seemed to give up in the freezing damp, but the third one caught and sent a blue ridge of flame creeping up the newspaper.

Willis stayed on his knees in front of it for some minutes, warming his hands and trying to coax warmth inside his jacket. Then he stood up and began to toast the backs of his legs.

He was standing opposite a full-length eighteenth-century portrait of a gentleman wearing a long coat and breeches and with a leggy dog, a wolfhound of some sort, at his feet. He was standing in the open air; behind him was a great expanse of grass and wind-blown trees. Very small in the distance there stood what looked like a great building in the process of being built.

Willis moved up closer to look at the face. He hated the assumption that policemen could sum up a character at a glance; the arrogance that said, 'I've been in the force twenty years and know a bad'un.' Willis had seen criminals who looked like angels, and some who thought they were. The kindest man he knew was a dead ringer for the stock Mexican bandit in a spaghetti Western.

Still, nothing better to do — what about this face then? The forehead was broad, the nose high-bridged and thin, and the chin small and rounded. The eyes were quite close set and must have impressed themselves upon the painter because they had been given a piercing glint. The mouth was shut like a scar. Not small necessarily, in fact quite full, but compressed into a thin red line. A mouth, Willis mused pompously, in which passion warred with reason, sensuality with self-denial. Taken with the eyes it created a strong effect of restlessness.

The artist had put all that into the hands. One was pushed carelessly into a waistcoat pocket, but the other writhed on the knob of a stick, which looked suspiciously like a cudgel. That brought him up with a start and set bells ringing.

But it was the ring on the finger that did it. The crest had been exaggerated and highlighted; the same crest he'd seen in Cherie's sitting-room. The ring with the family crest.

Suddenly Willis knew. The man was Ransom, the great landlord of the heath, the usurper, the murderer. Willis looked up at the face again. Sensuality and repression? Go jump in the lake, Willis. The man was crazy. He could see that now. See that now. See that . . .

A depth charge exploded at the base of his skull. See that face. You've seen it before. Seen it . . . lying under a layer of rotting vegetation in a suburban garden.

The same face. It had stayed with him. Even after the details had merged in the mulch and the whole thing had seemed like the most impossible optical illusion.

He struggled for a complete picture, tried to extract one clear thought from the wormy tangle of the shock of recognition; relief that he had not been unprofessional; horror that a part of him was being used as a channel. For what? By whom?

Willis's mind darkened and he saw the awful figure staggering like a scarecrow down the street, watched only by a lonely old woman who could not sleep. He saw it walk drunkenly on its way, stop, move jerkily up to every house with a cross pinned to the door or stuck in a window, crosses which were part of some ambitious local councillor's election campaign, but which reminded that wretched dissolving wraith of its past, of the crosses scratched on doors in the plague years of London, of God only knew what crimes committed with dagger and cudgel and buried under the turf of Blackheath.

What had happened? What was he doing? Trying to repeat old actions or *trying to atone for them, to warn them.* Willis felt dizzy as the thought hit him. Yes! And the next night what had happened? A series of killings so brutal and vicious that everybody was numbed by them. It *had* been an attempt at a warning. The thought made Willis feel even worse. The supernatural web now surrounded him seemingly on every side. He'd been brought in! There was no other answer. Except . . . except the old woman had talked of evil PLAYING AROUND. Did that mean he had to look beyond, beneath the surface to what lay underneath? Find out still more?

He looked up at the picture. The eyes glowed and Willis felt their influence like heat.

'Shit, shit, shit, shit — can't I have ONE clear idea?' he spoke out loud.

The key scraped noisily in the lock. The nun who had led him there was standing outside with Cherie, who was beckoning frantically.

Willis nodded politely to the sister, who in turn was staring hungrily at the roaring fire, and he followed Cherie to the jeep.

'Gotta get outa here. It's a madhouse. That woman!'

Cherie nearly skidded the jeep off the track and into a dyke. She drove on for about half a mile, then pulled into a gateway. She was shaking.

'That woman! I cannot believe it. She was foul. She

knew everything — I know it. I know it!'

'Steady on. Know what? I mean, what did she know?'

'She knew we'd broken into Ransom's house. It was like there were probes sticking in my brain. She knew that we were onto something. The last thing she said was: "Men make all the mistakes and expect our sex to get them out of it." What did she mean? Oh, Christ, I'm sorry. I just went in there expecting some little old nun with a shrewd expression and twinkly eyes and I met a Martian. She said some interesting things, though, like the fact that the place on the heath was called the Retreat, and it was a place where the nuns were pledged — that was her word — to go because, wait for it, they were meant to be watching over people's souls. Jesus! Oh, and they closed it down because they couldn't afford to run it any more and also she didn't hold with that sort of nonsense. Her words, not mine. It sounded like the lease had expired or something. I don't know, but I got the impression that she was holding out on something. I mean she made things pretty difficult, but she told me a lot. Perhaps she was holding back on something else.'

Cherie started the jeep and turned the lights on, then swung into the road.

There was a terrible screech of tyres and she swerved back onto the verge, whipping her head round. A car screamed past them, the driver's face turned towards them, white and drawn with shock. Cherie drew in her breath sharply. Willis swore softly.

They both saw Ransom. Willis saw the face he'd seen in the portrait; the same shape of the head, the same cast of features. Cherie saw her old next-door neighbour, but aged terribly, with lines of worry scored deep into what had once been a plump, bland face. It was over in a flash. The car fishtailed and accelerated away into the night.

'Get after him!'

Cherie started the stalled engine, engaged gear, but did not move. The rear wheels were skidding helplessly in a small culvert. She turned the motor off.

‘Well, at least you know what she was hiding. That was Ransom?’ Willis asked.

‘How did you know?’

‘They’ve got a whacking great portrait of him in the room I was put in. Not him — the ancestor. Same face. He must have been in the building the whole time.’

‘He’s changed,’ Cherie said. ‘He’s aged about twenty years. We must find him.’

‘Yep, I’ll see if I can push us out.’

Ten minutes later they were on their way back to London.

Chapter Twenty-four

It was raining. The roaring jeep followed its wedge of white light down the M11, the wipers thwacking the edge of the screen and sucking back across. Willis was driving, hunched over the wheel, peering down the tunnel of light.

'It's hypnotic, isn't it?'

'Huh?' Willis grunted.

'The noise. You're not falling asleep, are you?'

'No, I'm not falling asleep. I was thinking.'

'About what?'

'To be honest, I was wondering how you managed to get involved like this. You being an American and that.'

Cherie was silent for longer than was comfortable.

'When I said it was hypnotic, I meant it,' she said eventually. 'I was thinking about my parents.'

'Your parents? What have they got to do with it?'

'They died when I was young.'

'Oh, I didn't —

'Spare me. I've spent my whole life trying to get away from them, trying to get even with them — you know, for dying on me. But it's difficult to get away from them, to grow up, be yourself, when the only place they exist is inside your head. I suppose . . . I suppose it's the real reason I got married.'

'Uhuh, why?'

'Well, it was like my ultimate rebellion. They hated England. I don't mean personally. I mean what it represents, or is meant to represent to people like us. My father used to go spare when he saw anything that was meant to represent Old England. You know the sort of thing. He once caught me watching *Upstairs Downstairs* and grounded me for a week. He said it corrupted people — especially people like us.'

'What, Americans?'

'Old Americans. Old New England families. You see, it's even in the name. My father used to say, "We came over here to make a new England, a real new England, and all people ever do is . . ." I'm not explaining myself. His theory was that the older the family, the bigger the reason they had for leaving. I mean they had real reasons. Freedom. Freedom from tradition, the kind of tradition that stifled them in the old country, persecuted them, really forced them into leaving. In a way he was wrong, because New England doesn't owe anything to this place. Nothing at all. The tradition's good like that. But in another way, it has set up its own traditions now that are well, stifling in their own way. He thought people should remember their past. "Never trust an Englishman," he'd say to me. Never trust an Englishman. So I married one to spite him, came here to live, and look what happened. Daddy's always right. Ha! If he hadn't gone on about it so much I probably would never have come here at all.'

'So you're an old New England family?'

'Pretty old. My people were meant to have come over sometime in the eighteenth century. I don't know exactly when.'

'So he was creating his own tradition himself, really.'

'Yeah. And I was rebelling from it. Look where it got me, though. Up to the eyeballs in a pile of seventeenth-century shit. But to answer your question. The real reason I got involved is because I'm dumb.'

They drove on a few miles. Again Willis broke the silence, awkwardly. Whatever feelings he had held for Cherie (sexual, paternal, sentimental, or all three) had been subsumed by the greater issues that seemed to engulf them. Still, he felt the whole business had become so personal to both of them that talking about it seemed like divulging your deepest secrets, or probing someone else's, and that was something he had never been in the habit of doing — not in the pub to his friends; not to his married sister who lived in St Albans; not to the few women he picked up, or was picked up by, went to bed with, spent the weekend with, then didn't see again.

They were crossing from the M11 to the M25, heading for Dartmouth Tunnel.

'So what do you make of all this?' Willis asked after he'd negotiated the switch from one motorway to another.

'What? Your country's advanced road system?' Her voice was cold. Brittle.

'No, I didn't mean my country's advanced road system,' Willis snapped back, angry that she was making it so difficult. He swallowed his irritation. 'I meant . . . all the other things.' He was aware that he was unable to spell it all out.

'Frankly, I'd rather not think about it.'

'Don't we have to?'

'What's this "We" all of a sudden?'

Willis darted a glance sideways. Cherie was sitting hunched up with her arms tightly folded.

'I just meant —'

'You just meant ... What it's done to *you*? What's happened to *you*? Fuck all — that's what. Shall I tell you what's happened to *me*? Shall I?' Her voice was rising; splitting on the knife edge of hysteria.

Willis cut in, 'I know what's happened to you. I know it's awful. I'm doing all I can to get to the bottom of this. And . . . well, I want to help you.'

'Hep me? Oh, great. Perhaps that explains why you're always looking at my tits? Don't worry, I know. It's habit, and you don't mean to. Like the way my husband's friends used to grope me at parties. It's habit. Or perhaps you think Americans screw around a lot. Read that in some clever articles? Let me tell you, it's a symptom of every society that feels itself inferior to ascribe loose morals to any culture it feels is superior. Fact. So let's work out what your motives really are. Foreign widow, young, reasonably attractive when she's not hysterical, needs "help". Maybe a bit of comfort. We all know what that means in this fucked-up country.'

Willis winced. 'OK, OK.'

'OK, OK,' Cherie countered sarcastically.

'Look —'

'Look where?'

Willis felt real anger flare. 'Oh, just piss off, then. I'll leave you to it. You're just a silly little girl.'

'And that makes you a big wise daddy? So tell me, daddy, what do you want to do? Watch the silly little girl suck on a lolly? Spank her naughty bottie?'

'You little . . . bitch.'

'Oh, a bitch am I? At least I'm grown-up now.'

'Yeah, you are a bitch. A fucking mad bitch. That's what you are.'

'Bitch? Great. You know what bitches do? They bite.'

Cherie gripped Willis by the knee and stuck her nails in as hard as she could. The jeep plunged into a wall of fog.

'You know what *mad* bitches do?'

Slid her hand higher up his thigh, dimly registering the speed warning lights flashing by the roadside: 30:30:30.

'*Fucking* mad bitches? They grab men's cocks and they grab their balls and they squeeze as hard as they fucking can.'

Willis screamed. The jeep swerved halfway into the fast lane. There was a screech of brakes beside them and a car shot past, horn wailing. Through tears of pain Willis saw the lights of the toll-gates for the tunnel in front of them.

'Bitch! Fucking slag! I'll get you. I'll beat you fucking senseless. Goddamn ugly slut, I'll . . .'

Cherie loosened her grip. 'Better drive on, big boy. Daddy better do what the mad bitch says or she'll castrate him.'

She squeezed again.

'No! OK, OK.'

They were at the toll-booth. Cherie fumbled in her pocket and by chance pulled out the right change. He leant over to open the window, and slapped the coins in the startled attendant's outstretched hand.

'Now drive on.'

Willis obeyed. Cherie dropped across him, her head in his lap, and began to fumble with the zip of his trousers, still squeezing him with her other hand.

All Willis could think about was teeth.

'No, no. Please don't.'

'Don't argue with the bitch,' Cherie said, her voice slow and sleepy and terribly menacing. 'Remember what bitches do. What do they do?'

Willis was silent, just the hoarse rasp of his breath as the yellow lights of the tunnel flashed by above him.

'*WHAT DO THEY DO?*'

'Bite.'

They roared through the pale tunnel-light in a rocking tent of blackness. He felt her breath on his groin. He imagined her . . . teeth. Then her lips, her tongue. He felt himself respond. Felt an awful, terrifying twitching warmth begin to spread.

'Coming to see me, are you? I didn't think you liked the idea. I'm waiting.' She snapped her jaws.

'Get off me! Get off me! I'll get you. I'll get you! I'll . . .'

Something cold erupted in his chest. He felt a rush of tears in his eyes and a sheet of water gushed from them, curtaining his cheeks in wet, dripping onto his shirt. His voice slowed and thickened.

'. . . I'll slit you. I'll break your bones and skin you. *I'LL WEAR YOU.* Whore whore whore whore. AARGH —'

Cherie had bitten in, hard. He heard her chuckle in the back of her throat. The jeep exploded into the black of the night. Willis saw a break in the barrier and pulled the jeep round in a shuddering skid. It smashed through a wooden gate and thudded into a pile of sand. Cherie's head crashed into the steering-wheel. Willis — who had been trying desperately to pull her off with one hand before they crashed, before her jaws snapped — was thrown forward into the windscreen.

There was silence in the jeep as the traffic roared by behind them. Silence but for the tick-tick of cooling metal and the soft drip of blood.

Cherie woke first. She'd been thrown off Willis's lap and had ended up by the pedals, lying on his shoes. Her mouth was full of blood. Still groggy, she struggled out from the well and spat instinctively. Willis stirred, reached down to his crotch and gave a high bleat as his hand met some liquid warmth.

A napalm explosion of memory flashed in Cherie's head.

'Oh God. Oh God. Oh God.' She put her head in her hands.

Willis fumbled in his zip with relief. 'Jesus, it's still there.' His head jerked round and he stared at her. 'You were . . . you were . . .'

'I *know* what I was doing! Oh Christ, my head. I also know that . . . that thing got into my mind. It was like a big tongue licking me inside my skull, getting me to do what IT wanted, but making me want to, also. Anyway you wanted to kill me . . .'

'But you said you were going to . . .' Willis felt crippled by embarrassment as much as anything.

'Oh Christ, that's right. I remember. Oh, my head.'

'Yes, I wanted to kill you. Jesus, the things I was thinking. I wanted to . . . This is awful.'

'That doesn't sound like a real policeman.'

'I don't think I am any more. Ever since this started I've been getting . . . kind of mental flashes. Terrible thoughts. I feel like a nutter.'

After a minute Willis tested the engine. It started first time, and he found reverse.

'Well it goes, at least.'

'Ransom must be miles ahead by now.'

'Christ, I'd forgotten about him. We've got to push on.'

'On to what? I'm getting a very bad feeling. We're forty

miles from Blackheath, but we were still reached by . . . .'

'It wanted to stop us, damn it. IT wanted to stop us.

'Does that mean it wanted to ensure Ransom got there first?'

'Could be. Or maybe it had something else on its mind.'

As they turned towards central London, the roads narrowed.

'We call this thing "it",' Cherie said when they were halted at a set of traffic lights. 'But what is it?'

'A ghost?'

'That makes you think of white sheets with eye-holes cut into them.'

'Is it us?'

'There's a local legend about The White Man. He's a sort of local bogeyman kids have songs about. Ever heard of it?'

'Hello, dere, White Man! Wanna blow a spliff wid me?' Willis spoke in a cartoon West Indian accent.

'That's not particularly amusing.'

'Come on, it was a joke.'

'Coming from a policeman, it's not as funny as it might be.'

'What? Here we go. Little Miss Liberal Conscience. Listen, let me tell you —'

'Shut up! Stop it! It's started again. Can't you feel?'

'Listen, I'm not going to be insulted by some prissy little pious bitch with —'

Cherie leant over and slapped Willis as hard as she could across the cheek. Their eyes locked. Willis's eyes emptied: pupils wide and dark as a camera lens, and Cherie found herself looking into two black pits, empty but for flickers of white in their depths. She tried to look away, but wanted urgently to discern what the white things were. She saw her own white face, reflected in the pupils, then looked past it, and down to a place where there was no light, and white things moved slowly and persistently together on a bed of filthy straw.

Then a voice she knew was Ransom's spoke to her in a language she could not understand. It made her look more closely at the white things, and as she looked more closely, she saw them split in half and turn red, and she realised that she had been looking at human babies.

Then a new voice. It was inside her, but she heard it as if it came from outside, echoing in her ear. It was sexless, thickened with hatred. Though she could not understand what it was saying, Cherie knew that it was willing her to come to it, and that she wanted to come (again) again AGAIN?

New noises: a roaring and a braying. Voices filled with hate. Cherie realised these were coming from outside, rather than inside — then fading. She snapped her mind back.

Willis was driving again, and they were two miles further down the road.

He looked over to her and smiled. 'You dropped off — we both did, at the lights a mile or so back. Must be tireder than I thought. Must be the shock.'

'You didn't . . .'

'What?'

'Dream anything?'

'No.'

'I heard his voice, saying something. Who's the ghost?'

'Going on what we've got, it's one very angry . . . thing. Listen. I've been doing some thinking. At least I *think* it was me doing some thinking. Do you mind if I smoke?'

'Go ahead.' Cherie opened her window.

'There are two strands here. Take Ransom first — the original Ransom. A nasty piece of work, right? Reading between the lines, we've got him basically running a racket. There's a plague on in London . . .'

'You make it sound like a Torvill and Dean extravaganza.'

'Come on, you know what I mean. There are people lying dead and dying all over London. It's chaos. So

Ransom, a bit of an operator, starts off burying the dead on the heath. A nice little sideline. But it's not enough. Think about it. There are houses, empty but for people who are sick or weak or both. His gang starts nicking their valuables. Small things at first, then big things. Then they start killing people for their money, their possessions, all the things he confessed to that quack doctor, and tossing the bodies into the pits. Who'd go and look? Right. Now, the plague's over. His boss's son rumbles him, so, being the sort of guy he is, he murders him. Things move on: he marries the widow, the old master dies (how, I wonder?) and he's the new landlord after persuading the old man to adopt him. Then what?'

'He's haunted. The ghost: the white man. That fake doctor wrote it down. They were wedded in white, or something. That's the colour the spirit took. White spirit. Get it? Anyway, that's the story.'

'Yeah.'

'It's incredible really,' Willis continued. 'We're talking about a man who was a mass murderer, and yet because it all happened three hundred odd years ago —'

Cherie, who had been staring out of the window lost in her own thoughts, suddenly turned.

'What did you say?'

'I only said that just because something happened three hundred years ago . . .'

'That's it! That's what that nun said: three hundred years. What was the date of the plague?'

'1665.'

'1965.'

'So?'

'That's when she claimed the pledge expired. But they stayed on there for another, what, twenty years?'

Willis looked puzzled.

'Look, Ransom's ancestor tries to atone for what he's done. He establishes schools, like the Leaford school. He endows a religious foundation. Oh God, she said they were watching over souls. I just thought she meant souls in general. Suppose, just suppose, she wasn't talking about souls in general. Suppose she was talking about two souls in particular. The two which Ransom's ancestor murdered. But in 1965, when the whole thing was meant to run down, when it had run its course, *something else happened.* Something happened which, I don't know . . . which meant the whole thing started up again, so that they had to stay there. Does that make any sense? Are we looking too far into the past? But how can we find out?'

'We'll have to ask Ransom. The sooner we get back to Blackheath, the better.'

'I just hope we're not too late.'

Blackheath slept. There were no lights on in Ransom's house, and his car was nowhere to be seen.

Willis dropped Cherie off at her front door and got wearily into his own car.

He wound the window down. 'Are you sure you're going to be all right?' he called.

Cherie walked over to the car window and bent down. 'The way we've been going about things, I think it'd be better if we separated. Look, I'm sorry about all that . . . earlier on.'

Willis shrugged. 'It wasn't just you. I'll call you tomorrow. I've just remembered I've got a job — that is, if I haven't been given the sack meanwhile.'

'Good luck.'

'Sleep well.'

Cherie closed the front door, and Willis drove off.

Chapter Twenty-five

There were good days and bad days. Correction — there were great days and there were less great days. But on the whole, on balance, life was good.

His brain seemed to hum like a dynamo a lot of the time, and he found that he could turn it on and off quite easily, though it was a bit of a drag when it wouldn't turn off and he found that he was doing some really strange things and some really disgusting things. But he didn't think of those things; he just thought of the good things.

It was as if he could do anything he wanted. Like the first time in the toy shop. There was this fantastic yacht; he'd never seen anything like it — ever. The decks were made of real wood strips, just like the real thing. The sails were red, with proper rigging. There was a cockpit with a steering-wheel that turned, and it was all operated by radio control. She even had an auxiliary motor you could use if you got becalmed.

That time he'd just walked into the shop and asked to see the boat. Suddenly his head had started humming, and after he'd looked at it for a while he had said he would like to take it. The assistant asked if it should be wrapped, and he had said, politely: 'No thank you. I want to sail it right away.'

'You want to sail *her* right away,' the manager had corrected him jovially.

'He can't wait,' another assistant had said.

'Wants all his friends to see him,' a third had said. 'That's why he won't have it wrapped.'

'Goodbye, young man,' they had all said together. 'Goodbye'. Sebastian Lee had felt tears start in his eyes because they were all so kind, and he had walked out of the shop and into the street before remembering that he hadn't paid. He paused, then realised that the people in the shop had *wanted* to give him the yacht, and had wanted him *not* to pay. And that was nice because it was what he had wanted, too.

It was a brilliant boat. He had taken it to the pond on the heath and in one afternoon he'd learnt how to sail with the wind, with the wind to beam, how to tack, and how to goosewing down wind. A man had been there with his son, but soon he sent the son away and devoted all his time to Sebastian Lee. Whenever somebody else had come to the pond to try and sail a boat he had simply sent them away too. No problem at all.

Sebastian Lee thought of going home with this man, who seemed a nice sort of person, but it struck him that Gran might be getting a bit worried, so he rode — free — on the bus all the way home, while the bus conductor admired his boat and told him what a clever fellow he was.

The next day his grandmother took his mother off to her bungalow in Hove, leaving him behind. They agreed it was the best thing for all of them. Above all it seemed as if Gran had really *wanted* to go.

Eating presented no problem. At the hamburger place he had been given quite as much as he had wanted, and on top of that the manager had kept on coming to his table with snacks and new dishes which he said he wanted (wink, smile) *tested.*

Sebastian Lee liked that idea, and in the video arcade down the road the person who gave out the change agreed with him that quite a few of the games needed testing in there as well. So she handed over a tenner in ten pence pieces and told him to come back for more if he needed them. During the first few days he had gone to restaurants and video arcades quite a lot. Lewisham was best for that.

The woman in W.H. Smiths had been just as nice, and the first time he went in there he had walked away with a carrier bag full of car magazines. He had thought it might be nice to pick up a copy of *Playboy*, but had been too embarrassed to ask. Imagine his surprise then when he got home and he found it sandwiched between two other magazines. The assistant must have slipped it in while he wasn't looking.

But the magic only seemed to work on other people. When Sebastian Lee wanted to learn to cook he found that he couldn't. Everything burned and stuck to the pan and tasted horrible, so he asked Mrs Taylor from next-door to come in and teach him. Well, she'd tried to teach, but it soon became clear that what she really wanted was to do everything herself. So Sebastian Lee let her cook and clean all afternoon. And when Mr Taylor had come storming in that evening, after spotting her through the window, he was soon ready to help too. He had been upset at first because the baby was crying, but Sebastian Lee soon put a stop to that. In fact, they said, the boy was a marvel. They'd never seen the baby so quiet. It must all be Sebastian's influence.

They were very kind to him, and told him all sorts of nice things about himself he had never known, like how his parents clearly neglected him, and how they had been so worried over this, and in their heart of hearts would really love to adopt him. Perhaps they still could? Then the baby, Paul, would have an older brother, they would have a proper son, and Sebastian Lee would have some proper parents. At times like this he would feel warm all over, and a wonderful happy tearful lump would rise in his throat.

But after a few days things got a bit dull. One evening the three of them were watching a film on the video which had a lot of kissing in it but stopped when it looked as if things might get a bit interesting. Sebastian Lee was vaguely wondering what happened next, when Mr and Mrs Taylor got undressed and showed him.

Very disappointing. Embarrassing and rather boring, he thought. Not at all how Richard Rendall had described it to an audience behind the prefabricated hut that served as the art room at school.

On top of that, as Sebastian Lee got increasingly bored, he noticed that the Taylors began to grow edgy and look annoyed and talk about the baby. The whole *thing* only seemed to work when he actively wanted something. Then everything turned out as he wished. Quite honestly, thought Sebastian, I want them to go home. And so they did.

There were still a few matters he wanted to clear up before he . . . what? Buried somewhere in the wrinkles of his mind was the assumption that there was a before and an after, and he had better get things done *before*, because *after* things would be very different. The feeling was like trying to remember something which had never happened. Sebastian Lee both knew it and didn't know it simultaneously. It was irritating to say the least.

However, he felt there was a certain pressure on him to finish things off, and the most pressing matter was the business with school. The memory of his last day — the taunting from Scruby's gang, and his expulsion by the headmaster — still made him flush uncomfortably when it came to mind. He thought of lots of things he could do. One idea he had was to visit each of the boy's houses in turn and get made a fuss of by their parents, while the boys were sent upstairs to bed or scourged or something like that. But he did not know where any of them lived, so he shelved that idea. Anyway, it would be nice to teach them all a lesson at the school in front of everyone else.

Sebastian Lee woke early and got a lift down to the school. He was finding it increasingly easy to get people to help him as soon as he made eye contact with them, and this included car drivers. It was difficult to work out quite what happened. He would see the car as it hit the crest of Shooters Hill, and as it began to descend he would try to catch the driver's eye. After that it was a bit like grabbing a ride at the playground; he had to calculate speed, which was the way they were travelling, and height, which roughly corresponded to the type of person they were. His father had an automatic station search on his car radio. Getting the drivers to cooperate was a bit like working that, and a bit like finding where a strange dog likes to be tickled; the bit that always makes its back legs thump up and down uncontrollably. Sebastian Lee would just feel around the driver's brain until he found the reflex spot and then beam a corny old impression at it. Something like: there's a nice little boy by the road looking lonely; if I pick him up and give him a lift I shall go to heaven/feel great/save him from a fate worse than death/stop somebody else doing it. Occasionally it misfired. Once a woman stopped whose son of about Sebastian Lee's age had recently been run over. She cried and cried, and pawed him so much that Sebastian Lee was convinced the car would crash. But that morning it was pretty run-of-the-mill. A nice young businesswoman had wanted to take Sebastian Lee to the south of France for a holiday (Sebastian Lee had been flicking through holiday brochures and had discovered that some people didn't wear clothes on the beach there. Wicked!), and when he said he hadn't the time she gave him twenty quid and a business card instead.

By the time they reached the school, Sebastian Lee had pretty much worked out what he wanted to do. He walked into the playground unnoticed, but soon had a crowd of boys gathered around him admiring his new multi-function digital watch; the massive Akai twin-cassette music box with dub function and three-way speakers; the Reebok trainers; and the Italian leather jacket which, although it was a bit big for him, was pretty cool. He was standing in the middle of a competitively sycophantic crowd when Edward Scruby, the boy who had led the teasing on the day he had been expelled, walked into the playground with Steven Stubbs, his crony, in tow.

'Here,' he warned, 'you can't talk to him. He's been

expelled. You're all in big trouble already.'

Sebastian Lee's new fan-club all turned at Scruby's voice. Sebastian Lee felt his influence slip, dilute. He was getting good at detecting shifts in mood, and there was a distinct sense of surprise from some of them that they were standing around in the playground admiring a boy who had been expelled, and who had always been considered a bit of a creep anyway.

Pump up the volume

There was some surprise on their faces as they all turned smiling to Sebastian Lee, who had tentatively beamed — there was no other word for it — at them mentally. Now for the duel of wills.

'What's the matter, Scruby?' Sebastian Lee was annoyed that his voice was shaking. Old habits died hard.

'Nothing's the matter, Smeg-face. Except I've just seen the headmaster look out of the window. He's going to get you, and all the little Smeg fans talking to you.'

Control

like me like me like me like me like me like me like me like me like me like me

'He won't,' said Sebastian Lee.

Scruby turned to Stubbs. 'Come on. Let's leave the children to play.'

STAY!

'Hey, Scruby!'

Scruby turned, his face straining as if he had just been told something he didn't want to know.

'Sebastian Lee scrabbled in his mind for insults. None there. Come on, come on, come on. Suddenly:

'Your mother!' That was better. Voice sounded strong. 'Your mother . . .'

Pause as he projected a picture of Mrs Scruby: leggy, laughing, young deb turned perfect mum, and married to an older man who raced horses and had money. Amazement and joy dawning. None of them would have heard *this* one before.

'. . . sucks her horses!'

Got him! Even got the accent right: American and mean.

'And *your* mother —' Scruby was saved by the bell, but it didn't matter. Nobody had heard his voice rise like that before. He was wounded. Disgusted. Furious and humiliated. The playground began to empty as the boys streamed into assembly. The duty master looked in puzzlement at the hideously dressed boy left standing alone. He looked familiar. Good God, it was the Miles boy who had beaten up Knight so badly that he was still off school with dizzy fits and fainting.

He opened his mouth to shout: 'Here, you, what do you think you're doing. Get out! Get away from here at once!'

Then a strange thing happened. The teacher suddenly realised that he couldn't do it. He didn't want to. Thoughts came geysering from the bottom of his mind. Hysterically kind and loving thoughts about the Miles boy whose father had died and who had been cast out from the school into the . . . the wilderness. But what could he do? The expulsion had come straight from the headmaster. There was only one thing for it. The child would have to be taken back to him and allowed a second chance, a free hearing. Why, the teacher thought, I'd stake my reputation on it. Damn it, I'd stake my career. I will stake my career. I'll just go up to the headmaster and say: 'Sir, if there's any problem I will take the boy on. He's got potential. Great potential. He must be saved.'

The teacher found tears in his eyes as he thought of his own nobility and selflessness. The boy was looking straight at him, with a curiously, no, pathetically blank expression.

'Come on, my boy. Come inside with me. I think we've got to sort things out with the headmaster, don't you?'

'Just take me there and leave me, please.'

So brave, so independent, the teacher thought, as he knocked on the headmaster's door. He looked lovingly on as Sebastian Lee opened the door and walked in.

At lunch both staff and pupils were surprised to hear that all afternoon lessons and sport were to be cancelled and a general knowledge knockout quiz was to be held in the school theatre. Preparations for it would begin after lunch; the teams were posted on the notice-board. Forms Three and Four were to stay behind after lunch to help carry tables. There would be a cash prize of twenty pounds to the winning team.

Twenty pounds! The dining-room began to buzz. With teams of four boys, that would be a fiver each! Will you be in my team? Shall we get together with Simmons? Bit of a creep but he's brainy. No, old Hannibal said he'd chosen teams already. Did you hear? The losing team gets extra work.

Teachers frantically face-signalled to each other from the ends of their tables. Mouths half open, eyebrows raised: *Do you know what's going on*? Eyebrows raised, shoulders shrugged: *First I've heard of it. The old man's flipped.* Some went home. Some stayed out of curiosity. Some marched through the corridors, shouting and organising. But by a quarter to two the school theatre had been rearranged for the competition, and the boys were sitting untidily on benches. A festive and lightly anarchic spirit — as accompanies every pleasant surprise in the school day — prevailed.

Forms Three and Four had been busy. The stage had been set with black flats from the previous year's production of *Macbeth* (highlights from), and three tables had been arranged to make a rough L-shape. Two of the tables faced the audience; the other was set apart from them at an angle of about ninety degrees. Right at the back was a school desk piled high with encyclopedias, with a researcher, assumed to be the school secretary, almost completely hidden behind the heap of books.

The scrum around the notice-boards had been fierce, to find out who was in which team. Equally the jubilation and fury. It was plain that no attempt had been made to balance the teams. There were two outstanding ones, and one or two goodish ones. But the rest were obvious losers from the outset, and it was hard to work out why they had been chosen. Roughly half the school was involved.

The rules were simple: it was to be a straightforward knockout competition up to the semi-finals. The best loser from that round would then play the knocked out team with the highest score. Then would come the finals, and after that a last round, when the two finalists could nominate any one of their members for a singles match, the victor of which would take the title 'Honorary Mastermind of the Leaford School'. A final 'Sir-Prize' was promised for the winner.

Edward Scruby had a place in the front row. His team hadn't been called for the first round, so they sat back and tried to look relaxed. The questions weren't too bad. They were a mixture of remembering lessons (capital of Venezuela, chemical formula for water, the spelling of receive, and such), a bit of general knowledge (name of the Great Train Robber living in Brazil, is Venus a star or a planet?) and some pathetic 'school' jokes (if you heard Mr Willans shouting 'Whisky!', would he be looking for his dog or asking for a drink? Ha-bloody-ha). Everybody enjoyed themselves, especially the headmaster, who beamed periodically towards the researcher's desk behind him.

In the first round the teams were drawn out of a hat. Scruby's team was in the second round on stage, drawn opposite a team of complete no-hopers. After trouncing them, they went back to their seats to wild applause, obvious favourites to win eventually.

They sat through the next round, which was reasonably close-run, and then the competition for third place.

Scruby found he knew almost all the answers. It was going to be a breeze. It was fairly predictable who the other finalists would be; they were good, but had scored less than Scruby's team. At last came the call for the finals, and Scruby's team stood up and made their way forward to the stage.

There was an excited murmur as they climbed the steps, it seemed as if the school went wild. Boys stood on their chairs, clapping, and whooping like banshees. A huge wolf-whistle split the air, and Scruby turned round to see Mr Thomson, the taciturn and disciplinarian chemistry teacher, whip his fingers guiltily out of his mouth, then give him an enormous wink. It was a fantastic feeling. His team had no idea they were so popular; even Scruby couldn't work it out. He was the last up on stage, and on reaching the table, he turned and gave an ironic bow. More cheers, more catcalls. Even the headmaster gave him a grin. Scruby held his hands up in a thank-you-very-much-but-that's-enough gesture, just as he'd seen Terry Wogan do. For a second there was dead silence, then another burst of laughter. Scruby took his seat, feeling ecstatic. This is what it must be like to be a star, he thought — bloody fantastic. And, to celebrate, he put a showbiz arm around the shoulders of the boy sitting next to him. Shakespeare was a swot and a creep, but what the hell: he was brainy.

Then something made Scruby look towards the table where the invigilator was sitting. It was faintly spooky that the person sitting there was invisible. Suddenly a little wave of goosepimples travelled up his neck, bristling the short hairs at the base of his skull. There was a small gap between the books, like the gun-slit in a concrete pillbox, and two eyes were looking straight out — staring at him. Glinting. And the shoes! That couldn't be Miss Leach, the school's secretary. She didn't wear Reeboks. But someone did . . .

The headmaster was speaking. 'We now enter the penultimate stage of the competition: the team final. I'm sure you'll agree that all the teams have done splendidly up until now. So without further ado we'll launch straight into the first question. No conferring, and the first to ring gets to answer. Ready? Right.'

What is the name of the President of the United States?

Ring. Correct answer.

Who was the first man to reach the South Pole?

Ring. Correct answer.

What colour is indigo?

Ring. Correct answer.

What is the valency of carbon?

Pause. Suddenly Scruby felt his hand stretch out and ring the bell.

'Four.'

'Four is the correct answer!'

Applause. Scruby made a humorous face. Just a guess. But it wasn't. He had *known* with a certainty as complete as knowing that three and three made six, or that Kim Wilde was definitely fanciable. Except he didn't know previously – hadn't known until a split second before his hand snaked across the table to ring that bell. Still it was the right answer, and he received appreciative looks from the rest of the team.

The open round ended, and was followed by team questions. At the end of that round, Scruby's team was trailing by four points, but now, in the final round, the questions were worth five points each. The tension began to get to Scruby, who would answer last. If all the other teams got their questions right, it would make no difference how well he did. But if one of them muffed a question, the outcome of the match could well depend on him. Bloody tense, especially as the questions were getting harder. Still, he could have answered most of the questions fired at the others. Which Christian saint was depicted tied to a tree, being shot with arrows? that was quite easy: Saint Sebastian. What Confederate general in the American Civil War surrendered at Appomattox Court House? They'd just done that in history, and

Shakespeare got it without hesitation: General Lee.

And then it happened. The last one on the other team was asked for the temperature at which water froze in Centigrade. The boy thought for a second, then with a big smile said: 'Thirty-two.' A groan went up from his team, and sarcastic catcalls floated up from the audience. That was Fahrenheit. The moron! The wally! The boy looked horrified.

Scruby felt his heart leap: they now had a chance. They could win! It was his turn. Then, almost as quickly, he realised that they wouldn't win if *he* got his answer wrong. His mouth dried out, and his heart began to pound. Everything depended on *him.*

'Scruby, complete the following quotation . . .' The voice seemed to boom from the far end of a tunnel.

Scruby felt his concentration begin to slip, and his attention was drawn to the mysterious desk with the invisible person sitting behind it at the corner of the stage. Who was the saint shot full of arrows? *Sebastian.* Which American general surrendered at Appomattox Court House? *Lee.* Who was wearing Reebok trainers this morning? *Who was sitting behind the desk in the corner? Who?*

'Scruby? Scruby!'

'What? Oh, sorry, sir. I just didn't catch the question.'

'Very well. I'll repeat it once more, and once only. Ready? In the nursery rhyme "There was a crooked man", how far did the crooked man walk?'

Crooked man? Who was he? How far did he walk? God only knew. To Saint Ives? Into the Valley of Death? All along down along out along lee? Oh hell, I don't know. *I don't know.* I'M GOING TO LOSE US THE MATCH.

The team across the stage were now looking desperately expectant. He heard one of his own team mutter: 'C'mon, c'mon. COME ON.'

Scruby glanced round to the wall of books — to the eyes looking through. To the shoes fidgeting underneath.

Reebok trainers.

There was a crooked man.

Saint Sebastian.

Who walked a crooked —

What, though, what? What does it rhyme with? Quick! Quick!

General Lee.

He found a crooked sixpence

Sebastian Lee

Against a crooked stile

Behind the books: the eyes. The eyes.

'MILES!'

'Correct! Well, a mile. Not miles. But we'll give it to you. The crooked man walked a crooked mile, and that means that Scruby, Shakespeare, Gordon and Taylor are the winners by a single point! Congratulations to the losers who —'

But the headmaster was drowned out by a wave of cheering and shouting. The lights went down and Scruby found himself being thumped on the back by his team.

'Decent.'

'Brill. Wicked. Really ace.'

'Skill, Scruby. God I didn't know that answer. You got it, though.'

'Should have seen their faces. Twenty quid between four of us. That makes a fiver each.'

'And you're going into the play-offs Scruby. You're the best. Bet there's a brilliant prize for that.'

Scruby felt dazed. He had no idea where that nursery rhyme had come from. It had just started going on in his head. And the other thing: the thing with the names. That was just spooky. But it couldn't be that little rat Sebastian Lee behind the books in the corner. It couldn't be.

On stage the lights went down. Four of the stage-hands pushed the tables to the back. Two high spots from the front of the stage, both left and right, came on and focused on a spot right in the middle of the platform. From the wings came the sound of castors rolling, and the headmaster's voice hissing angry whispers. And the audience fell silent as the high-backed black leather chair that always stood behind his desk was wheeled onto the boards and positioned under the twin beams of white light.

In the audience a couple of the teachers began to mutter to each other about the strain this would put the two finalists under, but they fell silent as the headmaster beckoned the two highest individual scorers from the wings. These were Scruby and a boy called Watson, and he tossed a coin to see who would go on first.

It was Watson to start, who scored fifteen out of a possible twenty. He left the stage to polite applause, and then Scruby walked across to the chair. Again the audience erupted into cheers and whistles, but this time the house lights had been dimmed and Scruby was confronted by a screaming wall of darkness which seemed to dance and swim in front of him. The lights hurt his eyes, too. He felt sure that they had been turned up higher for him than they were for Watson. Only by lowering his eyes could he avoid their searing brightness. In front of him, and slightly to the left, he could see the headmaster seated at a table and reading with a small spotlight. Scruby turned back to the dusty, rustling darkness in front of him.

The first question came suddenly from nowhere.

'Which is heavier: a pound of feathers or a pound of lead?'

Trick question. Easy.

'Neither. They weigh the same.'

'Wrong. A pound of lead.'

WHAT? No. No. No.

'Who beat whom at the Battle of Hastings?'

'William the Conqueror beat King Harold.'

'Correct.'

'But the first one —'

'What colour does litmus paper turn in an acid solution?'

'Red.'

'Correct.'

'What object am I holding up?'

Scruby looked across. The headmaster had stood up,

holding something against the light. Scruby squinted. The light was so intense that tears started from his eyes.

'I can't see, I'm afraid, sir. I can't —'

Laughter from the audience. Laughter. Did someone say 'Cry-baby'?

'What object am I holding up? Come on.'

Scruby turned his head again and squinted. He looked out of the corner of his eye. It looked like one of those things that captains used on ships. The headmaster kept one in his study.

'A sextant.'

'Correct.'

'How many yards in a mile?'

George the something said with a smile

One seven six nought yards in a mile.

'One thousand, seven hundred and sixty.'

'Correct.'

A muttering from the darkness: 'Swot. Swot. Swot. Swot. Swot.'

'If I have five counters on the table, and somebody gives me three more but takes two away, how many are left?'

5 + 3 − 2 = 6

'Six.'

'Wrong.'

No. Right.

'How many elephants can you fit —'

'Sir.'

'You're wasting time.'

'But, sir, the answers —'

Swot swot swot SWOT SWOT SWOT.

'The answer's six.'

'Wrong. How many —'

'But, sir . . .'

But the noise from the audience was now so loud that Scruby's voice was drowned, and he could not hear the next question over the din. Scruby felt the sweat pour off him, onto the leather. His face was sweating, too, but the heat of the lights seemed to be baking it into a sticky crust.

'Sir, I can't hear what you're saying. It's not . . .'

Diddums! Poor little baby. Not fair, not fair. The creep can't hear. Scruby's a cocksucker. Your mother —

'Sir, please . . .'

But the headmaster was steadfastly reading questions, oblivious to the noise. Against the light Scruby could just see his lips move, stop, move again. The noise from the audience seemed to die down a little. Scruby struggled in the big chair, arms thrown across his eyes, skewered by the burning white light. Tears streamed down his face. The audience grew quieter. There was a sense of expectation. The headmaster droned on.

'What — that's the bell, but I've started so I'll finish. Here's the final question. Why do we all hate Scruby so much?'

There was a second's pause. The room took a breath. Then a voice said 'Lights', and suddenly all the house lights went up, the spots dimmed, and Scruby saw a room full of people rigid in a frozen sea of hatred. Some were half out of their chairs, as if they were about to rush the stage; some where actually halfway down the aisles, their faces caught in expressions of dreamy intent. Some were sitting, their mouths wide open, the tendons in their necks taut as if caught while they bayed their hatred out at him.

Scruby stood up, trembling, too scared to run, then heard a footstep. Sebastian Lee stood beside him. He seemed more interested in the audience than he did in Scruby.

'Hello, Scruby.'

'It was you! All the time, behind the desk. Why —'

'Shut up.'

'God I'm sorry, Miles — Sebastian.' Scruby's face was working terribly. His bottom lip felt loose like a dockleaf. His mouth filled up with saliva and he kept on glancing out towards the auditorium, where the audience still kept its grotesque stiffness.

'I didn't mean any of those things, Sebastian. I'm sorry,

I'm sorry, I'm sorry. Was it all for that?'

'Grow up, Scruby. It was an experiment. Now I think I'm ready.'

'Are you going to kill me?'

But Sebastian Lee turned and walked into the wings.

'ARE YOU GOING TO KILL ME?'

The crowd in the theatre began to move. Talking quietly among themselves they filed slowly into the aisles and began to move towards the stage. Scruby could not budge. He stood with his eyes closed. He felt his bladder open as the whispering grew closer, closer. He could feel them around him — ON HIM. Their words filled his ears with mad noises —

'... did hurble skull the cabbage ... silent nightly through heavy sister my come . . . fuckmass ctelphth-mongrom splitter increase . . . bastom suckles high thigh holes stucky . . . regal? kind albino sick pitty humour . . . into aggasm pronto . . . redeye fig sod yis nobbum . . .'

— and they were past him into the wings.

Scruby stood there, certain it was a trick, certain that if he moved, or turned round, he would see the whole crowd massed behind him on the stage. Waiting. Smiling. He felt cold on the back of his neck, and his damp trousers clung to him. There was complete silence around him, and a draught. Which meant ... the doors were open. They'd gone!

Scruby wheeled round and saw what he could not believe. The stage was empty. He was alone. They really had all gone. As quietly as he could, he followed them out.

Chapter Twenty-six

The Sixties. Free love and property booms, Cherie thought. Swinging London. Upstairs was a pile of Giles cartoon books going back twenty or thirty years. Peter once admitted that his first erotic fantasies had been based on the deep cleavages of the micro-skirted dolly-birds which seemed to crop up everywhere in the detailed pictures. Cherie had a sudden vision of that ghastly envelope of flesh, that hallucination, which had been draped on the bed upstairs in Ransom's house. That and the room in the basement.

Connections. Putting things together. The body — ghost, whatever it was — was linked to that room in the basement, was linked to some year in the 1960s when something happened to someone in it. But what? There were bolts on the door. Big heavy bolts. So someone had been locked in there. The girl. It had to be the girl. Left alone there with nothing but a few records to keep her company. But who was she? Where had she come from? *What had Ransom done to her?*

The ghost had floated off in the direction of the convent. That if nothing else linked it to Ransom. Another message. Another sign. Cherie's mind was swimming.

Outside the sitting-room window the heath looked unusually dirty. The colour seemed to have drained from the grass, and merged with the sky above. White. Grey. Both seemed to be doing their best not to have any colour whatsoever. In the distance she could see a tractor and trailer pulled up on the grass to clear up the rubbish. It couldn't be paper because the men were throwing things from some distance into the back of the trailer and paper would have just blown away. The telephone rang with a harsh jangle. She picked it up. Willis.

'Howyadoin?'

'Fine. And yourself?'

'Just trying to think. At the moment I'm looking out of the window at some park keepers cleaning up the heath.'

'You haven't heard?'

'Heard what?'

'I went to work this morning — well, basically I went in to plead overwork and incompetence and ask for some time to think about my career. I said I spent yesterday in bed with the phone off the hook. The superintendent jumped at the chance to get rid of me, believe it or not. Anyway, I was chatting with some mates and there was some incident here yesterday. Apparently a great flock of birds gathered, and then just started dying. Raining from the sky. And more came and more came, until eventually it became dangerous to walk there. A seagull falling fifty feet onto someone's head, beak first, can make a very nasty dent.'

Cherie looked out of the window and shuddered. She now saw clearly that the park keepers were throwing dead birds onto the back of the trailer. Seagulls, she guessed, because they were white.

'They're still picking them up.'

'They were estimating ten thousand in all. It only went on a few hours. They've been working through the night in case they're infectious. I mean they're not, but you have to make sure.'

'They're not what?'

'Infectious. The first thing that was done when the first reports came in was to do a few tests on them. Nothing. They're just dead. Then all the men from the Ministry came with air testers — this is all an official secret by the way just in case you felt like selling the story to the press —'

'Just get on with it.'

'Nothing. Nothing at all. No trace of gas, radiation, Nothing.'

'Oh.'

'Nobody's got a clue —'

Cherie felt a wave of panic overtake her. She knew what he was going to say next.

'— except us.'

'Yes.'

'It's the . . . thing.'

For a second Cherie almost put the phone down. She felt that was all she had to do to deny its existence. Saying anything would reaffirm it. Saying *yes* would commit her irrevocably to the idea.

'Yes,' she said, and knew it was the bravest thing she had done.

'So,' he said. 'What do we do?'

Cherie's jaw dropped. 'What?' she managed to stutter.

'I'm all at sea. And I think you've probably got a better grasp on this than me. There's one thing I'd like to do, though. I'd like to try and find Ransom's ancestor's grave. But I think one of us has got to tackle next-door again.'

'I've been trying not to think about that,' Cherie said. 'But it's hard. I couldn't face it, though I've got some ideas about the grave — or about *a* grave anyway.'

'You sure you're up to that?'

'It won't be difficult. But there's something you could do. When the demolition crew started on the convent there was a rumour that they'd found a really old coffin in the grounds. Can you check up on that?'

'I've still got a few friends left.'

'We'll meet here in about an hour, then. I imagine you'll want to get into Ransom's house then?'

'Yes.'

'Better wait till I'm back before you do anything. You can get over the garden wall and break in through the back.'

Willis laughed uneasily. 'Are you taking charge?'

'I think I've probably got a better grasp of these things

than you, dear,' Cherie repeated back at him in her sweetest voice. 'See you later.'

'See you,' Willis answered, sounding wary.

There was something nagging Cherie; something she now wished she had cleared up before. And the thought — or the thought behind the thought — was now pushing to the front of her mind with horrid persistence. She did not know what it meant; but had to find out.

The damp wind cut through her jacket more keenly than any wind she had known in freezing New York winters. Cold ate its way through the soles of her boots like acid. The skin on her face seemed to be shrinking as she walked towards the ruined building.

She stood outside the railings and tried to cast her mind back to a morning weeks back when she had stood waiting for the demolition ball to swing. She had been standing somewhere on the perimeter then. Deep in thought she walked to the front of the building, where the crowd had been gathered, and then attempted to retrace her steps. Remembering that she had seen a bulldozer knock down a shed, she kept her eyes open. Then saw it. It was later in the year and the undergrowth looked yellow and sickly as if it had died for winter. It would all make her job that much more easy. Taking a quick bearing she walked back the way she had come until she found a gap she could squeeze through. Then she made her way along the inside of the fence.

She almost tripped over the grave, the headstone was so low. It was strange to see the vivid white scar on the worn and lichenous surface, left when the bulldozer had knocked it and sent the little cross spinning through the air to land at Cherie's feet. She thought of the other grave, lying unmarked, that had been disturbed by the same bulldozer, perhaps, and wondered what Willis would be able to find out about it.

Then she knelt down, and taking a stiff scrubbing brush from her pocket began to rub away at the inscription. The vegetable mould of centuries began to come away, and though the name on the tomb was worn by the wind, and eaten by the clinging roots of lichen, it was still faintly legible. Cherie nodded thoughtfully. Taking the cross which had been knocked from the gravestone she tried to place it on top. There was no place for it to rest; no spur to mate with the hole drilled in the base of the upright. Left on its own it toppled into a tangle of flat wet grass and nettles. She picked it up, dropped it in her pocket and walked home.

Willis was waiting outside Cherie's house when she returned. He looked serious.

'What put you onto that coffin business?' he asked.

Cherie shrugged. 'I must be getting intuitive,' she said.

Willis nodded. 'I remember it now,' he said. 'Some of the lads down at the station were talking about it, but then the murders happened, and it was rather put to one side. You see, everybody assumed that it had all happened so long ago that it was low priority. We tend to think that when a cadaver's over a couple of hundred years old. I was surprised that it wasn't just cremated, but they seem to be waking up a bit and every body that was being brought in was given a full autopsy. This one was pretty gruesome. All the limbs had been smashed — I don't know if you knew that — and the coffin itself, which was lead, had this archaic inscription in the lid. "Here lies one who could not walk or crawl so others might be kept in thrall." Some nonsense like that.'

Cherie frowned.

'Well. My immediate reaction was: it's that old black magic. That lunatic Ransom had set about sacrificing people or something in an attempt to propitiate the ghost. I mean he must have killed hundreds before, and Lord Leaford's son, *and* his wife, so what difference would another make? Right?'

Willis was obviously expecting some sort of rise out of Cherie, but she kept staring steadily out of the window.

'Except,' he continued, 'he didn't do it. Whoever killed that person did it relatively recently and made damn sure it was going to *look* like an ancient corpse. I won't go into how.'

'No, do', said Cherie.

'I warn you it's pretty disgusting.'

'Just tell me.'

'Well, basically it's wind drying. That corpse was mummified near enough, which made everyone think it had been there for ages and kept dry by some freak of nature. But it hadn't. That body had been actually *dried out* to make it look like an ancient corpse. It was a woman; they could tell that. And they think, from the teeth, that she was quite young. God knows how it was dried out, but it was, after all the vital organs had been removed, of course' — Willis kept an eye on Cherie but could detect no reaction; it was almost as if she had been anticipating something like this — 'put into a lead coffin with that phony message cut into the top, and buried. So, now we've got another murder investigation on our hands'.

Willis paused. Cherie continued to look out of the window. After a while she nodded. The thought that kept on occurring to her filled her with such horror that utter composure was the only way she could maintain any semblance of reason or calm. Willis said: 'So what about you? Did you have any luck at the convent?'

Cherie shook her head. 'No. I mean yes. I discovered something totally negative which may prove to be conclusive. I don't know.'

'What?'

'The cross I found. Do you remember me telling you about it?'

Willis nodded. 'Of course. He stole it.' And he nodded at the connecting wall between Cherie's and Ransom's house.

'And I told you that when I found it I'd had this, like, vision?'

Willis nodded.

'Well I'd just assumed, taken for granted really, that it was all very significant. The way I found it. The way events turned later. Ransom's interest in it. All that. So anyway, I made up this little story that it had fallen off a tomb and somebody inside was screaming out for justice. Right?'

'I suppose I did, too,' Willis said.

'Well it's nobody's,' Cherie said. 'Correction. There is a grave near where I found it, only it belonged to a dog. I've read the inscription. There's no mystery attached to it. That cross didn't come from any grave or at least not from one in the convent. It's like a massive blind alley, or rather it's a symptom of the dumb stupid idiotic way we've both been thinking. Now if it had been on the tomb that the mutilated body was in, we'd have had a story. But it's like everything here. Nothing makes sense. Nothing.'

'But Ransom?' Willis said. 'He nicked it from you. You told me he'd shown an inordinate amount of interest in it.'

'He did both things,' Cherie replied. 'But God knows why. For some entirely unconnected reason. Perhaps he really was interested in it from some local history point of view. But I can't believe that. He's the sort of man who'd have a reason for everything.'

'Are you saying there's no mystery then, no ghost?'

'What? Like in Scooby Doo when you find out all along it's just been a gang of bank robbers with a few sheets?'

'And luminous paint,' Willis added.

'You watch Scooby Doo?' Cherie smiled for the first time in days.

'Only when I get the chance,' Willis replied. 'No, I've got a nephew and a niece of telly-addict age. I watch telly with them.'

'It'd be nice to do that,' she said.

Willis suddenly felt embarrassed. There was a pause. He broke it.

'You were saying?'

'You said it in the jeep.' Cherie said. 'Something about a mass murderer in the seventeenth century seeming somehow less awful than a modern murderer, though they shouldn't. In some ways you're right. There's no difference. I remember reading once that the mongol invaders of China tried to kill every Chinese peasant. Every one of them. They gave up at about thirty million. ... That should shock us as much as the Nazis' attempt to exterminate the Jews, or the Khmer Rouge's attempts to commit national suicide, but it doesn't. Those centuries in between make a difference to the way we feel because we know we couldn't make a difference to whether the Mongolians killed every Chinese man, woman and child or whether they just played a little rough. We're not involved. But we could, conceivably, stop what went on in Nazi Germany happening again in Europe, and we should know now how not to make the conditions that create a Khmer Rouge. What I'm getting at is this. There's something going on here that WE can make a difference to, I know it. And I know damn well that it's got nothing much to do with a madman who lived three hundred years ago. That might come into it, but it's like a blind alley. Is there anywhere that keeps old newspapers going back, I don't know twenty, thirty years?'

Willis sighed. 'I don't know what you're talking about. But, if you really want to look through old newspapers you could try the Colindale Newspaper Library. They have newspapers on microfiche there. But what are you looking for?'

'Anything, anything about Ransom. His past. His present. His future. Anything. It's him. I know. That foul upper-class slime-bag has done something and I want to find out what it is.'

Willis was silent for a second. 'Too vague. You could be there for days. You're talking about one name in God knows how many papers. Even if you limited yourself to one paper it's still a matter of luck. No I've got a better idea. One of my contacts. Every bent copper needs one.'

'What?'

'A reporter. Fortunately it's all local. Let me make

another phone-call.'

Cherie went back to the window. A couple of hundred yards away one of the men gathering the dead birds picked one up and held its wings outstretched before tossing it onto the white pile in the trailer. Was their death a warning or just pure malice, she wondered. What force could do that? Something under the ground. Something buried in the filthy residue of centuries. She smiled. No. It wasn't that. It was something that lived with them. She stared at the steps leading up to Ransom's front door.

Just you wait, she thought. Just you wait. I'll make you pay.

Willis's voice cut into her thoughts. 'Jack, Mike here. Mike Willis. Have you got a minute? Great. Listen. Just one question. Yes. Yes, I'll owe you. All right and there's a drink in it as well, you old lush . . . Listen. Can you help? Just a line of enquiry and you're the short cut as it were . . . As a matter of fact one is involved . . . Yes . . . No, far too classy. Anyway, let me shoot you a name. Ransom, as in Leaford, I believe.' There was a short pause. 'Really. Really? Hold on. Let me get a pen that works. Right, fire.'

For a minute or two Willis just scribbled away in fluent shorthand. Cherie had never learnt it and wished he'd say something so she could follow what was going on.

'Never married. And you can't remember her name? Tamara? . . . Tamsin Whitley. Something like that. OK. No, it's not important. Well it might be. And Leaford-Ransom just faded away. Never heard of again . . . All his friends clammed up, you say. Well, you're wrong there. He's living, in Blackheath. I'll give you the address when we have that drink. The last thing we want now is you poking around . . . Yes, I know there are phone-books. Good bloody luck. All the best, Yeah, bye.'

He put the phone down, and raised his eyebrows.

'It's a lead,' he said. 'Apparently there was a time when the young Lord Leaford was a sort of "Lucky Lucan" figure around town. Darling of the gossip columns. The sort of git who thought no evening was complete unless he'd nicked a policeman's helmet or crashed his E-Type jag. Nothing serious, as they say. Youthful high spirits. And he loved to gamble. Well, that was his downfall. The family had a big house down in Kent somewhere and first anyone knew about his problems was when he had to sell it. Apparently he'd amassed huge debts and had no real money — or certainly not enough to support him in that sort of style. The bloke I was talking to was a local reporter in Sevenoaks who covered the sale. It was his first real story so he did a bit of research and remembered it. Anyway, Leaford got serious all of a sudden. Started looking for work in the City and then had a stroke of luck. He managed to land an heiress, God knows how, but he did and all of a sudden the gossip columns were talking about him again. Not only an heiress but an orphaned heiress. Loaded she was. The date for the wedding was set, everything ready, he bought this house next-door to you around then, apparently, and then she disappeared.

'Disappeared?'

'She vanished.'

'But people don't do that.'

'They do. Quite often. Well, Leaford — now calling himself Ransom — was questioned, thoroughly. Really grilled. He seemed genuinely distraught, but you never know. Anyway he was questioned, but nobody could pin anything on him and that was that.'

Cherie suddenly felt sick. 'That means the body in the convent grounds could be . . .'

'Could be?'

'Oh come on. It must be her, the girl. That poor girl he was going to marry. *He killed his fiancée!* I've been living next-door to a murderer. I knew it. I knew it.' She felt her voice rise but could not stop it. 'It's been Ransom's fault all along. Nothing more. Nothing else. All those people dead . . . my husband dead. All because of him. We've got to get him. We've got to before something else happens.'

'And do what? We've got no proof.'

'Proof? What about that room? What about the bolts

on the door? On the outside. That must tell you something. He locked her in there. Now he's going to suffer.'

Cherie jumped to her feet. 'I'm going back inside that house. I'm going back. I don't care what's in there. It was trying to tell us something. I know it. That apparition. It was trying. Oh, my God. That poor girl. What did he do to her?'

Willis got up and tried to grab her. 'We don't know anything!' he said. 'There was something else I was told on the phone. About her. She's got her own story!'

Cherie rounded on him, eyes blazing. 'We know everything,' she hissed. 'Except where *he* is. I'm going to have a look and don't try and stop me.'

She wrenched herself free and ran out of the french windows at the back of the house.

Chapter Twenty-seven

Cherie scrambled over the wall between the two houses. Her anger had suddenly evaporated and she was left feeling very calm and clear in her head. She must avenge the girl that Ransom had killed. Everything would be better then. She knew too that this would be her chance to hit back at everything she hated about her life, and God only knew there was enough to hit back at. All her suspicions had been proven. It was up to her to put things right.

On Cherie's side of the high wall there was a raised verandah which made getting onto the connecting wall relatively easy. On Ransom's side a garden table had been pushed up against it. As she jumped off it she heard Willis following noisily behind her. Ransom's garden door opened straight into a passage which ran from the front of the house to the back. It had glass panels and Cherie could see, by twisting her head round, that the key was in the lock. She was casting around for something to break the glass with when Willis tapped her on the shoulder. He shook his head and pointed to the basement window which opened onto a small area below ground level. Lowering himself down, he pulled one of Cherie's metal knives from his pocket, inserted it between the top and bottom sashes and began to work away at the old-fashioned lock. After a couple of minutes' grunting he slid the bottom sash upwards.

It was dark in the cellar, though light was coming from the end of the passage, down the stairs. This puzzled Cherie. She decided that they must have left in such a hurry the other night that they had not turned the hall light off. She walked quickly towards it; turned to go up the stairs; flinched; nearly screamed as something white and fluttering dropped past her head like a stone and thudded onto the stairs. She flung an arm up and a querulous voice from upstairs quivered: 'Get thee behind me!

Out devil!' then broke and caught on a horrible dry sob.

Cherie glanced at the floor. Willis was carefully prodding a large leatherbound Bible with his toe.

Together they mouthed: 'Ransom.'

He was curled up against the front door, on his side, mewing with terror. Cherie was paralysed. It was like looking at a mortally injured animal. All she'd been taught suggested she should offer help. All she felt was that she wanted to get away and not to touch the ghastly wreck of life. Ransom's face, or what they could see of it because he'd folded his arms in front of it, was grey. His legs worked feebly to try and push himself further into the corner. Then the mewing stopped and he began to mutter to himself. Cherie forced herself forwards to try and hear. It sounded as if he was repeating the Lord's Prayer to himself in a fast and hysterical whisper.

As Willis approached the muttering stopped and he began to scream again.

'It's all right, sir,' said Willis. 'I am a police officer.'

The screaming stopped. It was replaced with sobs. Willis pulled Ransom to his feet. 'Whatever it was you were frightened of,' he said. 'We're not it.'

Ransom grabbed his arm. 'You're not her. She came for me. She came. She's been trying to send me mad.'

'Who?' Cherie spoke for the first time, Ransom started. He pulled himself free from Willis and staggered into the dining-room. 'Just let me pull myself together,' he said.

'Take him upstairs,' Willis said. 'I'll fix him a drink.'

In his sitting-room, Ransom collapsed into a deep armchair, clutching a drink. Cherie waited until the embarrassing silence grew unbearable. Then she realised that she would have to be the one to break it.

'We know about your fiancée.'

'You know . . . You know about that? Thank God somebody understands!' Ransom said. He looked at Cherie gratefully.

She stared back at him in horror.

'Understands? Wait a minute. We don't understand.

We understand you killed her —'

'NO! They tried to make me say that before. But I didn't! I didn't!'

'You killed her! You mutilated her! You buried her in the convent grounds with or without the nuns' permission! The body was found weeks ago and despite what you did to it, they know it was a young woman, killed about twenty years ago.'

'They know it was Tamsin Whitley!'

'NO-O-O-O!'

'God damn it, YES!'

Cherie was standing up. Veins stood out in her neck. Ransom was cowering back in his armchair.

'Now wait a minute . . .' Willis interrupted.

Cherie wheeled round. 'Don't you start!' she bellowed. 'We've got him. We can't let this go now.'

'We don't know anything!' Willis was shouting now. 'All we know is that *a* body was found.'

'CHRIST! What is it going to take to make you *do* something!'

Willis and Cherie were both standing, no more than two feet apart, each shouting into the other one's face.

'I was trying to tell you back there,' Willis said. 'Something came out when she disappeared. It was one of the reasons why they investigated Ransom so thoroughly. She was a blackmailer.'

'What?'

'Once she'd gone — disappeared, people started coming forward. It took ages because ... there was lots to hide.'

'What?'

Ransom stood up suddenly. He moved to the window, looked out then wheeled round to face them. 'She was evil!' he screamed. '*We* all did it for a bit of fun. *She* really meant it!'

Willis looked slightly embarrassed. 'There was a coven,' he said softly. 'She and Ransom were, well, in charge. It wasn't much, but she took pictures. A lot of the people involved were well connected. They would have lost a lot. Those that have most to lose . . .'

'*She was a witch, for the love of Christ. A WITCH! And now it's too late. LOOK!*' Ransom shouted.

Cherie staggered. She felt winded, as if someone had kicked her in the stomach. But then Ransom pointed to the window, his arm a rigid bar, his mouth slack.

'It's too late now,' he said. 'It's too late. See for yourselves.'

They all looked out of the window.

It had grown dark, a heavy brown darkness like a thick blanket. It pressed heavily against the window. They moved behind him.

The heath was alive with people, families, all streaming out of their houses and making their way onto the grass. They were well wrapped up for the most part: men and women in overcoats, children in anoraks and bobble hats.

Cherie looked up and as she did the sky seemed to change. It pulsed and flickered with a dead light that came from behind the clouds, an eerie whiteness that came and went like the irregular beating of a heart.

'It's started,' Ransom repeated. 'We'd better go and see what we can do.'

They ran downstairs. The pulsating glow was brighter now, a canopy of white that sucked colour from the sky and earth. A front door slammed two houses down and a man and woman began to shepherd three happy children onto the street. They hurried past them.

'Did you hear what they were saying?' Cherie asked.

'It was something about a firework display, wasn't it?'

'That's what I thought, but it's crazy. There have been no posters or anything. I'd have heard.'

Above them white veins marbled the sky briefly, then it settled down to its steady hypnotic pulse.

Willis pointed to a spot a few hundred yards away. 'That's where they're all heading. Perhaps we'd better go, too.'

Reluctantly they joined the flood of humanity pressing inwards towards the centre of the heath.

Chapter Twenty-eight

The firework display had been Sebastian Lee's idea. From somewhere an important thought had begun to grow in his mind: it would be nice to get as many people as possible on the heath that night. He was dimly aware of earlier abortive attempts, concerning birds and various strange happenings, but he knew that they wouldn't have impressed him much either. What did bring people out onto the heath? Well, there was the fair, and there was the Guy Fawke's night firework party, ususally sponsored by a local firm. If you wanted people to go onto the heath, you put on a firework display. Simple. There was, of course a slight problem with the timing. The Voice had wanted as many people as possible and had, it seemed to Sebastian Lee, started a bit on the early side. He now recognised that the impulse to move the whole school outside had come from the Voice: he just had not realised it. Actually, hearing the Voice was a bit like seeing fish in a river. First you would just see the shining, heaving surface of the water, then, clear as day, by altering the focus of your eyes the minutest amount, you would see fishes. But, as suddenly, they would be gone, as if the river had drawn a glittering veil over them.

So with the Voice. It took practice to hear it, to recognise it. Suddenly it would be there, curled in his thoughts like a kitten, and then it would be gone. Sebastian Lee would be thinking, aimlessly usually, and then would have a particularly *nice* thought. The thought would generally be pretty mundane in itself, but would fill him with a bubbling fountain of joy, so that he just had to follow it through.

Take them all outside, the voice would say for example, *but don't talk to them at all. Don't be their friend.* And, feeling happier than he had ever done before, Sebastian Lee would do whatever was asked of him.

Sometimes the Voice would reward him, but he felt an essential wrongness in that. Doing the thing was fun enough. The rewards were too much. (Just as drinking the dregs from the glasses after one of his parents' parties had been fun, while a whole glass of the stuff was pretty revolting.) And in some strange way, Sebastian felt the rewards, which were like warm fruity ice-creams exploding in the centre of his brain and dripping slowly down the bare dome of his skull, were a bit embarrassing. Too much. Basically, it was too much like being kissed.

Thinking back, Sebastian Lee realised that whenever he had had a particularly good idea in the past few days, it had probably been due to the Voice. All the times he had made people do things for him, the Voice had been giving him the idea in the first place — which, presumably, was why he had thought it such a good one. And when he questioned mildly *why* he had been doing all these things, the voice sent a laughing velvety feeling through his body and said: *Practice, chickie, Practice*.

'Practice for what?' he had asked.

Wait and see, dearest. Wait and see.

Practice. That made a lot of sense. Of course he would never have bothered to find out how many people's brains he could get into if he hadn't gone to school that day. And if it wasn't the Voice telling him to do so, then who was it? Perhaps bits of the revenge on Scruby had come from himself, like the way he had got the headmaster to tell him the answers were wrong when in fact they were right, and the way he had let Scruby half guess he was somehow involved without letting him be sure. But he saw now, it was all crystal clear, that the whole *point* had been to get the school together and see if he could make them behave exactly as he wanted. *All* of them together. What happened to Scruby now was massively uninteresting.

It had taken a bit of effort at first, but like everything else, once you got the hang it became easier and easier. He had found the wavelength by discovering, rather unexpectedly, that in fact while everybody pretended to like Scruby, underneath they really thought he was horrible. That had given Sebastian Lee the idea. As Scruby went on stage his popularity was apparent. All the other teams had been pretty uninspired and the audience desperately wanted to support somebody. So Sebastian Lee had amplified their feelings, but it took very little to do this, and after that they just sort of caught fire. But as the cheers and catcalls reached a peak, Sebastian Lee had sensed something else: feelings of hatred and violence, circling deep and slow like white blind sharks that never saw the light, and he was able to use these when he decided to break Scruby into little pieces.

After all that, getting the school to walk out with him onto the heath had been simplicity itself. But what then? Sebastian Lee looked at his watch. It was only half past three and would not be dark for another hour and a half. Did it really matter? *Yes.* What can I do? *Silence.*

Sebastian Lee looked out over the heath, at the little knots of people dotted on its flat surface, at the sheets of old newspaper and the fish-and-chip wrappers bowling over the turf. He focused on the headmaster who suddenly snapped alert from a state of near vacancy.

'Right,' he said, straightening up and rubbing his hands together briskly. 'Everybody gather by forms. Miss Livingstone, would you be so kind as to bring some dustbin bags. You'll find them in the caretaker's cubby hole; here are the keys. Now, listen, the rest of you. As you can see the heath is in a disgusting state, litter everywhere. I'm not saying that any of you are responsible, all I'm saying is that something must be done about it. Now then, when the bags arrive, everyone pair off into twos and we'll all see how many bags we can fill before it gets dark. Ah, here they are now. Form an orderly queue, an *orderly* queue . . .'

Sebastian Lee looked on happily. Once the headmaster had given instructions everyone would be obliged to carry them out, and while they were carrying them out he'd be too embarrassed to cancel them. Meanwhile the Voice was calling, calling for him to meet it. With a last look over his shoulder at his school mates energetically picking up rubbish, he scampered off to the old convent.

When he reemerged it was dark. He felt full of clear white goodness and power. His skin throbbed and tingled tautly and deliciously; he thought that if he so much as touched anything he would explode. If he wanted, he could spin light sticky tendrils from his mind that floated like spiders' webs and stuck like gum. He was the centre of a world of his own creation; everything came from him and fed back into him. It was awesome.

As he walked from the convent to the centre of the heath, he sensed rather than saw the aimlessness of the people who had already gathered there. Impressions came to him bittily; there was no consistence, no sense of the sharing which he liked so much. There had to be a reason for them all to be there, which was when he first started to think of the fireworks. Immediately he sensed a change. Everyone around him was suddenly waiting, not wondering. He looked up, sent a warm capsule of will into the sky, and detonated it so it showered the heath and everyone who was standing on it with his milky influence. A happy gasp went up from the crowd. Then he stretched out.

He soon found out that it wasn't enough to try and blanket the suburbs in thought. It became too diffuse and something more direct was called for to negotiate the distances and the space. The boy stood still for a moment and thought. He thought of front doors and steps, he thought of hallways and sitting rooms. He sent himself flicking into the corners of the big Victorian houses, into the cellars and converted attics, into white kitchens and chintz sitting rooms, TV rooms, studies and bedrooms.

He slipped through locked shutters. He darted up curving Georgian staircases as sure and fast as an anteater's tongue, probing, questing, testing and catching little ants on his sticky thoughts. And slowly he winkled them from their television, their books, their thoughts, their games and brought them to him with insistent promises of rapture which he knew he could make go on and on and on.

Chapter Twenty-nine

Cherie looked up apprehensively at the glowing white cloud that seemed to be getting brighter and brighter in the skies above the heath. A ripple of excitement passed through the crowd.

Come on, come on. It's about to start!

People were hurrying forward at a trot to the centre of the heath, brushing irritably past Cherie, Willis and Ransom.

Come on, come on. You'll be late. Join in. You're in everyone's way. Join in. Join in. Don't be spoilsports.

'What's going on? What's happened to everyone?'

'Beats me.' Willis shook his head. 'Either we're the only sane ones here or the only mad ones. Can't think what the hurry is.' He was holding Ransom by the elbow, but more to support him than restrain him. Cherie turned and gave him a suspicious look.

'Do you know what's going on?' she asked very slowly. He shook his head. Then: 'Look!' The light flicked off, leaving the heath for a second in pitch darkness. Then it restarted with greater intensity, glowing and flickering dully like a broken television. Everyone around them craned their heads skywards.

'OOOOOH!'

'AAAAAH!'

'OH!'

'It's lovely!'

There was nothing. Nothing at all. The flat light beat down on the upturned faces, on gaping mouths, on eyes wide with wonder. Eyes that looked at . . . nothing.

Oh. It's wonderful. Beautiful. Can we get closer? *yes everybody get closer move in move up come oncloseupcloserinfurtherinfurtherinininininininin* . . .

'They've all gone mad. They've all gone mad!'

Cherie started tugging at the arm of the woman next to her, who had her hands placed protectively on the shoulders of a little girl.

'There's nothing there! There's nothing in the sky! You're all being conned!'

'What's the funny woman doing to you, Mummy?' the little girl asked.

'I expect she's just a little bit unhappy, that's all,' the woman answered.

'But why is she unhappy?'

'Because she can't see the lovely fireworks,' the mother answered with unswerving logic.

'What can we do?' Cherie turned to Willis.

'I would have said call the police but . . .' and he nodded to his side where a young constable had taken off his helmet and was staring raptly at the sky.

Cherie felt herself close to tears. 'It's horrible! It's horrible! All those people. The heath's packed. There must be thousands here. What are we going to do? WHAT's GOING TO HAPPEN TO THEM?'

'Can we get to the centre?' Willis asked.

'What do you mean?'

'Let's try and find out where it's all coming from.'

They began to push themselves through. Everybody was almost rigid; their bodies stiff like sandwich boards. They did not give as Cherie tried to force herself between them, and Willis, now almost dragging Ransom along with him, was soon left behind. Many people almost fell over as if they had lost the ability to balance properly. The exclamations had stopped too and a great silence had fallen over the heath. Nobody took their eyes off the sky. As they struggled inwards, the crowd became tighter and tighter packed. Dragging Ransom along proved impossible and Willis left him behind to catch up with them later.

'What did you say?' Cherie asked Willis as he finally reached her.

'Nothing.'

'I thought I heard you say something.'

'Too busy pushing.'

They struggled on.

'There!' Cherie whipped round. A man's mouth had moved.

'What did he say?' Willis panted.

'I couldn't catch it.'

'*Big thigh wanked*,' the man said.

'Huh?'

'*Stump bled?*'

'Oh Jesus.'

'*Heinous pelvis pupod cezar in dido wetwet.*'

He stopped talking although his mouth continued to work, slowly, as if he was trying to read something.

Willis shook him by the shoulder. 'Are you all right?' he asked.

'Their minds have gone. Their minds have gone. Oh, God, look at them all.'

All around them the crowd began to sway in perfect unison. Cherie felt as if she were treading water in the ocean. Willis was snapping his fingers in front of the man who had spoken. There was no response. Then the man turned to him, opened his mouth and began to vomit steadily, as if a tap had been turned on in his stomach.

'OH, CHRIST!'

Willis grabbed him by the shoulders and turned him so the steady gush of thick fluid ran down the back of the person in front. Cherie felt as if she was going to be sick herself. 'Where's it all coming from?'

'Don't ask! Just move on!'

As soon as their backs were turned the man stopped vomiting and went back to watching the sky.

Then the voices started again. Great surges of nonsense rose and fell around them; noises as powerful and as meaningless as the sea that got louder and louder as they thrust themselves between board-like backs, hitting, tugging, screaming at people. Anything to get out of the crush. Cherie felt that if she stopped the crowd would start to press inexorably in towards her like the ice-pack and crush her until she was nothing. She felt her chest begin to heave; she had to struggle for each breath. The only way she could move forwards now was to force a hand through a gap in the crowd, wriggle it until the wrist and elbow were through, then using the leverage of her elbow and shoulder try to prise a gap open and squeeze the rest of herself after them. Then, if she could manage it she would hold the gap open for Willis. And all the time she was doing that, hands would be fluttering and pinching below waist level, stroking and holding her back.

Then suddenly she was free. She stuck her arm through a tiny gap and felt nothing in front of her. With an almighty heave she shoved two men in front of her over and stepped out into the open. Willis followed, panting, his face covered in a thin film of sweat. And stopped dead.

Both of them had been there dozens of times. Above them rose the little hummock crowned with gorse and the birch and ringed by a fence of stakes; in front of them lay thc little pond.

Or it should have done.

The pond was drained of water. On the black gravelled bottom perhaps a dozen men were stripped to the waist and digging energetically with spades and pick-axes. Another three or four were pushing wheelbarrows up an earthen ramp which crawled round the sides of the steadily deepening pit. The men's bodies glowed pallidly in the shadowless opalescent light. As soon as one grew tired there was always another to take his place. Already they were ten feet below the surface of the heath. Then behind them the huge crowd moaned. It was an indescribable sound, rising from thousands of stiff throats and spiralling upwards into the still air. And Cherie saw why.

A boy stood on the mound, looking at the sky, his mouth open. He seemed pathetically small and frail, and yet Cherie sensed that he was the cause of all this, if not the agent behind it. She recognised him immediately as the child she had first seen by this very pond, unconscious, and later in the old convent when he had given her the ring. Her hand felt its warm heaviness in her jacket pocket. She gripped it without thinking, half realising that she had no idea how it had got there because she was sure that she had left it in her dressing-table drawer. Then she slipped it on.

Immediately she understood what held the crowd. The boy was singing. Not words or sounds, but shapes, shapes that left his mouth as pale strands of ectoplasm and rose like flowers in the air where they spread and blossomed and fell. Some shot upwards like rockets, spiralled like honeysuckle, tumbled like clematis, then glowed and expired like dragon's breath. Some gathered themselves into globules and spun about the heath like mad things, weaving in and out of the greater tendrils of white like mischievous sprites before exploding joyfully and showering everything in gentle white rain. And there were others. A great bridge arched across the sky, pulsating milkily, dripping vast and writhing stalagtites beneath it. Sharp jagged lines darted hither and thither in a blinding ever-changing grid of magnesium intensity that seemed to crackle with energy and threatened to melt the delicate tendrils it crossed. Soft billowing shapes like giant jellyfish hovered and shimmered high above them, flapping diaphanous umbrella membranes in glutinous waves, barely staining the greater dome of darkness behind. And the colours: it was impossible to conceive that so many shades of white existed.

Pearl, mother-of-pearl, moonstone, bone; cloud white, ash white, ivory, mist.

Eyewhite

Mucus

Tripe

Graveflesh

AND

A hundred thousand skeletons began to dance across the sky,

They put on flesh.

Bones grew layers of fat and flesh, then slipped into loose folds of skin that floated in the ether. The new forms writhed briefly in the constricting folds of tissue, then stretched and felt new elasticity and strength. They raced screaming over the night sky and swooped down above the upturned heads of the humans on the earth. They shot into the air like fountains, exploded, scattered like starlings, then re-formed into firm new shapes. Some lay with thighs apart and others raced hungrily into the giggling bodies, up them, through them and out into the still cold air, themselves to be sucked into long ecstatic phalli, swallowed, and defecated in streams that glowed across the night.

Cherie watched as shape merged with shape, body with body, flesh with liquid, bone with mucus, and she longed to be a part of it. She could feel the liquids in her flesh pulled as water in the sea is pulled by the moon. She felt her blood gently tug her heart, her womb, her breasts forwards, backwards, up and around, always following the epicentre of the ecstacy above her. Without realising it she began to croon.

Willis was unaware of all this. He was looking, as people do, at the men sweating and toiling in the pit below him, but something was bothering him and he could not drag it up from his subconscious. Their mouths opened and closed, their faces twisted and moved into familiar shapes. It was as if they were talking from behind thick plate glass; no noise came from the pit, and they were lit by the dull dead flicker of the sky above them. The men stopped. They put down their tools and waited, heads tilted slightly on one side like dogs listening.

Willis grabbed Cherie.

'We've got to get out of here!'

There was no response from her. 'Cherie? Oh, for fuck's sake, woman!'

He shook her, and felt sweat break out on his face again.

'Come on, where are you? Cherie? Cherie!' He shook

her. Then his eyes strayed down to the pit and he felt her move in his arms. The men, now streaked with mud, were on their knees and were scrabbling away at the earth with their bare hands. Cherie was feeling a strong, almost irresistible desire to approach the pit edge and take what they were about to offer. It was going to make her better and stronger and a part of some great whole, all bound together with the great army of figures in the sky who were now waiting patiently for her to join them.

Willis felt her push him forwards. Her arms kept on stretching out to the pit where the men were now digging frantically in the mud. He turned and looked down, feeling the strange swooping emptiness of fear as he saw the tangle of white bones lying like branches in the mud. Not all the bones were bare of flesh; some had shreds of dark tissue hanging in strips from them. He saw one of the men take a shin bone and gnaw it delicately before passing it on to the next man who did the same. Cherie grew restless in his arms, as she tried to move closer to the pit. It was like holding a baby; there was the same unreasoning determination in her movements, the same lack of awareness.

The bones from the pit were now being passed up and into the crowd. People grabbed them eagerly, often touching them to their faces before passing them back. Cherie was getting more and more desperate. She saw only glittering shards of white that glowed with soft radiance. She wanted one so badly, but something was stopping her, something was holding her back. She brought her arms up to fight, and as she did so Willis saw the ring on her finger and with a stroke of pure intuition tugged it roughly off.

Cherie was standing on the edge of the pit, and as the ring came off she fell. But not into the pit.

She was falling down a long cold well shaft and as she fell she looked upwards at the disc of light above that shrunk and shrunk to nothing. She hit the water with a smash, and plunged on down into its stinging depths. She could not breathe; water pressure squeezed her lungs and every time she struggled she grazed her arms and legs on the rough stone of the shaft. She was sinking to a place where hairless people with no eyes scurried to and fro on a bed of slimy stones, waiting for her . . .

Then she was being pulled sideways out of the water and she came to under the dead neon shroud of the night sky. Willis was yelling at her.

'. . . away! We've got to get away! Don't you see? That's a plague pit! He's giving everyone the plague. They're touching the bones. They're all going to die. Get away! WE'VE GOT TO GET AWAY!'

'What? Oh, my God.'

A skull was pushed from the pit at Cherie's feet and toppled over towards her. She kicked it away instinctively, then bolted into the crowd. Willis was able to trace her progress by the swirl of action in the forest of inert and rigid bodies. He followed her slowly, avoiding the bones that were still being passed out of the pit. Cherie was fighting her way round to the hillock where the boy was standing.

'HE'S DOING IT! WE'VE GOT TO STOP HIM!' she yelled over her shoulder.

Willis surged up behind her. She scrambled over the fence which surrounded the hillock, ran up the slope and grabbed the child.

'Kid. Hey kid! Wake up! WAKE UP!'

He wasn't there. Cherie felt that she was holding something empty and alien.

'You carry him!' She pushed him at Willis.

'Carry him?'

'Fireman's lift. Anything. Get him away. Anywhere.'

Willis stooped, gathered the boy around his knees and lifted him. Sebastian Lee stayed upright and rigid.

'Can you bend him?' Willis grunted.

Cherie folded him like cardboard.

'Poor kid', she muttered.

The poor kid opened his eyes and drooled.

'Will you get that stuff off me?' snapped Willis, who felt

the wet on the back of his legs.

Cherie plucked a clump of long grass and began to rub. The child opened and closed his jaws rhythmically.

'Eeeaargh!'

'What is it?'

'It's coming from his mouth. Drop him! Drop him!'

Chunks of foam were now falling from Sebastian Lee's mouth. As each one hit the ground it swelled like a great soft pod and grew with horrifying speed.

'DROP HIM AND RUN!'

Willis glanced over his shoulder and saw a quivering wall of whiteness. He let the child fall and ran. The crowd seemed to part around them as they panted across the heath. A terrible roaring drowned out all other sounds and Cherie risked a glance behind her. Above her.

A vast frothy tidal wave curved above, taller than she could ever have imagined, and horribly smooth, blanking out the inky sky. Its surface gleamed dull white like polished soapstone and was flecked with dirt picked up from the heath as it rolled towards them. The ground in front was quivering with its weight, and wrinkling like a carpet. Heads would emerge from its milky depths and disappear. Now and then a great arm of foam would appear on the left or the right forcing them to change direction. Her lungs burned, each breath she took was agony now and she felt that her wobbling legs could hardly carry her another pace. But the ground was rising ahead and she knew it was their only hope. Glancing sideways she saw that Willis was stumbling up it too. But it was crazy. There were no hills on the heath. And especially no hills with buildings on top of them. Willis got there first. He dived through a hole in the wall and darted down a narrow cavity which led off to the left.

'NO!', she gasped. 'Not there!'

But it was too late. The whiteness crashed above her and she fell after Willis down the narrow tunnel.

Chapter Thirty

Sebastian Lee Miles felt awful. Empty and drained. He found that he was lying on cold grass while a light but penetrating drizzle drifted in dreary sheets over the heath. The first thing he saw was legs. A motionless forest of them. A crowd stood like an exhausted army on the heath, staring at the sky. Sebastian Lee looked up at the faces. They were empty and blank. In the sockets of sightless eyes the rain pooled and trickled down the faces like thin tears. Others had their mouths open and the rain dribbled over their lower lips. The fretful wind tugged at the clothes a little, but nobody moved.

Sebastian Lee got to his feet. The stiff, motionless crowd was as blankly menacing as a field full of staring cows. There were no gaps between the people. He climbed to the top of the hillock. In the distance he could see the acid glow of street lamps, but between him and them was this desert of empty faces. He knew he had to get through.

He stood in front of one of the crowd, the biggest man he could see, and pushed. The man rocked on his feet, backwards, forwards, backwards, hung for a second, then toppled into the figure behind which in turn took down two more. Sebastian Lee ran back up to the top of the hillock. The human domino chain gathered momentum; as he watched a great swathe was opening out and widening, fan-shaped and dark. Out of his control. It made him feel sick.

'Stop! Please stop. I didn't mean it! I'm sorry. Please, I *want* you to stop!' he shouted.

But his voice was drowned by the terrible dry thudding

rustle of tumbling bodies.

Suddenly he knew he had been left. His power had gone. He was alone. Completely alone? Something remained, a dim, scratchy insistent idea that there was still something he had to do. Finish off. The gleam of a light caught his eye and he saw that it was coming from a tall row of houses that jutted into the heath like a dark pier. A beacon. Scrambling over the slippery landscape of stiff limbs he made his way to Ransom's house.

The door was ajar and banging gently on the latch. Sebastian Lee pushed it further open with a shy hand and waited uncertainly. There were noises and they came from the basement. He walked slowly to the stairs and tilted his head to one side, listening. Someone was crying. There was a picture in his mind of how that person looked and how he had to be led up and out and . . . away.

Ransom had his back to the door but he whipped round as a floorboard creaked behind him, his face drawn into a sudden rictus of terror. He relaxed as he saw the boy.

'What are you doing here? How dare you? This is a private house. Get out this instant.'

But the boy just stood there. Ransom's face suddenly puckered. And collapsed.

'Where? Where for God's sake, where? Tell me!' Ransom was not sure if the words had come from his mouth or if someone else had said them, but once said they seemed to become what he meant.

The boy turned and walked from the room. And Ransom followed him.

Chapter Thirty-one

They were somewhere in the convent. Ahead stretched a long vaulted hall. Cherie was sure it was underground but it could have been any place, any time. Or limbo. There was a slow, silent pressure all around her, and the cold musty air covered her like a sheet. Willis was standing next to her, his chest heaving up and down. He was looking around in what seemed to Cherie a ridiculously detached manner.

'Can you remember what happened to Ransom?' he said.

'I thought you had him.'

'No. I dropped him. Had to.'

'On the heath. All those people.'

'He'll be here.'

'Where's here?'

'The convent. Must be. We were forced in here. Ransom will be somewhere around.'

They both heard it. A quick scream, cut off. Sharp and high like a rabbit's.

The echoes scurried down the hall and back again.

As their eyes became accustomed to the gloom they saw a deeper patch of blackness, two thirds of the way down on the left-hand side. It was the only break in the dull monotony of stone that surrounded them. They walked towards it, their footsteps clicking loudly in the silence.

'Oh, God help me!'

It was Ransom's voice.

The doorway in the wall led onto a landing. There were stairs, going up into the light and down into thicker darkness. Ransom's voice came floating towards them from upstairs.

'Please! Somebody!'

Willis took the lead. The stairs wound round themselves. He found himself standing in a great hall. Cherie recognised it. She had found the boy there. He had given her the ring there.

How had she forgotten that?

There had been the boy who had given her a ring, the ring in her pocket, and a ... thing, a figure that moved towards her. The walls spun around her and she felt a deep sense of hopelessness. The ring had led them to Ransom. They had led Ransom to the heath. And Ransom . . .

Ransom was standing in the middle of the hall. He was staring wildly around, his body caught in an unnatural stillness. He started when he saw Cherie and Willis emerge from the door in the wall.

'Save me!' was all he said.

Willis stepped towards him, but Cherie held out an arm.

'No,' she whispered. 'Don't you see? He's got to suffer. She has to realise he's here. We can't escape it. Not this time. Neither can he.'

'You can't mean that we're going to —'

'Listen! It was because of him my husband was killed. That monster is personally responsible. The past isn't working through us or the boy or anyone else. It's working through him.' She paused. Swallowed. 'Mr Ransom, you must admit your guilt.'

'NO! You don't understand.'

'Oh, I do.' Cherie willed herself on. 'Why deny it? I accuse you of —'

'You? Accuse me? By whose right. By what right?'

'My right. *Her* right. And for all those people out there. I accuse you of — of causing all this. It's all your fault.'

'What is?'

'EVERYTHING!'

The word crashed around the hall in diminishing flat echoes. For the first time Cherie noticed that Ransom couldn't move because his legs were tied in glowing gossamer strands that grew from the floor like ropes of mould and his wrists were bound in front of him. Every time he tried to walk towards them they twitched and pulled him back, like living manacles.

Willis grunted: 'I can't stand this.'

He ran towards Ransom and began to pull at the writhing strands. They broke easily, and evaporated quickly, leaving only a memory of searing cold and numbness across his hands, but they had already eaten through Ransom's trousers and left deep red weals on his lower legs. Ransom was only prevented from collapsing by Willis who caught him round the waist.

Willis half carried him back to where Cherie was standing. Ransom shook himself free and collapsed against a wall.

'Why did you do that?' Cherie hissed. 'Why? It's him she wants. It's him! And he deserves it! It's either him or all them outside.'

'I couldn't just leave him there, and you know it,' Willis answered. 'And neither could you. We have to fight it.'

'Not it. HER! It's the ghost of your fiancée! Isn't it, Ransom? Isn't it! We saw her! Upstairs on the bed. And we went into that room in the basement. WHAT HAPPENED? If you admit what you did, it might all end, mightn't it?'

He pulled himself upright, his back against the wall, and seemed to regain some of his old arrogance. 'Frankly, I doubt it. I'm just part of it. All those people out there can rot as far as I'm concerned. That's not my business.'

'She wants you!'

'It wants all of us, you simpleton. Listen . . . if you know so bloody much, why not try me. It's what an idiot like you would want, after all. So go on, put me on trial. You can be the bloody judge and the bloody jury and the bloody hangman for all I care. We've got a stalwart officer of the law here to ensure fair play. Go on, if you're so confident, ask me what you want!'

Cherie looked at him. 'Don't do it,' Willis said. 'Not here. Not like this. For heavens sake, he's trying to set you up. Somehow — I don't exactly know how. Let's all get out now. Think about this.'

But Cherie was staring at Ransom with cold hatred. She brushed off Willis' hand that was gripping her forearm.

'I don't care what he says,' she said. 'We'll do it. It's our only chance.'

Willis felt utterly drained, all will to resist gone. Cherie and Ransom seemed to be feeding off some elemental source of power that he couldn't tap. He knew he should put a stop to the terrible travesty of justice about to unfold in front of him but could not. Then Cherie spoke.

'You are William Ransom, previously Lord Leaford, descendant of Thomas Wainwright who took the title you have since renounced?'

'Yes.'

'And can you tell us why you stopped using that title? There was a scandal, wasn't there? Tell us about that.'

'We were being blackmailed. The details came out. I did what anyone would have done in the circumstances.'

'What circumstances?'

'The circumstances surrounding the blackmail. My dear, you'll have to do better than that. Why not let the policeman ask the questions? I'm sure he's used to beating confessions out of prisoners.'

'You can't provoke me, Mr Ransom. Cherie, if you must do this, clear up the loose ends first.' Willis suggested. 'Ask him about the nunnery in Lincolnshire. Then ask him about this place.'

Cherie screwed her eyes tight shut.

'Wait a minute. Tell me about that wooden cross I found. The one you were so interested in. The one you stole back from me.'

Ransom looked at her thoughtfully, 'Ah, yes, I made rather a cock-up over that, I'm afraid. You see — no, let me think. You see in spite of your pretending that you'd had it for years, I knew exactly where it came from. I practically gave it to you the day you found it.'

'You mean it was yours?'

'I didn't say that, did I? No, it was hers. That's why I was trying to get rid of the foul thing. Something of her lingered in it. I was trying to bury it near her. I was actually standing in the nunnery grounds the day they started to knock it down. The problem is I've never been good at throwing, so my feeble attempt to get it buried by the bulldozer backfired. It slipped in my hand, I saw it bounce off the scoop, and then, I imagine, you picked it up. Then they found the bloody coffin. How, I don't know. She must have been working away even then. But you must admit it was clever, the coffin I mean. You know, the inscription and all that. An elaborate piece of fakery on my part.'

'But why go to all those lengths?' Willis asked.

'In case the coffin was found. I just assumed that everybody would associate it with my mad ancestor.' He paused. 'That retreat. It was a vile place. Its architecture. Those dogs. Do you know, I think they all went mad sitting there. Silent. Waiting. But for what? It must have been like being sent to the front. Just sitting there and waiting for the unimaginable to happen. Perhaps the place got to them and corrupted them. Perhaps they just grew complacent.'

'So how did you get into the convent grounds?'

'Easy . . . My family, as you know, has an historical relationship with the convent. Anyway, there was always one nun on duty here who was delegated to deal with outsiders. Buy the bibles, that kind of thing. It wasn't too difficult to bribe her, but just my luck it was the delightful Sister Mary — the one you met in Lincolnshire.

Cherie held up a hand. 'She told me something about a pledge lasting three hundred years. I —'

'Three hundred years! That bitch. She was always good at covering her tracks. They were pledged to stay there forever! And they'd be there still if I hadn't . . .' He shook his head. For a second he looked pleadingly from Cherie to Willis. 'That's why I was up at the convent the day you were there. I was begging them to return! I realised then the frightful . . . But it's too late, isn't it?'

'Tell us about the girl,' Cherie said quietly.

'Sister Mary and I came to an understanding. For a small payment she would let me and my chums into the grounds, lock up the dogs and look the other way. The way we saw it it was completely foolproof. I mean who would go looking for a body in a nunnery? And who would have been able to identify it? So everything was fine. Until a couple of years ago when sister Mary was appointed head girl of the order, realised the place was a priceless asset to her sisterhood of impoverished penguins if sold and developed, and sent me a letter reminding me of a certain object she saw me bury twenty-odd years before. She didn't want money from me — she knew I didn't have any. She just wanted to get out. And she guessed I had contacts. Funnily enough, a rather pompous young merchant banker had just moved in next-door and I began to try and raise capital for the development of the old convent through him. That's where your husband came into things, my dear. Incidentally, what did happen to that ring I gave him?'

'I have it,' Cherie whispered.

'Hang onto it,' Ransom said. 'It's worth a bit.'

'I can't believe you're talking like this. You're admitting that you murdered a young girl, mutilated her to make it look as though a mad ancestor had done it, buried her —'

Something whispered in the back of Cherie's mind. A voice,

helphelp me help we can help we can beat can beat canbeatthembeatthem

She had a momentary vision of miles of tunnels underground and a tiny figure (no shape) moving through them.

I'm coming I'm coming I'm coming comingcomingcoming.

'You're evil,' she said. 'Evil. Tell us about the girl.'

'And you're a smug little foreigner with no idea about anything at all. What do you know about evil? Oh, I've been bad. I admit that. Selfish. Greedy. But not evil. Let me tell you about evil. And don't interrupt me again with your pathetic little vicarage platitudes.' He paused. 'Actually this is harder than I thought. You see we all do things when we're young that we might regret later. You, Mr Policeman, did you never lean on an innocent suspect? Frighten him half to death, threaten him, taunt him until you got what you wanted? When you were a kid did you never half kill a bird with your catapault and leave it twitching on the ground to die? Did neither of you cut a worm in half to see what would happen? Are you evil? You see, it's all relative. This is the story. You'll just have to take my word for it. Now, listen. Me and my chums, school chums mostly, lots of money, not much to do, well we knew a few girls — this was after we'd all been chucked out of our various universities — we'd all slept together at one time or another and decided to formalise it. We had a little club, a circle, a little orgiastic circle. It was quite fun at first, then that got pretty boring too so we made it a rule that each month one of us had to introduce a new member. Fresh blood. Sometimes it worked, sometimes it didn't. Sometimes they ran away screaming. Sometimes they joined in. Anyway, about this time I met a girl. She was pretty, sweet, rather innocent and hugely rich. I was hugely broke, and decided to marry her. It wasn't difficult to persuade her. I was good-looking then, had a title, that sort of thing. But first I decided it might be fun to introduce her into the circle. I should have waited. It was a disaster. She was one of the ones who ran away screaming. Not only that. She threatened to go to the police. We threatened back. Said we'd tell her guardians, the newspapers, her friends. We said we had photographs . . . Then I got clever and said that if she agreed to marry me, we'd let the whole thing drop, and she had better join our little club just to show willing. You know she went along with it? Well it turned out that she wasn't that innocent after all. Things got a bit wild, someone brought out a camera, only the next day we found that the film had disappeared. It didn't take long to discover who had hidden it. So we locked her in the room, our little clubhouse, and said we'd leave her there until she told us.'

'So you locked her in that basement room of your house,' Willis said.

Ransom nodded.

'And how old was she?'

'Seventeen.'

Cherie thought she was going to be sick.

I'm coming. I'm coming. That thing underground coming closer and closer. Cherie felt her scalp begin to tighten.

'Anyway. One night I thought I heard noises. The food I'd taken her wasn't touched. Eventually I got worried. I thought she might have gone mad. I went in. She was lying there. On the bed. I don't know what had happened. What could have done it. She was all bent. Broken. And her skin. She looked as if she had been dead for weeks, I . . . just thought I was going mad. It was the only explanation. She was there. That was a fact. But I hadn't killed her.'

'Oh, so that's OK. You just blackmailed her, corrupted her, locked her in a room where she just happened to die, but you have no guilt,' Cherie said flatly.

'Listen to me, you stupid girl! She — she called something to her! I know! She would never have come back if you hadn't started your infernal meddling!'

'NO! NO! NO! Stop trying to get out of it!'

'YES!'

'Oh, you bastard. You killed her! You locked her down there, and even if it wasn't by your hand, it sure as hell was your fault.

'You'll understand.' Ransom gave a private smile. 'Responsibility, not guilt. And not even that much responsibility. That's hers.'

'You gave her to — something! You evil bastard!'

Ransom looked strangely defiant. 'Like I said, it's all relative.'

Something changed.

The moonlight in the room grew brighter and there came a sound as soft as a spring breeze blowing through tender young leaves. Cherie felt her body respond with a deep yearning that reminded her of summer days as a child, the last days of the school holiday, first love,

then —

nothing. A vacuum smacked her insides out. Empty. Left. Reject. Somehow she knew that she'd been tried and found wanting. Greyness filled her.

The rustling, gentle yet insistent, grew louder. Harder. Dryer. It was the sound of a million hard-clawed cockroaches moving through black stone canyons. It was the sound of white bones rubbing together, of leaves moving on a grave when no wind blew. The sound grew fainter and died away. Then —

THUD

THUD

THUD

Footsteps?

Knocking?

(oh do come in)

A signal.

Then she felt its presence. A sort of bulk that filled her head, tried to press her brain against the sides of her skull to make a space for itself.

Do anything! Talk!. Talk to Willis. A ghastly thickness took her tongue and throat. There was a mass of thick damp fur that lay in her mouth, pressed against the back of her throat, forced up against her teeth, gagging her.

Willis, Willis, her mind said.

'Nobber slipunt?' her mouth said.

Willis looked round at her.

'Blagobshit!' he said. Then looked desperate.

Then it began to probe. It was unlike anything she had

felt before. It wanted her to realise. Wanted her to know. But it wanted too much! Suddenly Cherie began to understand what Ransom had been talking about. IT WAS TOO MUCH! It (she?) didn't want her help, it wanted all of HER!

She felt it questing for each of her senses. She tried to hold it out. Closed her eyes. Blocked her ears. The smell. NO! NO! But the smell was there, clinging in her nostrils. There was a thickness, a ripeness to the stench, and yet it was simple. Blood and mould. Blood as rich as fine chocolate; rich and thick and dark, laced with delicate tendrils of mould. And the smell so vivid it ran gleaming down the back of her throat and pooled heavily on her tongue. She thrust her hand in her mouth to try and sluice it out. The smell stuck to her fingers. Suck them. Yum yum yum.

GOAWAYGOAWAYGOAWAYGOAWAYGOAWAY GOAWAYGOAWAYGOAWAYGOAWAYGOAWAY GOAWAYGOAWAY

If only that voice would stop

stop

she stopped screaming

silence

The silence was much worse.

The sound was gone. The smell was gone. The taste was gone.

All sensation gone.

There was nothing.

Cherie opened her eyes. There was a brief confusing moment when she saw a vast shape that seemed to be made of thousands of compressed bodies, grey, and swollen and broken, a shape that had a specific size but at the same time must have reached the stars and filled the horizon it seemed so huge. Then, as she looked, the shape suddenly shimmered down into human form, small and white. It was a woman. Very small, neat, with a face that seemed to shift as if it were being projected onto the form from a long way away. And at first Cherie thought it must be dressed in wedding clothes. But the longer she looked, the clearer she saw that it was a field of energy that was flickering around the figure like a mantle of light, the cold dead light she had come to know so well.

Suddenly the spell was broken by the boy. Sebastian Lee had brought the old man to the horrible place, and had crept away to hide. Then the sound of human voices had pulled him from his hiding place and he had come to look.

'NO! NO! You're wrong. You can't do it. I don't LIKE you any more. I HATE YOU. You made me do things. You're not my friend. I HATE YOU.'

'Oh, no,' Cherie moaned. She sensed he was in terrible danger. Why the child had been used she couldn't guess, but she knew he could be destroyed with one thought. She tried to get to her feet but couldn't. Her legs and arms seemed to be encased in lead. Her guts had dissolved and were slopping around inside her.

Dimly she was aware that Willis was moving slowly and painfully and that he too was trying to get to the child. A part of Cherie realised that the thing that stood in front of them was trying to win the child over to it, and that while its attention was on that, they would be safe.

'Go back. Go back!' The child was shouting now. Cherie thought he was shouting at her and Willis but he wasn't looking at them at all. She realised that Ransom had disappeared again. 'GO BACK!' and it was clear that the boy was shouting at the wraith still hovering in front of him. It dissolved, as if the pretence was no longer worth the effect. Now there was just a grey quivering pillar in front of them, ready to take on whichever shape suited it.

Cherie saw ideas shoot through it, ideas which took the form in shapes of incredible complexity and beauty; human, geometric, organic. It was reaching out to her.

It was beautiful, she saw that now. Beautiful and wronged. If only they could grow together, become one with each other. Without realising, she took a step forwards. It was her destiny. She saw that too. It had been wrong to try and fight it, like all those others. They had paid the price. They had tried to fight, they had been punished. They —

Cherie's thoughts collapsed. She shook her head, and saw Willis doing the same.

Then she noticed Ransom. Somehow he had managed to drag himself towards it.

So . . .

And the voice was like razor blades and blood

So . . .

and the word dropped into the silence like dead meat into mud

SO

Cherie whimpered and tried to drag herself back. Terror reasserted itself.

How could I have been so stupid? she thought. This is Ransom's fault. He can stop it if he wants. He's got to! He's got to!

And she willed him on.

Ransom was crawling towards the boy now, had reached him, had managed to push him to one side and had staggered to his feet. He stood for a second upright as the shapes hovered in front of him.

WHO?

There had been no sound but the question echoed round the hall like a thunderclap.

There was a brief flurry of activity. Inside the membraneous envelope, Cherie could see ectoplasm swirl in grey vortices. Time froze. Cherie's hand groping in her pocket found the ring. Without thinking she tossed it to where Ransom stood. It fell short and rolled to his feet. He bent and picked it up.

A blunt limb floated from the shape and absorbed his hand.

You!

First one voice, a girl's. Then another. And another. Men's, women's, children's, blending, merging, piling on top of each other in a mad song of hatred, that soared, that spiralled upwards to the roof, that crashed against the glass, roared around the hall in a mad cacophony of echo.

Then silence again.

Ransom dragged his head round to face Cherie. He said very quietly in the silence: 'You'll see. It's not just her. It's them. She planned all this at the very end. Everything. The cross. The film. She hid it inside. Look at the negatives. The last pic —'

Is there a moment in every heroic act when the martyr, or the victim, has a sudden intimation of his end? Ransom's face collapsed in terror, and a high girlish laugh, delighted, playful and intent floated around the hall.

He stood still. Willis was crying. Cherie was crying too because something had exploded inside her head with the intensity of a flashbulb. Whirr . . . click. She understood the last joke now.

Now a pale cloud surrounded Ransom, blanketing him in silence. The onlookers found themselves holding their breaths.

The noise started slowly, at first nothing more than the sound of tiny bubbles bursting. It grew louder and louder, and then, finally, a terrible, unimaginable sound of tearing as every membrane in Ransom's body was ripped apart and every cell penetrated by the essence of the wraith.

For a split second the cloud glowed pink and then, incredibly, it imploded. There was the minutest gasp as molecules of air rushed to fill the space vacated by the cloud. A moment later, nothing.

The three of them walked slowly from the old convent. The heath was empty; the air clear. There was no moon, and the stars were already retreating as the morning began to dissolve the night's blackness.

Sebastian Lee Miles was talking excitedly.

'I understand now. It chose me. You see it really liked me. I don't think anyone had ever really liked me before. That's why I was taken in by it. A bit sneaky really. I think it needed me as well. It couldn't do that much on its own. It sort of used me like a radio. To talk. Gosh. I'm glad all those people have gone from the heath. I don't know what it wanted to do with them but I'd have got into trouble if anything had happened to them. It didn't really have a clue about much. Are you really a policeman?'

Cherie was staggering from exhaustion. Nevertheless something the boy said caught her attention. 'It?', she said. 'You said "it". Surely you mean "she".'

'I don't. Honest. I don't think it was a she. I mean, I thought so at first but I don't any more. Are you American? Why do you live here?'

'I really don't know,' said Cherie.

Chapter Thirty-two

SECOND PLAGUE OUTBREAK
Polluted Water Supply Blamed

Local GPs and Lewisham Hospital have been secretly coping with an outbreak of a virus that has all the symptoms of bubonic plague, an anonymous source claims. An area health authority spokesperson said that though the disease is serious and highly contagious, it is treatable with antibiotics. So far, no fewer than fifty patients have been admitted for treatment in local hospitals.

Causes for the outbreak are unknown, it was stressed. But officials are stating privately that the most likely cause is a freak access of the virus to the water supply. All water supplies are now being closely monitored and have been declared safe. So far it has not been conclusively established that the virus can be communicated like this.

Allegations that the police are investigating an incident during which vandals opened up a plague pit dating from the seventeenth century in the middle of Blackheath, were dismissed as 'rubbish' and 'unverified'. The alleged site, which was an old pond, has now been concreted over, apparently because there was a danger of subsidence.

South East London Gazette.

And is it really over?

Cherie was sitting at a window table in a riverside pub. The bar was crowded with Sunday lunchtime trade, and the conversation rose and fell around her in steady, good-humoured waves. She looked out of the bay window at the river. At Greenwich the Thames is tidal and the river was high and wide, though ebbing fast. It flowed swiftly past her to the sea, its quiet power only showing when a piece of driftwood broke the surface and was whirled helplessly downstream, or when the coiled muscle of an eddy burst and writhed briefly on the silky surface of the water.

'Vodka and tom-ar-to juice. We've just got to get you speaking English properly.'

Willis sat down with fresh drinks from the bar. Beer filmed the outside of his straight glass and dripped onto the table.

'Cheers, good health and all that.' He raised his glass and took a swig.

Cherie smiled. 'Cheers. And thanks for the tom-ay-do. I've decided to go back to the States.'

She hadn't meant to say it like that, but had not been able to work the conversation round to the subject naturally.

For a second a shutter seemed to go up in Willis's eyes. She saw hurt, and surprise. Then it dropped down. Good old Willis. Always jovial. Never phased. Sometimes Cherie wanted to hit him.

'Here's looking at you, kid. Why?'

'It's over. My time here. I'm just hanging around, killing time. More than that though, I want to go home. I've thought it all through, and I'm not running away from anything. I'm certain of that now, and I had to be certain.'

That's it then, she thought. Now I've said it, it really is over.

Willis looked at his beer for a second or two.

'I was thinking of moving, too. Seeing if I could get a transfer. I'm sure what you're doing is right. I'll miss our drinking sessions though.' He smiled at her then grew serious. 'What's going to happen about your house?'

'It's being sold. It's got to be done. I'm going to have a lawyer handle the whole thing. All the good furniture was Peter's and that's gone back to his parents. I'm selling most of the rest. All I've got do to is pack my bags and go.' Her face closed down and she shivered.

'When?'

'Tuesday.'

'What? The day after tomorrow?'

'First thing.'

'Whew, you move fast, Ha ha.'

Willis couldn't hide his surprise, but said nothing. He hoped she couldn't tell how hurt he felt.

None of my business, he thought. Even so, we shared a lot.

'Packing up tomorrow?'

'Yes.'

'Could I pop round?'

'Would you? Please?'

'When do you want me?'

'Come for a last lunch. It'll be the last meal there. I'm leaving in the evening — I couldn't bear the thought of getting up in a completely empty house, so I booked into the Heathrow Holiday Inn.'

'OK, I understand. I'm sure it's the best thing,' Willis said.

He looked at his watch. 'Well, I'd best be off if I want to get any gardening done while it's still light. See you, when, one-ish?'

'Great.'

They finished their drinks and left.

Outside they walked the few yards to the *Cutty Sark*, the great tea clipper, resting in its empty concrete dock by the waterfront. Cherie paused to look at the masts, wheeling across the sky against the backdrop of high clouds. On the paved apron around the ship two young tourists, lovers, were standing, looking up at the sharp black prow and the brightly painted figurehead.

'You know who Cutty Sark was originally, of course,' Willis said, anxious to break the silence. 'She was . . .'

But Cherie was no longer with him. She had stopped walking and was staring with a look of blank terror at the young couple. The man had positioned a small camera on a bollard, pressed a button, then another, and then ran back to his girlfriend. Whirrrrr. Now they were wiggling, striking poses, grinning, laughing. Then at the last moment the boy grabbed the girl round the waist and folded her in a mockingly passionate embrace — *click*.

Cherie's sharp intake of breath was drowned by the girl's scream of laughter.

Willis shook his head, blessing providence that he hadn't finished the sentence. Cutty Sark — as he had read in a whisky advertisement on the tube — had been a witch.

He offered to drive Cherie home, but she declined. She wanted to walk back, try and fix the place accurately in her mind. She knew she'd never forget it but wanted an accurate last picture to resist the distortions of memory. But no photographs, she thought. She had to carry it all with her. Emotional baggage, locked. Because suppose there were photographs. Suppose one day she had children. And suppose one day they came across the shoe-box or the dusty album in the old trunk in the attic and looked at the funny pictures of the funny English houses. And suppose they came running to her with the box or the book one day shouting: Mummy, Mummy, what's this place? Daddy doesn't know. Did you live there? Why did you leave it?

What would she say?

Could she say: That's where Mummy fought the big bad ghost?

For then they would say: Like the ghosts on Hallowe'en? Did it go WOOOOOOOH! Was it dressed in white? Did you kill it?

And she'd have to remember and say: No. A very bad man who made the ghost in the first place, just for one second became very brave and killed it.

Or was that really the story?

How did he get brave? Because Cherie Simpson gave him no choice, even though, in the very last fraction of a split second she understood.

And just suppose these same happy American children, unburdened (Oh God let them be) by history, came upon a certain roll of negatives curled in the bottom of an old wooden chest. Suppose they'd bothered, as she had not, to actually unroll the film that Tamsin Whitley had kept hidden in the hollow upright of the old wooden cross, what would they have seen? Thirty-five funny images, hard to make out at first, with the white where the black should have been and the black where the white should have been, thirty-five images of men and women in odd positions, convoluted, twisted, one on top of the other on top of the other.

And they would ask: what are the people doing, Mom? And she would have to answer: just something grown-ups do when they're bored and perhaps not very happy.

But suppose then one of the little children said: So what's this last picture meant to be? It's just a funny woman with no clothes on, smiling, and anyway the negative's all blurry, all misty round her waist and legs.

Then she'd have to confront the fact that Tamsin Whitley, blackmailer though she might have been, had not in fact suffered a fate so grossly out of proportion to her crime that it left you trembling anger at the injustice of it all.

For Tamsin Whitley had died happy, secure in the knowledge that vengeance would be hers. And indeed vengeance had been hers. And the thought had made her so happy that in the few seconds before the rather formless wraith she had summoned took her, entered her, penetrated her, joined with her and absorbed her hatred, her energy, her vitality . . . In those few seconds she must have walked naked from the bed, pressed the timer on the camera, lain back and actually *willed* the spirit to enter her — all in that tiny crack in the fabric of time when all could be frozen, white on black, black on white, forever and ever, whirrclick . . .

She thought back to the couple embracing by the *Cutty Sark* and shivered, then emptied her mind of thoughts and walked slowly up the steep hill that led to the heath. On her right was an irregular row of beautiful old houses, representing every style of English architecture from Jacobean to Victorian. On her left lay Greenwich Park. The low, slanting rays of the winter sun bathed the grass in gold and the noble oaks and great chestnut trees, stripped bare of their leaves by the first gales of winter, spread a delicate lattice of shadow on the ground.

It's beautiful, thought Cherie. No kidding.

The road steepened, then became more gentle, flattened and opened out. Now the heath lay before her. She paused, taking it all in.

This is how I want to remember it, she thought — green and golden. A clean wind swept across the turf and tugged her headscarf. Clouds chased across the greyish-blue country sky. Her feet crunched over a pocket handkerchief of frost that lay in a dimple on the turf. Families were out strolling, flying kites, walking their dogs. Her eyes swept across the great expanse, trying to fix the fine old houses, windows glowing as the panes of glass trapped the afternoon sun.

It was my home once, she thought. Never forget it.

She started, as she always did, when she saw the gap where the old convent had been. Everything had gone. Barely forty-eight hours after the night when Ransom had died, the demolition work had started again. This time there had been no protests; there had not been time. Reports said that as the demolition ball swung into the split flank of the building, on the very first blow, there had been a deep, threatening, rumbling sound. The ground had started to quiver; people felt it a mile away, and the demolition crew had jumped from their lumbering machines and run.

When the dust cleared the convent had gone. It had fallen in on itself and into a great pit that had opened beneath it. The whole structure had been unstable. They said the ground beneath must have been so riddled with holes, with vaults and cellars, that the shock of demolition had started off some subterranean chain reaction. It was still too unstable to build there, and anyway the Council had refused planning permission. It was going to become an Enterprise Park. Unemployed youngsters were going to plant trees and flowers there. Landscape it.

There had been a macabre footnote. When the district surveyors had been poring over the rubble, one of them had seen a hand sticking up from the ground. It had belonged to a body, later identified as William Aloysius Ransom. Though the corpse had been horribly crushed, a distinctive signet ring had made identification possible. It had proved impossible to establish the cause of death, and what the elderly man had been doing in the convent remained a mystery. Recently his sole surviving relative had come forward and though Ransom had died intestate, it looked as if the estate, or what was left of it, was going to him.

Cherie walked up the steps to her front door, paused and took a long last look around. A gust of wind made the estate agents' signs outside her and Ransom's houses rattle and she went inside. In her sitting-room she checked the answering-machine for messages. One. It was from the boy, Sebastian Lee Miles. They had kept in touch, or rather he had made a point of keeping in touch with her. He had even brought his mother — a quiet, watchful woman — round for tea once.

The message stated that his mother was out so he could use the phone. He just wanted to say that she seemed better now and his old school was going to let him back because he had had an interview with the headmaster who had decided that he had been under a lot of stress and was really all right. There was something at the end about how a boy called Scruby had been caught cheating and been expelled. Cherie couldn't work out what that meant. She wondered at how quickly he had recovered and at how grown-up he sounded. No 'adjustment' problems there, she thought.

She wrote him a quick note with her address in the States and went upstairs to sort out clothes and suitcases.

Chapter Thirty-three

On Monday morning the removal firm came and took away the few large items that Cherie was shipping to the States. By midday she had finished putting her clothes into two large suitcases, so she walked to Blackheath village to buy a French loaf, some wine, cold meats and cheese for her lunch with Willis. Just in time she remembered the paper plates, plastic knives and forks, and plastic beakers.

The weather turned nasty as she walked back. A vicious little gusting wind made her eyes smart, and flung freezing spurts of rain in her face. Heavy banks of cloud rolled across the sky; she had to turn the lights on indoors when she got back.

Willis was a few minutes late. He'd wasted half the morning trying to find a going-away present for Cherie to take back to the States, and had been able to find nothing. As he walked up the steps he reflected that it was probably because he had no idea of what her tastes were, her strong likes or dislikes, or whether she had a sense of humour. It was strange to have gone through so much with somebody and yet still know nothing about them at the end of the day. The idea that sharing some great traumatic adventure brings people closer is one of those misleading clichés, he thought. All it means is that you know how they react in a set of circumstances that will never be repeated.

But, he thought, if ever I need to go ghostbusting again, I'll know who to call on.

Cherie opened the door for him and planted a relieved kiss on his cheek.

She led him through the empty hall and into the sitting-room, bare but for a couple of armchairs that had been sold to a neighbour who would pick them up later.

'Thank God you came. I was going spare in here.'

'It's good to see you. God, but the place looks funny without furniture.'

'It reminds me of when Peter and I moved in,' Cherie said. 'Two years ago. And here I am, back again right where I started.'

'Older and wiser,' Willis said encouragingly.

'Washed out and cynical. Damn, I didn't mean that. Let's have a drink. Oh no!'

'What?'

'The corkscrew.'

Willis smirked and produced one from his pocket. 'I don't know what made me think about it, but just as I was leaving my flat this morning a little voice whispered in my ear: Take a corkscrew.'

Cherie grabbed it and pulled the cork.

'Here's to little voices,' she said with a smile. Then the smile froze on her face. 'Or not, as the case may be.'

'Here's to *some* little voices, at any rate,' said Willis.

There followed a pause which became a bit embarrassing. 'It's difficult to talk about, isn't it?' Willis said. 'When you've gone, there'll be no one to share it with. I know we haven't talked about it at all — perhaps it's impossible to and always will be, but . . . but just seeing you has kept me in touch with the whole thing, even if we always skirted around it.'

Cherie hugged herself. 'I know. I think I'm to blame mostly, but I just can't . . . talk about it. But there's something you might want. It was partly why I asked you round in the first place, and then I thought you wouldn't want it, but now I think maybe you will have it. It's entirely up to you. No pressure on you at all.'

'What?'

'It's at the top of the house.'

They walked up the two flights of stairs, through the

empty junk room and into Cherie's studio.

The picture was propped up against a wall and Willis remembered it immediately. He'd seen it the very first evening he had come round to investigate a break-in. Seeing the picture shot him back through time. He remembered the young American woman, with, as he had thought then, the tragic, strained face and the wide sensual mouth, and as he remembered it he got a sense of how he had been then. Everything had been so different, and between them and now was a . . . something like a vacuum, a horror both in him and out of him that he had to fight not to think about for fear of getting pulled into its cold depths.

'It freaked me out when I saw it again,' Cherie said. 'I was doing it when things were really bad. I can't take it with me. I don't want anything like that. But I can't destroy it. It's yours if you want it. If not, I'll just shove it up in the roof space. Who knows. Someday I might get famous and someone will discover it. The mystery of the Cherie Simpson picture in the attic. That sounds very flip, but I really would like you to have it, even if I understand perfectly why you mightn't want it.'

Willis snapped the light on and studied it. It was smaller than he remembered it, and less detailed. Now as he looked it seemed strangely bitty, disjointed. Whatever the artist had seen in the relationships between the various groups, he couldn't. They were linked by a way of seeing things he didn't understand. Or was it that he was simply blocking it out? No. There was no reason why the sky had to take up so much of the canvas, and having taken up so much of the canvas should have been left so blank. There was no point in putting a group of schoolboys in the middle of the heath playing some bloody silly little game. But there was something there. The painting posed a question. It was asking the viewer to find the missing element which would make sense of it all.

Willis made up his mind. 'I'd love it,' he said. 'Really I would. And I'll treasure it.' His stomach gave a loud rumble. 'But after lunch.'

They ate with plates on their laps, beakers of wine balanced on the arms of their chairs, and chatted about the future. Cherie was going to stay with her friend Jennifer who, with her husband, ran a Manahattan art gallery, a loft in SoHo and a house in the Hamptons. They would be based in New York, where they sold art, she would be based on Long Island where she would produce it, or so the story went. Willis was going to stay in the police force and thought he might even go for promotion. He called it the flying pig syndrome. Now he knew anything might happen.

Then Willis got up to go and they hugged each other, and perhaps it was that, or the carrier bag with the remains of the lunch that Cherie insisted he took with him, or perhaps it was the wine which seemed to have gone to both of their heads that made Willis forget about the painting he was meant to take and made Cherie forget to remind him.

He drove off in his car, the exhaust smoking in the cold air, and suddenly Cherie felt as if she were going to burst into tears. She crammed the plates and plastic knives into a plastic bag she'd been saving for the purpose, then threw herself down into a chair, a great lump in her throat and tears building up in her eyes. She cursed the wine she had drunk for making her feel like this. What was the phrase? Tired and emotional. She reached for the telephone and asked for a minicab to call for her.

Her eyes wandered round the room, then she closed them and let a kaleidoscope of images flicker across her mind. She could picture the furniture as it had been: the sofa against one wall; the dining-table under the window; the pictures on the wall and the carpets on the floor. People — ghosts really — took up positions, snatches of conversations echoed through her mind. Evenings she had spent with friends, evenings alone with her husband, evenings alone . . .

Then, through her closed eyelids, she suddenly realised

that it must be later than she thought. It was growing dark outside, and time had been spinning past. She forced herself awake, pulled on a jacket, checked she had keys in her pocket and picked up the bag of rubbish from lunch. There was still a bit of time to kill before she had to leave; she could put the bag in a litter-bin on the heath.

The wind had dropped to a fitful breeze, but there was a still, clammy chill in the air. The first bin she went to was full to overflowing, and scraps of paper were being tugged hither and thither on the grass. The second bin had been ripped off its stand by vandals and was lying flattened on the grass about ten feet away. That left one more that she knew about, which stood quite near the old convent.

Checking her watch she walked quickly towards it.

The site of the old building still looked unnaturally flat. Almost shaven. Cherie dropped her bag into the bin, crushing it down so it didn't fall out, then caught a quick, furtive movement out of the corner of her eye. She whipped her head round.

Nothing. Double nothing. No movement. No building. Then, remembering an old trick, she turned her head to try and catch whatever she had glimpsed in her peripheral vision.

Yes! Something! It was like a wrinkle on the lens of her eye: a shimmer against the darkness, low down. Or was it something else. Kids? Kids playing on the old site. It was supposed to be safe, she knew that, but she didn't altogether trust it. The ground underneath could, for all anyone knew, give another lurch, collapse a bit more.

She glanced once more at her watch. Five minutes. She could give it five minutes. Then she'd have to make tracks back to the house to meet the minicab.

Nearer now, she saw the movement more clearly. In the shifting twilight it was still impossible to make out clearly what was going on, but now she was nearer she could see that there was more than one figure there and it almost looked like they were playing some sort of game. Voices floated towards her; high, childish voices, singing. Her heart stuffed her ears with noise. She stopped and held her breath.

NO NO NO! IT COULDN'T BE!

She was running now and getting closer and the words and the tune sat in her head

Ring a ring of roses
A pocketful of posies
Atishoo! Atish —

Almost close enough now. Crossing the line where the fence stood.

'Stop it! STOP IT!'

The dark air shimmered in front of her like a curtain, like a wall. Cherie tried to pull up. Screamed.

A BUILDING WAS RISING IN FRONT OF HER

But no longer the old convent. That was gone and she saw now, in a flash of comprehension, how subtle its design had been. Saw how the builders had sought to conceal its true shape: a marvellous geometric grid of planes and angles that both locked in what lay around it and set up its own mysterious lines of power that generation after generation of silent nuns had maintained and guarded. Saw now that the tunnels and vaults it had fallen into had been a part of this great design, and now some force, older and greater than anything she could have envisioned or imagined had taken its ruined, collapsed bricks and beams and was thrusting into the cold night air a hideous structure; a blind and sullen lair, dark and foul.

She felt a sense of sickening impotence and shame. She had not simply been misguided; she had been completely, utterly, irrevocably wrong. And why? Because deep down she had been so obsessed, or so programmed by her own pathetic domestic problems, she had failed to grasp the real significance of the succession of foul occurrences.

And in the moment she realised this she had burst through its dank miasmic walls. The singing stopped.

Silence like a held breath. A waiting. A moment of judgement and truth. Above her the crazed architecture grew relentlessly upwards into the night sky. Great black galleries opened onto nothing. Beams thrust outwards into the gloom like broken gallows. It all seemed part of a vile, logical, organic whole. The walls quivered and pulsated, swelled and cracked, oozing dark liquid that fell to the ground and burned like acid. Burned a pit.

Wrong all the time.

A roaring shook the ground at her feet. She turned round to grab at . . . anything, but there was nothing. The walls had retreated and she saw that she was standing not on the edge of a pit, but on a tiny pinnacle of earth that rose from the centre of an abyss. Beneath her the sheer sides of her tiny platform plummeted down into the dark. Helpless, she waited.

A dense white fog, acid strong, began to form in the pit. The ground trembled. The pinnacle swayed. She flailed her arms to keep balance, fell humped on top of the tiny platform, its point thrusting into her belly, arms and legs dangling helplessly over the edge, fingers scrabbling desperately for any sort of grip.

The mists cleared. A stench like a liquid flicked up and curled around her. Vile trendrils took her head, tried to lick their way into her eyes, her ears, her nostrils, her mouth.

They burned off her eyelids and forced her to peer down into a chasm where a forest of bones glowed white, bathed in a transparent yellow liquor. Figures moved below her. Tiny foreshortened figures like ants. They came and looked upwards. And a voice, thick and slow and dark, roared at her with formless, hate-filled and triumphant sounds. It was mocking her. It was down there. She could sense a presence hurrying through ancient passages.

Below her the figures shifted: broken marionettes, victims of plague, of murder, of greed; each victim, each dead person feeding the monster that they then became, adding to the whole their hatred, their resentment of the living. And as the thought came to her those broken, crawling figures stood upright, raised their arms and flew apart. Their torn bodies formed a gigantic tower of flesh that crept upwards, ever upwards. There on its trembling apex, enthroned in gore, sat the smiling girl. And there in Cherie's mind was the fact. The girl had surrendered to a great force that had lain dormant for centuries; had given it a thought, a single identity to focus its rage, had shown it how to rip, to tear, to kill — dear God, had shown it how to play! Together, they, it, she had played with her. And she had given them Ransom.

He was there; she had sacrificed him, allowed him to be taken, thinking that it would lay the ghost, not realising that she was feeding a force which was older than the plague, older than history, not the White Man, not the White Lady, not even the whiteness of death, or the whiteness of oblivion. It was the dancing essence of hatred that played above the graves of untold victims, like marsh gas among the pathetic creatures who scurried on the surface of its world. It had played with her. It had played with Willis. It had played with the boy. All it did was play. Endlessly. Eternally.

And now she was the game.

There was a terrible baying. The girl stood up, reached out with soft, white, tiny hands. Touched Cherie. The sound grew, rhythmic and strong. Strong. Horns! Horns! A blaring of horns to herald her end.

A horn.

A car horn.

With a scream Cherie jerked herself up from her chair, leaving behind in her dreams a tiny voice that spiralled like a wisp of smoke to nothing.

I'm with you now

The room was dark. Outside, in the street, a cab waited, its engine panting, its headlamps boring smoky tunnels in the light mist. The driver saw her come to the window and he raised a hand. She acknowledged him feebly.

Suitcases in the hall. Handbag by the door. The cab waiting. It was a dream, thought Cherie. Just a dream. Time to go. The cab driver picked up the cases for her and dropped them in the boot. Cherie closed the front door, double-locked it, paused then dropped the keys back in through the letter-box.

The cab sets off and Cherie remembers the picture Willis forgot to take, and she remembers the light she forgot to switch off. Craning round she sees the light glowing like a yellow eye set in the roof of her house. And as the cab pulls further away she sees the light grow fainter and fainter, dimmed by distance and the steadily thickening mist.

Upstairs in the attic a draught from a badly fitted window catches a bulb left burning. It swings gently to and fro, and the shadows move across the wall. The light banishes the darkness from dusty corners then lets it swim back. The light plays upon the surface of a forgotten picture left propped against the wall.

And the light brings a white sky to life.